THE RETIREMENT QUILT

By

Dr Ronald Lee Gaudreau

Thanks and Salutations

The cover images were designed by Anita Bradshaw, well known American quilter Email: accounts@eastex.net.

The production of this book would not have been possible, if it were not for the design and editorial assistance of Andrew Caird.

I would not have started this book were it not for my PT, Euan Murray's challenge in mid-March 2018.

They say that a journey begins with the first step but at every step along the way you find and meet people, who add to your happiness and well being and to them I dedicate this book.

In Australia

Tim, Kelly Ned and Pippa Benjamin, Derek, Kate, Tamzen and Siobhan Burrell, John and Fiona Cole, David and Margaret Emerson, Dr Bruce and Sue Greig, Maisie Houghton, Vippan and Dimple Kumar, Yung-Ok Oh, Sam, Naomi and Paddy Ryan, Ray and Judy Sinclair, John and Billy Tsilinikos, Peter, Claire, Jason and Steven Vernados

In the United States

Jill Berman, Marge and Mike Brennan, Manny and Marina Dimondo, Bill Fobert, Di Gaudreau, Steve and Kym Magnelli, Kevin MacCarthy and Michael Weiss and to my little brother, Gerald Philip Gaudreau, whose zest for life is worthy of its own book.
Finally, to William T Goldman, who was a mentor and inspiration.

Other Countries

Mirelle MacCarthy, France, and Jim and Carolyn Murray, Scotland

1. PROLOGUE

* * *

An idea is like dropping a pebble into a quiet pond, its ripples spread out from the centre, changing the surface as well as disturbing the plants and animals beneath. It was a series of single events that involved a small group of people but affected a small town in unexpected ways. True, the seeds that inspired these events were planted previously but their maturation was nourished by commitment and love by those involved. These were not earth shaking events but for those involved, they helped define who they were and shaped their future lives and the town in which they lived.

These events unfolded in the year 2016 in Morton, a small Australian town located along the Hunter River in the Hunter Valley, the traditional lands of the Wonnarua people, in the state of New South Wales. The very names of streets and buildings reflected the 200 year old history as a farming and a coal mining area. The main street in 2016 was named Elizabeth Street but was once a bullock track known as Colliery Road, one of the principal roads leading to the mining areas until the arrival of the railroad line, Haulage Street, Farmers Road, Harvest Road and Coal Dust Street. Other names reflected the nationalities of those 1800s immigrants — Scots Street, Dubliner's Road, Dutchman's Way, Paddy's Crossing, Roman Hill and also reflected the Wonnarua people's heritage — Baiame's Valley. Kelly's Paddock, the town's largest pub and hotel was named after the football field created in the 1880s by early Scottish coal miners. The pub was a virtual museum of sporting history of the area. In 2016, the town still retained enough historic buildings to retain its unique character and good planning help to control the design of new buildings, so that they complimented the historic ones.

The early settlers were not only farmers, vintners and coal miners; they were entrepreneurs who founded flour mills, breweries and soap and candle making and salt stores. They were ironworkers, blacksmiths, saddle makers, tailors, hairdressers, wig makers, dressmakers. They were teachers, solicitors and priests. The entrepreneurial spirit still exists in Morton, many of those shopping in town are still farmers but many who live there travel to the more commercial centre - Newcastle. Morton's role as a regional tourist centre is increasing. This will change the dynamics of the town and impact on its residents. Those whose lives were most affected by the events in 2016 were 50 to 75 year old men. They were not ordinary people but they did reflect the values and history of Morton and they were individuals who had reached a watershed moment in their lives. During those 12 months, each of them interacted with one another and others in ways that could not have been predicted.

The catalyst for this interaction was a quilt. The idea was making the **quilt** and the event, the creation of the quilt.

What is a quilt?

"It is a multi-layered textile, traditionally composed of three layers of fibre: a woven cloth top, a layer of batting or wadding, and a woven back, combined using the technique of quilting, the sewing together of the three layers."

The history of quilting in Australia includes quilts made by convicts, governors' wives, Gold Rush immigrants, wealthy shop owners, dressmakers, church ministers, WW1 diggers, people forced off the land during the Depression, WWII Australian prisoners of war, rabbit trappers, bushmen and finally everyday mothers and daughters. The earliest quilts were utilitarian — bed covers or ceremonial — christenings, weddings. by the 21st century they retained their utilitarian role but added a non-utilitarian role as works of art that told a story.

Without realising it. the creation of the quilt in Morton became a metaphor for the healing process that each of the participants underwent and from which they would emerge stronger. It also served as an example of the therapeutic value of such projects, highlighted the value of sensitively directed philanthropy and illustrated the power of love and friendship and the commitment that people can make to one another without any thought of gain. Finally, it reflected the basic decencies that we hope to find in others and ourselves.

Life would go on in Morton after 2016 but nothing would be the same for another pebble was dropped into the pond and would send out new ripples.

2.   GEOFFREY'S LAST DAY

* * *

On Wednesday the 20th of January 2016, Geoffrey Hamilton the 69 year old CEO of Robotic Solutions was waiting on the steps leading to the circular drive of North Grange, as the company car arrived promptly at 7:15 AM, as it had for the last 12 years.

His driver for the past 7 years, Charles Lewis greeted him:

Charles: "Good morning Mr H. Isn't it a beautiful morning?"

Geoffrey: "It is but it is a day filled with mixed emotions, since it will be the last time you will drive me to Robo."

Charles: "It has been a pleasure driving for you and Mrs H. I was saying to the wife this morning that my day will not seem the same. Although, I am happy to have the extra hour of sleep."

Geoffrey: "That goes for both of us but change is an inevitable part of life. I trust that the arrangements we made for you are satisfactory."

Charles: "When I heard that the new CEO preferred to drive himself, I thought that I would be out of a job, but Mr Haines took your advice and they are using me for special assignments requiring a vehicle. It will actually save them money, since I will replace some of the couriers and hire cars that they have used in the past. It will also mean that I will be able to retire in 5 years with a generous monthly pension. I took your advice and continued to buy shares in Robo, which pays a good dividend. In addition, the value of my shares over the past years has doubled.

All next week I wil drive the investors from overseas back and forth between Morton and Newcastle. Alice has organised for a regular run into Newcastle 3 days a week in the morning to collect the mail from the GPO and 2 regular pickup and returns to the University each week plus other deliveries."

Geoffrey: "I'm glad things worked out. With Australia day coming up, what are your plans?"

Charles: "Since it is an extra-long weekend, I am taking a few days holiday. The Mrs and I will be visiting our son and his family in his new home in Bondi. It should be a relaxing weekend and an opportunity to spend time with our grandchildren."

Geoffrey: "I don't envy you the drive, but it will be good to be with your family."

Charles: "We are not driving, since traffic would be a nightmare. We will take an early morning train on Friday from Newcastle to Central Station in Sydney and then a train to Bondi Junction where our son will collect us. What about you?"

Geoffrey: "On the 26th, I am going to an Australia Day ceremony at the Morton Cenotaph and then having lunch at the Club. On the weekend, I am taking a long ride in my new car, playing tennis on both Saturday and Sunday and catching up on some paper work. Alice and Michael Saas have invited me to a barbeque on the 24th. So for me, it will be a busy social weekend." As they talked, they drove down the tree shaded road, across the new iron bridge that straddled the Grove River, a tributary of the Hunter River which flowed from the Hunter Valley, split forming Stone Creek, and encircled Morton on both sides before re-joining 6000 metres later and then flowing into the Tasman Sea. Geoffrey enjoyed these morning drives, when the fog was lifting, the trees and grass were wet with dew and sparkled in the early morning sun and the air was clean, often with the fresh smell of seawater. The town was quiet except for the sound of birds, vans making their deliveries, a few early commuters heading for Newcastle and the school bus. The coffee shops, the newsagent, the bakery and restaurants were open. The smell of fresh bread reminded him of how Margaret used to bicycle into Morton every Saturday at 6:00 AM to buy the weekend papers and often something from the bakery, if Mrs McMillan had not baked the previous day. This, so often reminded him of the music of Peter Sculthorpe's 'Small Town' or Aaron Copland's 'Quiet Town'.

They drove into the drive that led to the entrance to Robotic Solutions' offices. He was pleased to see that the new landscaping was completed. The over 100 year old brick building was steam cleaned and the windows recently painted, as part of the modernization and rebranding program. This would be part of his legacy.

Charles: "Mr H, I won't say goodbye, because Alice has arranged for me to drive you home this afternoon around 2:00 PM."

Geoffrey made a mental note to remember to give Charles the envelope he had prepared.

Although it was the last day that he would be in his office, he arrived at his usual time, wearing a navy blue blazer with brass buttons, grey slacks and a striped blue shirt with his favourite red tie, both gifts from Margaret on his 65th birthday. This "uniform", as many called it, was a variation, in one way or another, of what he had been wearing for most of his life. Even his close cropped hair, 20 years ago an outdated style, was now back in fashion. Those who saw him for the first time would characterize his look as "preppy". There were those, like Michael Saas, who jokingly said he was born wearing a tie. "Partly true", he would reply, "I was born with my umbilical cord wrapped around my neck." He did not expand on this and say that it almost killed him and that by saving him it did kill his mother.

He entered his office for the last time. The prints and photographs removed, showing their silhouette in the space they had occupied for the past 12 years. The painter would remove them the following week. Even the tread marks of his movements through the space would be gone, since a black industrial carpet would replace the worn blue wool carpet. All memory of his presence would be gone in less than a week

He removed his jacket and hung it on the door handle, since the coat hanger was removed in preparation for the painter. As part of his early morning ritual, he opened the window and let the morning breeze bring in fresh air that always delivered different earthy smells - today of fresh grass and soil – and the raucous noise of the native birds nesting in the branches of the three 100 year old "Ficus Macophylla", otherwise known as Morton Bay Fig trees. He smiled at one of his two idiosyncrasies, the first the need to identify the genus of plants and animals by Latin names and the second the measurement of people by height and weight when first meeting them.

He recalled happily many staff parties under those trees. Those 3 trees and some 20 others gave Morton its name. Beyond the trees, he could see the Grove River that in the floods of 1955 and 1999 reached the trees but had never reached the Robo buildings nor the buildings on Elizabeth Street, all of which were situated at the top of Colliery Rise, a name reflective of the area's coal mining history. However, the town was isolated in the flood of 1999 because the 100 year old wooden bridge was destroyed and the bridge over Stone Creek was under water. That was the time when the Robo building and Kelly's Paddock, the historic pub, provided shelter, accommodations and food for those stranded in Morton for 5 days. He recalled how Margaret had taken her canoe and crossed the Grove River with a basket of fried chicken, a salad and a good wine. He should have been upset that she had risked being washed away in the swollen river but it was so like her to do the unexpected. Her first words were "I am not spending our wedding anniversary alone, so don't yell at me or I will paddle back. Now tell me that you love me and that you are glad to see me and, for God's sake, get me a towel so I can dry myself and change into dry clothing." He had not forgotten the date nor a gift, the poems of her favorite poet, Emily Dickenson that he had bought months previously; while her gift was a pair of gold cufflinks. That night they ate by candlelight on his office floor and later made love.

Returning to reality, he could see on the other side of the Grove River, North Grange and Hawthorne Manor now a retirement facility, where Margaret spent her last few days and the Bigelow cemetery, her burial place. He turned and saw Margaret's photograph sitting on the 80 year old highly polished walnut desk. The desk and the matching file cabinet had been, his predecessor, David Smithe's prize possession. He died at that desk at the age of 75. Because of their association with his death, his wife, Karen, had given them to Geoffrey, who was then CFO. He could have taken them with him, since his successor, James Hunter, wanted a more modernistic décor – glass, chrome and black, but they were too big for his home office and his new mantra was "Less not More." He was certain Alice, his longtime PA, would find a good home for them.

Since all corporate papers had been removed, all that was left were personal items accumulated over the years. He decided to have 2 boxes, which he labelled – *Take Box* and *Discard Box*, he thought he might have a **Maybe** box but discarded that idea – "Less not More", he thought. Although, he recognised that what was left represented a significant part of the last decade, he was determined to be ruthless in his culling. This was uncharacteristic, since he tended to be a "bower bird". The plan was to tip the contents of each of the nine drawers on the desktop, which he had covered with an old sheet provided by Alice and then sort through them. He hoped to be finished by noon in time for lunch with Alice, and the Acting Managing Director, Larry Abbott, who had been his CFO for the past 7 years and a good friend. The 3 draw file cabinet held no surprises and no challenge to his sorting plans and most of the contents were placed in the *Discard Box*, with the exception of two ties, well-worn athletic shoes and shorts, some medical records that he had misplaced and the long lost draft of his Will. The desk did produce some surprises. Into the *Take Box*, he put two diaries that recorded his daily activities for the preceding 2 years; on second thought, he dumped them into the *Discard Box*. He discarded the Christmas and birthday greetings from several years back, although he read them with a degree of nostalgia. He saved more ties and some DVDs, a few pens and gifts from friends and clients that he thought he had lost. The tin of sardines that expired on 3 February 2010 definitely was discarded. There were several certificates for completed courses and some pictures of staff at various office parties. These could join the others he found the previous month and could be framed. He had a sense of achievement, when he placed the last item in the *Discard Box* and he was pleased with the speed and his adherence to his resolution to discard anything unnecessary. He looked once more in the *Take Box* and discarded the old shorts, his old medical records and his outdated Will.

He knew it was 1030 because Alice arrived with his morning coffee and a piece of her signature lemon slice.

Alice: "Morning Geoffrey. Here is your coffee. Please drink it while it is hot. I made the lemon slice especially for you and have wrapped two extra pieces for you to take home, one for you and one for Mrs Mc. You must be pleased with yourself, since you have that Cheshire cat grin on your face."

Geoffrey: "Thanks for the coffee and the slice. I am certain Mrs Mc will appreciate the thought. I am chuffed with the results of the clean up. Alice could you do me a favour? I have decided not to take the desk and the cabinet. Do you think you can find a home for both?"

Alice: "Matter of fact, Murray in archives, asked if he could have them, if you decided not to take them. It will fit into his plans for the conversion of the old basement storeroom into an archive room tracing the history of the company and the building. I will have Eric take the **Discard Box** to the trash area and place the **Take Box** in the boot of the company car."

He remembered that he had an envelope for Eric, as well as Charles. A gesture of appreciation for his help over the years.

Geoffrey: "Alice, you might find some things in the **Discard box**. If so, please keep them."

Alice: Alice looked into the box. "I don't want the tin of sardines! However, I do like the paperweight but I am discarding things rather than accumulating more. We should keep your diaries for the past 2 years, at least for another year, and I would suggest I shred your medical I records and your old Will. Everything is arranged for lunch in the executive boardroom. Larry Abbott and I will join you at 12:30. I have ordered the wine chilled and waiting for you, if you arrive early."

Geoffrey: "Alice, what will I do without you?"

Alice: "It will be a change for both of us. You become accustomed to the way in which a person works, his habits, his likes and dislikes. Michael teases me and refers to you as my office husband without fringe benefits. However, thanks to you, I have a new job as Personal Assistant to the Chairman."

Geoffrey: "I knew that Bradley Haines needed a Personal Assistant and that you would be ideal for the job. James Hunter wants his own secretary; I suppose to match his new décor."

Alice: Laughingly, "I guess I wasn't chrome and glass enough."

Geoffrey: "However, you are good enough to work for the Chairman of a large corporation and in a position of considerable influence. Brad did not pick you because of my recommendation; he picked you because you were the right person for the job and for him."

Alice: With a catch in her voice. "Thank you! I had better go before I start crying. I will see you at lunch."

Geoffrey wondered if he had done Alice a favor by suggesting to Bradley that she would be the ideal PA. It would be a different relationship. Bradley liked to be the boss in the traditional sense, it would be Mr Haines and Mrs Saas, not Bradley and Alice, and she would have far more personal things to do for him. However, he knew that she would work things out.

With a shake of her head, she picked up the **Discard Box** and left the room, leaving in her wake the smell of Essence of Rose a scent that Geoffrey had always associated with her. This brought back memories of their first meeting 12 years ago when she arrived for an interview for the position as a replacement for Miss Lafayette, his predecessor's secretary and possibly mistress. She discovered his body slumped over his desk at 7:00 PM, the apparent victim of a heart attack. At the time of his death, there was rumor that there was more than work performed on that desk that night and that David, who had a history of heart trouble, died as a result of over exertion.

This might have been reason Karen was happy to give the desk to Geoffrey. The Chairman and senior staff members had pulled ranks and discouraged any speculation as to the cause of death. At that time, while having dinner with Alice and her husband Michael, Margaret said, "Why not just say that he died on the job and leave it at that. This will save Karen and his family any further embarrassment."

Michael: "Dear Margaret, you have given a whole new meaning to the phrase dying on the job."

She was known as Miss Lafayette, because she was one of those prim and proper secretaries of the Miss Hales College type, who dressed for the office wearing a dark suit with a white or pink blouse and a broach on her label with proper shoes and matching handbag and gloves and dark stockings. When Geoffrey first met her she was 160 cm and weighed around 50-55 kgs. She had a husky voice, the result of too many Gauloises. When Margaret first met her at a staff function when she was in her 60s, Margaret commented that she was attractive in a Duchess of Windsor way but she could not see her as a femme fatale as rumored.

When Geoffrey became CEO, he knew that his relationship with her would be fraught with conflict. It was! Both were set in their ways! However, she contrived to do whatever Geoffrey wanted in her own time and in her own way. It was fortunate that she had decided to retire after 3 months with Geoffrey. She was intelligent enough to know that her position was not secure, so before Geoffrey acted, she resigned and did it in her own way. She sent the letter of resignation to the Chairman, Bradley Haines, with a copy to Geoffrey noting that "The differences between his style and that of his predecessor makes it difficult for me to continue to work for him, therefore in the best interest of all concerned I tender my resignation."

The Chairman called Geoffrey and said that her resignation was a blessing, since both had discussed the difficulties in finding her another position within the company. The Chairman's secretary, Carole Freemen, organized a luncheon to mark Miss Lafayette's retirement. Most of the older executives and their wives, including Margaret, attended. It was noted, although invited, David Smithe's wife Karen did not attend. The Chairman presented Miss Lafayette with a round trip first class ticket to Paris for her long service to the company. Margaret arranged for her to stay in their apartment in Paris and bought a gold and silver broach for Geoffrey to give her. Geoffrey had thought of giving her a plant as well, but Margaret thought cactus was not appropriate. "It's too pointed", she joked. When the company car drove her out of the drive for the last time, there was a collective sigh of relief.

3. ALICE

* * *

Geoffrey had allowed himself to digress from his original question "Why did he engage Alice 12 years ago?" He knew he did not want another Miss Lafayette. He needed someone who would challenge him and not merely agree with him. He knew that he was opinionated and liked things done in a particular way, but he also knew that if a better way were presented that would accomplish the same objective that he would agree to it. At that time, 12 years ago, he was more a process person than a people person, which made people think that he was uncaring. This had been less so now because of Margaret's and Alice's influence and example.

In assessing his work habits, he believed, he was an orderly person, both personally and professionally. His desk was usually neat, although in the middle of a project he could live with chaos, although as he told Alice it was organised chaos. He could still fill the office with paper and even leave it there until the project was finished. He did the same thing at home, while Alice would ignore it, since she lived with someone whom she said was "orderly challenged"; Margaret was more organised and more direct, "Geoffrey Chaos, your wife Orderly Chaos wants to clean the study." Margaret's input into his choice of a secretary was thoughtful. "Choose someone who will reflect the best in you and who will represent your ideals and values. She or he should be able to challenge you when they think you are wrong, knowing that you are encouraging them to do so, but who will support you once a decision has been made and finally, they must be loyal."

Alice had worked at Robo for 10 years, the last 4 years in public relations. She applied for the job as soon as Miss Lafayette announced her retirement. Although, they had met at various company and social functions, they had had no direct contact at work. However, Geoffrey's observations were that she was a warm, open, competent and friendly person.

After interviewing a number of outside candidates, most of them in their late 20's with good experience and credentials, none seemed to fit his requirements, which he had to admit he could not define. It was more a feeling then the experiences and references. It was like falling in love, you cannot define it, it just happens and you know it is right. That was how he knew that Margaret was the right person for him. Jnlike his first wife, they were sole mates, lovers and best of friends and when she died a part of him died as well, although a part of her was always within him and he constantly thought about her, what she would do and how she would handle a problem.

Alice arrived for the interview early and sat in the outer office with Miss Lafayette. When the time for the interview arrived, Miss Lafayette knocked on Geoffrey's door, entered and deposited some completed work and mail in his IN Basket.

Miss Lafayette:"Mr Hamilton is there anything you have for me to do, if not, I am leaving for lunch. Alice is here. You won't like her."

Geoffrey: "No thank you. On you way to lunch, would you please deposit this letter in the post box? Please send Alice in."

Miss Lafayette left without any word and did not take the letter.

Geoffrey thought "What a Bitch." He smiled at this, since it was very unlike him.

Alice could not have been more of a contrast to Miss Lafayette. She was 34, 170 cm tall and weighed 45-50 kg, she was blond and had a round cherubic face with prominent green eyes and a wide smile. She was a local girl and had married a local boy, Michael Saas, whose family were involved in coal mining. He was a mathematics and physical education teacher, which, when Geoffrey met him, established a rapport based upon the same mode of thinking and the same distorted sense of humor. They had two girls, 6 year old Jane and 8 year old Susan. She exuded quiet confidence. She had an engaging and bubbly personality, which Geoffrey immediately liked. They exchanged greetings and before Geoffrey had a chance to say anything.

Alice: "Mr Hamilton, I would like the position as your secretary because I know that I can be an asset to you. This is also a step up the ladder for me, since I know that I can gain experience from you that I could not gain in the public relations department."

Geoffrey: "Alice, I have a copy of a letter of recommendation from Bruce Spencer your boss in Public Relations and he praises your work but does not want to see you leave the department. What is your response to that?"

Alice: "That is a difficult question to answer. If I answer it truthfully, it might be misconstrued as being disloyal to Bruce but ...." Before Alice could finish Geoffrey interrupted her.

Geoffrey: "You need to leave the interpretation of your response to me, I can see that he does not want you to leave but knows that you are considering doing so. Obviously, you did the right thing to advise him that you were applying for this job. He did the right thing, knowing I would require a reference and did so without my asking and without your requesting. So, please continue."

Alice: "Thank you, this will make it easier for me. Bruce is a wonderful man and a good person to work for but he relies too much on me. I felt that he undervalued my contribution, especially when he hired John Crammer, who I had mentored for one year, for a position that makes him my boss.   Now, I am doing a portion of John's work, as well still helping Bruce. I think that both Bruce and John realize that they will struggle, if I leave. However, I believe they will be able to cope with the work and it might be to our mutual benefit that I do leave."

Geoffrey: "Would you leave Robo, if you did not get this job?"

Alice: "I like working at Robo, but I do want a job with greater challenges and one where my contribution is not only rewarded financially but is appreciated and from which I receive self-satisfaction. Ultimately, if I did not find that satisfaction here, I would seek a new position elsewhere."

Geoffrey: "Alice, those were both thoughtful and diplomatic answers and I understand and appreciate your candidness. Now, what do you know about me?"

Alice: "Since you keep pretty much to yourself, there is no gossip about you. You are happily married to a wonderful woman, who I have met on several occasions, and who does volunteer work at the Wilson Community Centre and supports the arts and the Rehab Hospital. You have no children, no dog or cat.   You have a housekeeper, Mrs McMillan, who I know. You live in an early 1930's 3 bedroom stone cottage on a large acreage that was part of the Bigelow estate. Aside from playing the piano and the harmonica, you have no hobbies, but you read and have a good classical record collection. You and your wife are regular theatre supporters and theatregoers. You do not particularly like office parties but you always attend, usually with Margaret. You drink alcohol sparingly. You exercise regularly and run in the Summer Park and you play tennis. You are a member of the Morton Improvement Club and the Bigelow Racket Club. In addition to your support of the arts and health programs, you and your wife support programs for disadvantaged children. You spend 3-4 weeks in Europe in late August to mid-September and ....."

Geoffrey: With a laugh "Stop! You know more about me than most people. How did you acquire this knowledge? Did you have a detective follow me or did you work for ASIO?" They both laugh.

Alice: "I confess to being an Agatha Christie maven, especially her Poirot, and a Sherlock Holmes addict! I also did my homework and found out from various sources about you and pieced the rest together. I know something of your work habits and have been in your office when you first arrived, so I have some insight into who you are and what you might require from me."

Geoffrey: "OK. Impress me!"

Alice: "You like tidiness and orderliness but not to excess. You dress for comfort less than style. You are what we call a "Preppy". You always wear a dark suit or blue or black jacket with grey or black trousers, a tie, button down white or blue shirt with French cuffs and cuff links and well-polished black lace up shoes. You like fresh air in the office first thing in the morning, so you open the windows. You like a set routine, for example you arrive an hour before anyone else and take your coffee around 10:30 and biscuits and tea around 2:30 PM and you generally leave at 5:30 PM."

Geoffrey: "I am impressed. Now, tell me why I should hire you."

Alice: "Aside from the fact that I have excellent secretarial and computer skills and am well organised, I have good research and PR skills and can read and interpret financial reports. I am someone who will respect your personal lifestyle and enhance your professional work. I am very forthright and, if I disagree with you, I will tell you so and I will expect you to listen to what I have to say. However, I will support whatever decision you finally make. I can act as a sounding board, if you require one. I am discrete, since I recognise that your position requires someone who will not discuss what goes on in this office. I do have several requirements; I need to leave at 3:30 PM twice a week to pick up my children and once a week at 4

PM to leave for the university where I am completing my business management degree. In exchange, I can come in at 8AM and can stay until 6 pm from time to time and, if necessary, come in after 11:30 AM on Saturdays."

There was a moment of silence, one that communicated more than could be said. It was the recognition by both that there was a connection and that their professional life could be mutually satisfying. On Geoffrey's part, he sensed that this woman would provide him with the support he required and that he could trust her, in the same way he trusted Margaret.

Alice felt that this honest decent man would treat her with respect and appreciate what she knew she could do for him and reward her accordingly.

Geoffrey: "Based upon this interview, I believe that we could develop a mutually beneficial relationship, if you decide to take the job as my Personal Assistant."

Alice: "Personal Assistant? I thought the job was for a secretary?"

Geoffrey: "It was but if you are going to do everything you say you can do that is a PA's job. Frankly, I need a PA more than a secretary. The job comes with a higher salary and a certain amount of cache. In addition, I agree to your leaving early three days a week and accept your offer to come in at 8 o'clock and occasionally on weekends."

Alice: "What can I say?"

Geoffrey: "Say yes or no! Or I will consider it."

Alice: "Of course yes, when would you like me to start?"

Geoffrey: "Miss LaFayette leaves in 3 weeks. Let's wait until then and we both can begin with a fresh slate. It will also give you a chance to work with Bruce and John on the transition. I will advise Bruce of our decision."

There was a handshake and Alice entered his and Margaret's life. Now it was 12 years later and they had formed a strong bond of respect and friendship. She and

Michael had become close friends, more so when Michael inherited the Leasehold on East Grange from his parents. She had been there throughout Margaret's short fight with pancreatic cancer, reading to her and sharing "girl talk", while Michael, at Margaret's insistence, involved him in various sporting activities. Along with Robyn Coleman, they helped organise Margaret's funeral arrangements, the memorial service and the lunch following. Aside from seeing Alice every day, over the last year, he saw them socially at least once a week and he and Michael often rode their bikes down to Lake Macquarie on weekends.

"So many good memories." Geoffrey said to himself.

4.   THE GOING AWAY LUNCH

* * *

Through the one-way glass separating his office from the Executive Conference room, he could see the waiter laying the silverware and placing the glasses for lunch. The room was part of the 2 year $5 million modernisation of the building and part of the company's rebranding. It also reflected the needs of the computer age, which required raised floors and lower ceilings throughout the building to accommodate computer cabling and air-conditioning ducting. His office was left until the last, since he could not bring himself to part with its club like feeling. The only change he did permit was the removal of the wall between the executive conference room and his office and the replacement with a half-wall of one-way glass and a new chrome and frosted glass door. The one-way glass gave the CEO privacy while giving him views of the park, the river and the distant mountains. Next week, his office would be blended into the new décor and feel even more spacious.

He entered the conference room at the same time that Stephen from Executive Caterers arrived with his favorite white wine, a Marchand & Burch Chardonnay. He had acquired several cases for the company at a considerable discount. He had been tempted to buy several case of the Chateau d'Yquem, a wine Executive Caterers had given him on his last birthday. While he was not a wine maven, he did appreciate a good drop. It was Margaret who had the palette for distinguishing good wines. As a result, their wine cellar was the envy of many of their friends, largely due to the fine wines Margaret inherited from her father, her relationship to the Tyrells and her ability to select wines that cellared well. He recalled happy candle lit evenings sipping wine and eating assorted cheeses in their wine cellar at North Grange.

He was jolted out of his thoughts by Stephen.

Stephen: "Mr H would you like a glass of wine now or wait until your other guests arrive?

Geoffrey: "Thank you Stephen. I will have a glass now."

Stephen: "I guess this is a big day for you. Mike and I were discussing you this morning. Mike reminded me that had it not been for you encouraging us 10 years ago, we would never have started this business. You gave us our first gig, paid on that day and then gave us a 2 year contract to supply all the food and wine for the Robo. It was that contract and your and Mrs H's recommendations that secured our bank loan and new clients. Now, we are a $6 million turnover company.

As a thank you, Mike and I wanted to give you a small token of our appreciation. Since you like good wine, here is a bottle of Chateau d'Yquem and 2 extra for your cellar."

Geoffrey: "Stephen thank you and thank Mike. This is a totally unexpected but appreciated gift, as was your supplying the wines for Margaret's Remembrance Day luncheon last August. I was just thinking of that very wine a few minutes ago. Please open the bottle and join me in drinking a glass. A good wine deserves to be shared with good friends." Stephen opened the bottle, produced 4 crystal glasses and filled 2.

Stephen: "Cheers Mr H and our best wishes on your retirement."

Geoffrey: "Cheers."

It was the first time that the word retirement had a contextual meaning and Geoffrey was not certain that he liked it!

The Chairman, Bradley Haines, walked into the room.

Bradley: "Good afternoon Geoffrey. Hello Stephen. Geoffrey, I wanted to stop by and bid you good-bye on this your last day here. However, you are always welcome to drop in and see us. I expect I will see you at the Club from time to time. Of course, we will expect you at the annual general meeting in December. If there is anything you need, please let me know."

Geoffrey: "It is good of you to drop in like this. Would you like a glass of wine?"

Bradley: "I would love one but I am leaving for a meeting at the club and am already running late. See you soon." With that he was gone.

Stephen: "Talk about a whirling dervish."

Geoffrey: "That's Bradley."

Geoffrey never felt comfortable with Bradley. He felt he was never totally honest and sought the easiest and least controversial option when confronted with a problem. Margaret's assessment was more direct: "He is a bully and always has been. Don't trust him. If you get into a confrontation with him, hit him before he hits you. Throw him off balance; you will see that he will back down."

He certainly was enthusiastic, a remnant of his soccer days. However, many found him intimidating but that was probably due to his physical size– 198 cm almost 90 kg and his rapid fire delivery. He was a skilled negotiator and, as one supplier said "one mean sonofabitch". His style was not like Geoffrey – confrontational rather than conciliatory. He knew that Bradley felt he had no **coglioni**; although he also knew that Bradley praised what he had done with Robo in the last 12 years, taking some of the credit himself.

Alice and Larry arrived together, each bearing a large rectangular package. Their parting gift, he thought. Even though he had asked that no one give him any gifts, he would accept this from these two old friends.

Stephen, pointing to the Chateau d'Yquem asked in a conspiratorial voice: "The good stuff or the other."

Geoffrey: "Of course the 'good stuff'".

Stephen poured two extra glasses and Geoffrey raised his glass, as did Alice and Larry.

Geoffrey: "To my good friends, my thanks for being there when I needed you and for you daily support on whatever hobby horse I was riding."
Alice/Larry "To good health and long life."

Alice: "Geoffrey this is a great drop. Is this from your personal cellar?"

Geoffrey: Looking at Stephen he said,   "No, it is a gift from old friends and I wanted to share it with you."

The entrees arrived followed by the main course, smoked quail stuffed with scented rice and vegetable compote. The conversation flowed easily as it does with people who have so much history.   The dessert was a special cherries jubilee, which everyone knew Geoffrey loved and served with a small glass of brandy.

Alice: "Geoffrey, we know that you did not want any presents, but we thought that you would not mind a small token from us, one that is more a memory than a gift."

Larry: "Consider these as a way for you to remember us."

They handed him the packages. He unwrapped them carefully. He had always unwrapped presents in a manner that would exasperate the giver and as if he would save the paper for future use. They were large framed collages of the photos that he thought he would frame. Geoffrey could barely control his delight, so touched was he by the thoughtfulness and generosity of his friends.

Geoffrey: "I cannot tell you how touching this is. Only recently I was thinking of doing something with the pictures I had collected and you have done it."

Alice:	"I am glad that you like them. My only worry was that you would look for them and th nk you lost them or they were included with the corporate papers. We think that Jean, the graphic designer, has done a great job in arranging the pictures and choosing the matting. We matched the frames to those you framed last year, by going to the same framer."

Larry:	"Alice will arrange to have them brought down to the company car, along with the other things you are taking, when you are ready to go. Charles will drive you home and help you unpack." Alice left the room to make arrangements.

Larry:	"Geoffrey, what are you going to do with yourself? I assume that you will get rid of you~ ties and settle in to a comfortable retirement – travel, spend time at your apartme~t in Paris, take up a hobby, take a course or other activities, since I cannot see you sitting around the house reading or listening to classical music all day and you are not a gardener.

You have done a great job, since becoming CEO. You moved the company from being a supplier of software components to a manufacturer of 3D printers. You changed the company's image. You raised revenues from $40 million to $175 million and you have left the company with a healthy surplus for future investments or distribution to shareholders. With your background and experience you could be a director of any number of profit and non-profit boards."

Geoffrey:	"Thanks for the kudos Larry but, frankly, I don't know. I have had so many projects to wind up that I had not considered the future. Six months ago retirement was not on the agenda. I suppose I will discard what you people call my uniform and be more casual in my dress but I have made no plans other than to cull things from my home office and closets, install computer wiring and learn how to use the internet. I have a few housekeeping jobs and I need to discuss the garden with Mr McMillan and plan my visit to Paris in late August. Perhaps in 2 months I will have a plan."

Larry: "Any regrets?"

Geoffrey: "My major regret is that the Board and the University did not follow up on my proposal that they play a more active role in post sales support to the educational sector. Not because we want to sell more 3D printers but because 3D printers represent a new tool for learning and we supplied the tool without the support and I believe we should rectify this. The company and University, using their R&D capabilities and small seed money - $1-$2 million, could develop software that would better manage 3D network printers and we could train teachers to use this.

When I was last in Paris, I had the opportunity to visit a company called Iconem and found that they were using drones to take aerial photographs of historic sites before they vanish and transforming them into precise 3D models, in a process known as photogrammetry. We should be involved in this stuff.

I also think that the company has not fully explored Artificial Intelligence, which I foresee as having huge potential."

Larry: "It seems to me that you should seriously consider putting your talents and ideas into some research project. Perhaps, this is the time when Geoffrey Hamilton does his own thing, runs his own course. You have the time, the enthusiasm and the motivation, not to mention the money.   Let me raise it at the next meeting of the Executive Board, now that I am a member. Who knows what direction James Hunter wants to take the company? He is not an engineer like you but more an investment banker."

Geoffrey: "Thanks for your comments but I am still under contract until December, so it would be inappropriate for me to make any moves until then. In addition, I have been a corporate person so long, I am not certain I could function on my own and I am not certain I want to.

As for James Hunter, don't underestimate him. In my 3 discussions with him, including his initial interview by the selection Committee, I found him very knowledgeable about the potential of 3D and AI. He seemed open minded and willing to listen and, more importantly, to learn. His mandate is to build on our successes and expand the company's reach into international markets. His 4 years in China and 2 years in the USA as CEO of like companies has given him both an international perspect ve and contacts that will be invaluable to the company. That's why he is overseas and that is what he should be doing."

Larry: "I am glad to have your perspective on James. If you want to talk or have coffee or a meal, please contact me. You know Barbara and I love you and expect you to remain part of our extended family. I am sorry I have to rush off, but I have a meeting with our accountants to review last year's figures, which thanks to you are looking good. See yeah."

Alice: "Geoffrey everything is in the car and Charles is waiting for you."

Geoffrey: Laughingly, "Are you trying to get rid of me? Can't wait for the old man to leave?"

Alice: Laughingly, "Exactly. Now let me walk you to the car, since I want to make certain you leave and not go wandering around the building."

Geoffrey: "See you do want to get rid of me."

Alice: "No, but I don't want to delay the good byes, otherwise I will start crying."

Geoffrey: "It is not as if you won't see me again. To show off my new culinary skills, you and Michael are invited to dinner early next month."

Alice: "That is something I want to see and taste."

They hug as Geoffrey leaves the office and Alice, with tears in her eyes, waves good bye.

As the car pulled out of the Robo Headquarters for the last time, Geoffrey had mixed emotions; sadness at leaving and relief that the burden of running a large company were no longer his. It was the same feeling you have when you have run a long tough race - tiredness but exhilaration. He thought of Larry's comments. He remembered the pleasure he had when the company was smaller and he was running a small R&D team. The excitement he shared with his team when they had created the algorithm that unlocked their first 3D breakthrough. Perhaps another time and another place, he thought.

5.   ROBYN

* * *

It was mid-February before he decided he better answer the last letter from his best friend. Fred Russell.

Dear Fred,

I apologize for this long overdue letter. My last correspondence to you did not convey the details regarding my "retirement". In truth, I accepted retirement as the inevitable and best alternative to the political situation in which I found myself. The Board did not have the same future vision of the company that I did. After considering the personal events over the past 2 years, my lack of enthusiasm for the job and my unwillingness to fight their decision, I took the easy option and offered my resignation. This was accepted all too hastily and without discussion. Frankly, my initial reaction was that it was a little insensitive, however knowing Bradley Haines, who always took the easy options, I should have known that he would jump at the chance to avoid a boardroom brawl. On the surface, it appeared it was handled with great sensitivity and good will. The retirement party was very gratifying and the customary speeches were very complimentary. The new 45 year old CEO elect, James Hunter, gave a short but impressive speech, which congratulated me on my work and at the same time invited the staff to "join me on a new and dramatic growth of the company." I think that he will be good for the company and I told him so. Technically, I am still employed but am taking both my accumulated annual leave and my long service leave. My final benefits will not be announced until the Annual Board meeting proceeding the AGM in December. In this way James could start ASAP and I am on call should the Board or James require my assistance. He is off to China and the US to negotiate supply agreements and reestablish contact with executives he knows there.

I appreciated your observations about the most stressful events in people's life — death of friends and loved ones, serious illness and change of jobs. I can tick 2 of the 3 boxes. Had it not been for my job and friends, I would not have survived Margaret's death. Not having a job has been an adjustment for both Mrs McMillan and me. The first week, I still awoke at 5 o'clock, was up and ready to have breakfast and then go to work. The first two mornings I actually shaved and dressed before it dawned on me that I had no place to go. Mrs McMillan still had my breakfast ready. I now bicycle to the newsstand to get my morning paper each day. This has the dual purpose of securing my newspaper and getting in exercise, especially the ride back up the hill. The second week, I adjusted to not going to work, stayed in bed an hour later and dressed more casually. Mrs McMillan was still there for my breakfast. I did not wear a tie. (There seems to be some conspiracy among friends and acquaintances to have me discard my ties or is it just the retired person's look.)

Last month, I cleaned out my desk at the office and for the past three weeks I have been culling through my wardrobe and drawers and donated clothes, including all Margaret's, with the exception of a few of her favorite scarfs, since they smelled of her. I put the scarfs in the bag with my 60 ties, each containing a small memory, including my prep school tie and a tie you gave me in college.

I hired a technician to help me set up my internet and broadband system, which required me to upgrade my telephone plan. I also plan to move my office into Margaret's office/sitting room, which is double the size of the space I have in the library. I will need to take a course to help me maximize my use of the internet.

I bought a used car, an old yellow MG TD, which is great for this area, but perhaps a younger man's car, rather than someone my age. However, it is something I always wanted to own and I saw it and bought it. This may be the new me. I am going to the gym and working with a PT. Last week, I went to the theatre with Michael and Alice Saas, who you met and who now live in East Grange. I had lunch with several people from the office but I have not gone to the Club. Otherwise, my social life is quiet and my days are not too busy. More and more, I realize that my life had been defined by my work and more so before Margaret and after Margaret died. God, I do miss her.

I have an invitation to meet Robyn Coleman, you may have remembered her as the Maid of Honor at our wedding and for the very touching words she gave at Margaret's funeral. She is now working at the local senior citizen Centre, where Margaret did volunteer work. God! I am a senior citizen? She thought I might be interested in the Centre's programs and might be able make a contribution of time not money. I plan to follow up on this early next month, since she is someone who Margaret and I love and is part of our family.

Please consider visiting me in late July or early August, since the weather will be fine. I plan to be in Paris in late August – early September, which will be the first visit since Margaret died. If you do decide to visit, you can bunk here, since I have plenty of room. I cannot believe that Alex and Charles are both in their 20s and fathers. It seems like only yesterday that they were babies.

My love to Jane the boys and their families. Mrs McMillan asked me to send her love.

Geoffrey

20 February 2017

It was not until the end of February that Geoffrey made contact with GoGo/Robyn and arranged for them to meet. On Tuesday the 1st of March, Geoffrey found himself at the Wilson Senior Citizen Centre, a place that an acquaintance unkindly described as the waiting room of a funeral home or the hospital. For years, he had struggled to remember her real name, since Margaret always called her GoGo. This reflected the amount of energy she generated. She was always on the go.

She and Margaret had shared rooms at Pembroke Hall at Bryn Mawr in Pennsylvania USA in the 1970s. GoGo (nee Robyn Coleman) was not who Margaret's great grandmother would have thought was "the right person" to room with her great granddaughter" but the freshman student adviser thought that it would be a good match for both girls. Robyn was loud, opinionated, and argumentative but a loyal and true friend. She was tall 173 cm and 70 kg, had wiry red hair, bright blue eyes and a an oval face; while Margaret was 168cm and 45kg with long blond hair, green eyes and Grecian face. Margaret did ballet and yoga classes; Robyn did gymnastics, basketball and Lacrosse. They both were in the debating team. Robyn gained entry to Bryn Mawr through an academic scholarship; Margaret through the alumna program and old money, although her grades at Frensham would have qualified her for an academic scholarship. Both excelled academically and finished in the top 10 of their class, Margaret at number 3 and Robyn at 8. There was never any competition between either for grades, friends or boys. Robyn used to say, "Margaret there is no competition between us for boys, because I like bad boys and you like good boys."

After Geoffrey first met GoGo, Margaret asked him how he liked her.

Geoffrey: "Honestly, Margaret she is someone you love; she is part of your history. Therefore, I am predisposed to like her."

Margaret: "Geoffrey, that is a pompous response, unworthy of you."

Geoffrey: "OK, I was being flippant. GoGo is not someone that I would choose as a friend. However, she has a fine mind, although a vicious tongue, and a good sense of humor. She talks too much and swears like a sailor on leave and she tries to impress people. She does love you and I can see that she would be a loyal friend."

Margaret: "That is better and what I expected of you. I can understand your reaction to her. My reading is somewhat different, since I have known her for over 10 years. She was the scholarship kid with no clothes sense, no allowances, no cultural background and no friends. Girls at schools like Bryn Mawr can be very cruel to those they consider outsiders and they were. We bonded immediately when in response to my question "Who are you?" she said "I'm nobody, who are you" It was a quote from Emily Dickenson, as you know my favorite poet and it was GoGo's as well. In Emily's honor, we often wore white muslin dresses to classes much to the annoyance of some of our classmates and teachers and in violation of the dress code. GoGo encouraged and shared my first taste of rebellion, which only strengthened our friendship.

We protected each other. No one dared say anything about me or do anything to hurt me, because they would have had to answer to Robyn and vice versa. She had to be the best in whatever she did to earn the respect of our fellow classmates and she did in the classroom, debating, theatre and athletics. Although I was class president, it was Robyn who they chose to give the valedictorian address at graduation."

Geoffrey: "I understand that but …"

Margaret: "Geoffrey, she is still protecting me and she sees you as someone who could hurt me, because she knows I love you. You must try to win her respect and trust, as she is trying to win yours."

Geoffrey did accept her and grew to respect, admire and love her. They attended her wedding in Sydney in October 1985, a simple affair attended by only 2-3 of her friends and 8-9 of his. George Lacy, the groom, was a tall handsome Qantas pilot. Margaret as her gift to Robyn hosted the reception at the Royal Sydney Golf Club. At the reception, Geoffrey and Margaret had the feeling that this marriage would not last. This was prophetic, for less than 12 month later, a crying and pregnant Robyn arrived on their doorstep. Robyn said the marriage was over, George had discovered another love – Simon.

Robyn miscarried and for the next 2 months she recuperated in Morton, first at the Bigelow Rehabilitation Hospital and then at North Grange, where Mrs Mc was happy to have someone she could take care of. At the end of 2 months, she decided to return to Sydney. She divorced George and started work in a large community centre as Director. She and Margaret communicated regularly and Margaret saw her whenever she went to Sydney on family trust business and they saw her together when they stayed at the Bigelow Trust's unit at the Astoria on Macquarie Street. She visited at least four times a year and often joined them in Paris. She was here for a month, shortly before Margaret's death and the following month at her funeral where she spoke eloquently of Margaret and her life.

Geoffrey had regular emails from her and spoke to her by telephone at least twice a month. He last saw her in Sydney in November, when she accepted his invitation to "Tosca". Suddenly, she was in Morton. When he received her invitation to meet her, he was delighted and here he was.

He arrived around 11:00 AM and immediately saw GoGo standing in the foyer, wearing a colorful kaftan and large earrings. She saw him and came barreling across the floor and embraced him and kissed him on the cheek.

Geoffrey was not used to public demonstrations of affection, but GoGo's enthusiastic greetings were always the exception.

Geoffrey: "GoGo it is so good to see you."

GoGo: "Geoffrey can you skip the GoGo and call me Robyn."

Geoffrey: "Of course Robyn! When I last spoke to you in November you did not mention this."

Robyn: "In November you were wrestling with your own problems and I was happy to act as a sounding board, so the possibility of my being accepted for this job was not important. In addition, I had been approached last year for this job but I had not completed my studies and my contract had another 6 months to go. However, in October I was free of all my Sydney obligations when I met Mrs Henderson, a Wilson Board Member, at a Conference in Melbourne. During an informal discussion she said that they had not filled the position and that she would be delighted if I could visit Morton and meet the Board again."

Geoffrey: "Yes, I was preoccupied with the situation at Robo, so I apologize for not being more attentive to what you were doing. Now that you are here, what are you doing?"

Robyn: "I am the Wilson Centre manager and resident occupational therapist. I completed my graduate course last October and obtained my certification as an OT. In addition to administrative duties, I am the principal fundraiser and program developer. Wearing my OT hat, I direct a team of professionals who work with clients who are struggling to relate to other people because of mental, physical, developmental or emotional issues."

Geoffrey: "But why Morton?

Robyn: "When I saw Margaret 2 months before she died, I had been approached by the Chairman of Wilson. I discussed it with her and she said I should advise the board that I was interested but wanted to obtained my OT and finish my contract in Sydney.   She felt that while Wilson Centre was small, it was doing new and innovative things and she knew I could develop the potential of the Centre and serve the community. You know how persuasive she could be!"

"Yes I do know", Geoffrey thought.

Geoffrey: "I think that you will be great for the Centre. How do you think I can help? Or (laughingly) do you think I need help?"

Robyn: "Do you?"

Geoffrey: "Spoken like a therapist"

Robyn: "If you'll excuse the pun it is an occupational hazard. In addition to wanting to see you again, I knew that you had left your job and I wondered if you needed something that would exercise your brain and provide you with a rewarding challenge.   That is why I called. I would like you to walk around with me and see what challenges might be of interest?"

Geoffrey: "I am all yours. I have allocated the rest of the day to my adventure here. In addition, I would like to see the place where Margaret spent so many hours. In truth, I have nothing better to do."

Robyn handed Geoffrey a map of the 4 floor facility, which was clearly marked with what activities were scheduled on each floor.

Robyn: "Is there anything in which you have an interest? If not, we will take the elevator to the third floor and work our way down and by 1:30 PM we will reach the cafeteria and you can have lunch or Devonshire Tea."

Geoffrey: "That's OK with me."

The third floor was devoted to quiet areas – library, a reading room where a book club was in session reviewing the Jane Austin novel "Persuasion" and focusing on the character of the Elliot family. Geoffrey's entrance sparked a degree of interest, since all 6 participants were over 50s women - men were seldom present at book club sessions. He impressed them with his response to a question about the character of Sir Walter Elliot.

Geoffrey: "I found him superficial and vain. He lived beyond his means and jeopardized his family by attempting to maintain the fiction of nobility and judging people on their looks and lineage. Not at all someone I would like as a friend."

As they left, Robyn, with a laugh, said, "Geoffrey you made several conquests there."

Geoffrey: "That was the last thing on my mind."

The music room contained many old records that Geoffrey did not have but knew he would enjoy. A portion of the room was for live performances and included a baby grand piano and a harp. A soundproof glass partition separated the library from the performance area and a draw curtain that could give additional privacy to those rehearsing.

Robyn: "We have recitals for chamber groups – once a week and a major recital in December."

There were 2 quiet study rooms and another room with three tables. Two covered with unfinished pieces of fabric and the third empty.

Robyn: "This is the quilting and sewing room and there are 3 classes per week run by Maisie Cunningham, who is a gifted quilter and designer. She was in the building earlier, so we might run into her in the cafeteria, since she has class at 2:45."

The final room was for English language classes and speech therapy classes for those who were trying to regain speech after some trauma or surgery.

The 2nd floor was devoted to crafts and computer technology classes, which Geoffrey thought he might attend. He was particularly interested in the woodworking and the block printing class.

Robyn: "Several in this class are in a prison supported program. They are learning the tools of lost trades in the hope that they can find work. Last year two of the pieces they produced won awards in our Annual Crafts Show. We are proud of this part of our crafts program."

Geoffrey: "If I remember, Margaret bought an inlaid table in 2014. It's now in my office."

The 1st floor was devoted to more active classes – a Pilate's class, a Zumba class, and a general exercise class. There was a small room for cards and chess, a bingo room and a large room where a bridge tournament was underway. The ground floor was devoted to the administrative offices, counselling rooms, a reception/large meeting room, and a large cafeteria. The gym, basketball court and weight lifting and boxing were in the basement.

Geoffrey: "This is impressive, I didn't realise the extent of the facilities nor the quality of the equipment. It also seems very busy."

Robyn: "More impressive is the staff and their devotion to the members and the programs."

Geoffrey: "You say members not clients!"

Robyn: "When the founders, who included Margaret and Mary Bower, proposed the Centre they felt that being a member would be more meaningful and friendly than being a client. It meant that people made a commitment and applied to join the centre and accepted the Terms and Conditions of Membership. However, no one applying for membership is rejected because they cannot pay their annual fees."

Geoffrey: "The cost of running these programs must be high. The Bigelow Racket Club, which charges annual fees of $3000 and has 200 members and only has 4 tennis courts and 4 squash courts, finds it difficult to meet its annual budget."

Robyn: "Because of the founders' generosity, we started with a healthy investment fund, regular donations and support from the town, the State and the Federal government and we have joint programs with both Newcastle and Northup Universities, AIDS and aboriginal support groups."

Geoffrey: "I might be interested in this area."

Robyn: "Then you would be following in Margaret's footsteps. She and Mary Bowers had the passion that inspired so many others to participate and donate. They were far more persuasive in their ladylike ways than say Bradley Haines, who I understand served as Chairman for 2 years and alienated many people and donors."

Geoffrey: "Bradley would not have been my choice for the Centre. However, he was the perfect choice as AFL Regional chairman." They arrived at the cafeteria.

Robyn: "Devonshire Tea? My treat."

Geoffrey: "Definitely!"

Robyn: "Hi Maisie! May Geoffrey and I join you? I am getting Devonshire tea for Geoffrey. Would you like some?"

Maisie: "Delighted to have the company. Nothing for me, thank you. Tell me Geoffrey … are you a lover, a writer of psalms or a warrior or all three?"

Although surprised by her question, Geoffrey immediately liked Maisie, who had a kind and open face and startling blue eyes and a wide smile. She wore no makeup but had a ruddy complexion. She spoke with a slight Scottish accent. She was dressed in a blue blouse that almost matched her eyes. He guessed that she was in her 70s but looked like she was in her 60s, although she was sitting, he thought she was about 155cm and weighed between 45- 50kg.

Geoffrey: "You put me on the spot Maisie. It would be bragging to say I was all 3, let alone 2 out of 3, so I would have to say a writer of psalms."

Maisie: "I already heard you are a reader and impressed the reading group. Why are you here?"

Before Geoffrey could answer, Robyn returned.

Robyn: "Geoffrey has Maisie already asked you whether you were a lover?

Don't answer her. She is a great flirt"

Geoffrey: "Too late, I already did and said I was a writer of psalms."

Robyn: "Then you're safe! Maisie, I asked him to visit because his wife, Margaret, who you knew, was a good friend. He recently retired and I thought he might be interested in our little Centre."

Maisie: "Well Geoffrey what are your thoughts. Aside from me, what does the Centre have to offer you?"

Geoffrey: "I am not certain what I want to do, here or anywhere? In the past two months, I cleaned out my office of 12 years of accumulated "things" and I have been decluttering my home and donating "things" to Vinnies. However, I could not part with old ties and my wives' scarfs, since they carry happy memories - part of who I am"

Maisie: "Many people in similar positions convert those memories into something else – a picture, a scrap book or a qu lt. Since it is fabric, why not join a quilting class and convert those ties and scarfs into quilting blocks and then sew a quilt."

Robyn: "That's an interesting idea!"

Geoffrey: "It is interesting and I would like to think about that."

Maisie: "There is no need to rush.   There could be other ways of preserving the memories."

Robyn: "Why not come back next week and we can talk further."

Maisie: "The 8th would work for me. If you do decide to go ahead with the quilt idea, bring the bag with you. I can then review it and we can map out a production program."

Geoffrey: "Either way, I will be back on the 8th."

Robyn: "Let me walk you to your car."

Geoffrey: "Thanks Robyn but I am fine. See you next week."

He left and when he reached the lobby doors, he turned to see Maisie and Robyn in animated conversation. They turned, waved and he left the building.

Maisie: "He really is a hunk. What do you think?"

Robyn: "I am not certain Alice was right, he does not seem lost and seems to have kept himself busy. I like the quilt idea. The quilt could become the resting place of his grief over the loss of Margaret. It may represent closure."

Maisie: "He may be still holding on to the past and the ties might be the connection."

Robyn: "You may be right. I know that his job and Margaret defined who he was and now he may be struggling to find out who he is without them. After all, they were married for 30 years and he worked for Robo for almost 40 years. However, you can't just stop remembering and I am not certain that is what he should do.

We need to work with him to help him find the new Geoffrey. This was the promise I made to Margaret before she died. During her battle with pancreatic cancer, I saw her regularly. She asked me to look after Geoffrey, who she described as her best friend, as well as her one true love. She felt that he would bundle all his pain and retreat into his job. She knew that he was no longer happy at Robo and would probably resign within a year, if so, he needed something about which he was passionate and to which he could devote his energies and talents."

Maisie: "And then this job opened and you returned here?"

Robyn: "There is more to it than that. Four months before her death, I received a telephone call from the Chairman of the Board of Directors of Wilson, Mr Patraca. He said that an anonymous donor had donated $450,000 to the Centre. As a result, they had a position open within 12 months, which would provide a 4 year contract at $80,000 per year plus a car. In addition, the donation included $100,000 to develop the Centre's programs. Would I be interested? I said I was. We arranged for an interview. I spoke to Margaret who was enthusiastic and said I should accept but that I should request a delay in taking the position until I finished my university graduate course and my contract at the Centre. I met Mr Patraca, the Chairman, Mrs Henderson and Mr Azzaz, who represented the NSW Department of Community Services. I liked them and, apparently, they liked me because I received a letter acknowledging their interest and an invitation to contact them later in a year. The rest you know."

Maisie: "Do you think that Margaret was the anonymous donor?"

Robyn: "She could have been. Margaret had money of her own and she inherited money when her parents died. It is possible that without Geoffrey's knowledge, she arranged for the funds to be donated."

Maisie: "What a lovely story."

Robyn: "Yes but it does place certain obligations on me to fulfil my commitment to Margaret to look after Geoffrey and not tell him."

Maisie: "Well it is up to Geoffrey to decide what he wants to do."

Robyn: "Yes, if he decides to commit to a memory quilt, I can provide funds to support the quilt project from the discretionary funds left to me. However, I doubt that this will be necessary, since he has his own money."

6.   THE THINKING SEAT

* * *

After the meeting, Geoffrey decided to drive his MG through Summer's Park, since it was a warm day.   A visit to the park always helped him think.   As if by its own accord, the car stopped near a spot that Margaret had regarded as her own, a large Weeping Willow tree planted by her great grandfather and located on the bank of the Grove River.   Margaret said that she often came there as a young girl to read and as a young women to avoid the constrictions of her great grandmother, grandmother and mother and to write and read.

Margaret: "It was my sanctuary, my special place. Aside from my reading and my writing in my diary, I came here whenever I felt the need to be alone or work out a problem or when I was faced with a major decision – choosing Bryn Mawr and when I decided that I would marry you, if you asked me."

Geoffrey: "When was that?"

Margaret: "Two weeks after I met you."

The Weeping Willow was on land that once extended from the Bigelow property to the Grove River. Her grandfather had donated the land and funds as part of the Bigelow commitment to the Summer Park Trust to preserve the natural habitat for local birds and wild geese and native plants and animals.   Owing to erosion, the tree's roots settled into the river and one of the branches was low and wide enough for two to sit over the Grove River and dangle their feet.   Geoffrey proposed under this tree and she accepted his proposal and his grandmother's engagement ring, which he had sized for Margaret's fingers.

Margaret: "It fits perfectly. When did you do this?"

Geoffrey: "Four weeks after we met."

Margaret: "We did waste a lot of time!"

Geoffrey: "But it was worth the wait."

Margaret: "My gift to you is this branch. Will you accept it?"

Geoffrey: "Yes. Let's make this official."

Geoffrey then pulled out his father's penknife from his pocket and carved their initials on the branch. Margaret called it Geoffrey's Thinking Seat. They came here often, alone not with friends, since they considered this their special space. Geoffrey called it their "Sylvan love nest", since they had made love under its shade and secluded by the pendulous branches which drooped to the ground.   One day Alice and Michael asked where they went earlier in the day and Margaret jokingly said "to our sylvan love nest."

Alice: "Where is that and what did you do there?"

Geoffrey: "We communicated with our nature."

Alice: "What?"

Michael: "They were bonking in the bush."

He came here, much like Margaret, whenever something troubled him or he needed to think something through. He still felt Margaret's presence whenever he was here, it was as if the tree had absorbed a part of her. This reminded him of the "Tree of Souls" from the 2009 movie **Avatar**. They came here after she was diagnosed with inoperable pancreatic cancer and he came here after her funeral, where he sat for an hour in quiet contemplation and left with a calmness that he had never experienced before. When he decided to retire, he shared his concerns with Mrs McMillan, who said, "Go to your "Thinking Seat" and I know that you will find the answer". As soon as he was seated, he felt Margaret's presence, which seemed to be saying, "Geoffrey now is the time to leave; now is the time to move on to something different and exciting."

Today, he sat quietly as the setting sun reflected the light off the river and the leaves moved to the gentle caress of the afternoon breeze and he discussed the events since his retirement. If you were watching from a distance, you would have thought that he was talking to someone. He fingered the initials on the tree, with a laugh and smile slid off the branch, and made his way back to his car.

Before he reached the car, he heard a voice:

Mrs Mc: "Mr Geoffrey, we were on our way home and saw your car and wondered if you were OK."

Geoffrey: "Never better, thank you for asking."

Mrs Mc: "Since it is a warm evening, I have left two chicken and avocado sandwiches and lemonade and some brownies in the refrigerator.
There is lettuce, tomatoes, cucumbers and carrots for a salad, if you like."

Geoffrey: "Thanks Mrs Mc. Remember, don't bother to come in until after 8:30 tomorrow morning. Have a good evening."

Mrs Mc: As they drove away, she turned to Mr McMillan "He is always better after he comes here and has a talk to Margaret."

7.   NORTH GRANGE AND THE BIGELOWS

* * *

Each time Geoffrey pulled into the circular drive of North Grange, its simple beauty struck him. It was one of the 4 stone houses that had been built in the late 1930s by Margaret's great grandfather, Nathaniel Hawthorne Bigelow, using local labourers, including 4 Italian stonemasons. The design for both the Manor house and identical cottages had been selected by her great grandmother, Maud Adams Bigelow and was in the Tudor style. One for each of their children and one for the surviving spouse of the previous inhabitant of the Manor or when it was decided that the next heir should occupy the Manor. The name "cottages" was a euphemism that Maud adopted from her summers in Newport Rhode Island with classmates from Bryn Mawr.

Hawthorne Manor was a large house built at a time when guests stayed for extended periods and activities to entertain their guests were created by the hosts. Both men and women changed attire several times a day and women travelled with their maids and men with a valet and often a chauffeur. It was 26 rooms with fireplaces in most formal rooms. It was warm in the winter and cool in the summer. It had 8 guest bedrooms, 2 master bedrooms with toilets and bathing facilities, a 2 story library, ballroom. reception areas, billiard room, smoking room, small theatre, school room and nursery and a large office. There was also two small rooms for the housekeeper and two additional rooms for other staff. The house had a staff of 7 for the main house, 4 for the stables and 4 for the flower and vegetable gardens. There was a large chicken coop which provided both chickens for roasting and eggs and fertilizer for the gardens.

The original stable accommodated 4 horses and 2 carriages, with rooms in the loft for the stable hands. In the 1960s the stables at each cottage and the Manor were converted into garages for the "horseless carriages" with an apartment above.

It had a Pavilion and a pool house with change and amenities rooms. A path led from the formal grounds through the woods down to the Grove River and a boathouse with two canoes and 2 rowboats and a large deck for casual entertaining. Guests could also fish off the 12 metre jetty. The 4 stone cottages had access to the pool house along a path that did not pass through the Manor's formal gardens.

The Manor was located on the highest point of Morton Hill. It had views of each of the four cottages, the family cemetery, the orchards and vegetable gardens, as well as a view over the Grove River, the town of Morton, the Bigelow factory, the Divinity School, later Northup University, and the distant mountains. Margaret's grandfather, David Kendall Bigelow, was given South Grange, his sister, Mary, West Grange and his other sister, Katherine, East Grange. It was Katherine, who insisted that Maud was always spying on her, since she saw her each morning on the widow's walk with binoculars looking at each cottage.

At 45 Margaret's grandfather with his wife, Katherine, and two sons, 18 year old, Nathaniel Hawthorne Bigelow II, and 15 year old David Kendall Bigelow Jr, moved to Hawthorne Manor. When he married, Nathaniel, moved into South Grange. After the death of his father and Maud's decision to move to North Grange, which until that time had been used as a guesthouse for relatives and friends, moved his infant daughter, Margaret, and his wife, Elizabeth, into the Manor.

On the death of their father, Nathaniel and his brother David became the Trustees of the Bigelow Family Trust. In 1979 they decided to sell the family's interest in the Bigelow plastics business and factory, which for over 70 years had

smelled its age. However, Geoffrey did not mind this, since it reminded him of his grandmother's home in Toorak.

Mrs Springer, the rental agent, had said that the owners were less concerned about the amount of rent then they were about the kind of person who would live in the house. She said, "They want someone who will respect the house as it is and love it as they do".   It had not been advertised, but the Chairman of Robotic Solutions had suggested that he contact Mrs Springer. He was obviously an acceptable tenant for he was offered a 3 year lease. Since he was a widower, Mrs Springer suggested that he interview Mrs McMillan who had worked at Northern Grange for the past 5 years and previously at Hawthorne Manor, before it was converted into a retirement home. He met Mrs McMillan, a tall women, 173 cm and 70 kg, who was in her early 40s. The Bigelows had employed her family for 3 generation. She interviewed him not the reverse. She was Scottish and her family had arrived with the wave of Scottish coal miners in the 1800s. She was definitely a no nonsense person and he knew immediately that she was the right person for him. They agreed upon the terms and conditions of her employment. She advised him that her husband was the gardener and handyman and would be in at least once a week to tend to the grounds and to make any repairs needed; however, the Bigelow Trust would pay his wages, since he also tended the grounds of the other 3 Granges and the Bigelow Family Cemetery.

His mind drifted back to when they met. Little did he know that Margaret not only represented his landlord, the Bigelow Trust but that she was the Trustee. She inherited the Trusteeship from her father, who she had nursed through his seven year long illness. It would be a meeting that would change his life forever.

8.   MARGARET AND GEOFFREY IN LOVE

* * *

As a result of heavy wind and rain, many of the old trees at North Grange suffered wind damage. Mr McMillan arrived with Margaret, to assess the damage and to arrange for the cleanup of the property. Geoffrey always remembered how he first saw her. She was in her 30s, 166cm tall and weighed 50kg. She had an athletic figure and moved with a dancer's grace. Her light brown hair was tied in a ponytail revealing an oval Grecian face with blue grey eyes, a lovely smile and full lips. She wore a plaid shirt tucked into jeans with a brown suede belt, brown work boots and suede driving gloves. Mr McMillan introduced Geoffrey to her.

Mr Mc: "Mr H meet the representative of your landlord, Margaret Bigelow."

Margaret: "I am also your neighbor and live at South Grange. I hope that you are enjoying North Grange, although I think the interior requires a fresh coat of paint and more interesting pictures." She walked to the piano and played a few chords, which were from Bach. "The piano needs tuning. Mr Hamilton, I am afraid we have neglected you."

Geoffrey: "Please call me Geoffrey. I had meant to have the piano tuned but I have been busy with the new job."

Margaret: "I can see by the sheet music that you do play and some serious works."

Geoffrey: "I do play but only for my own amusement."

Margaret: "You wouldn't play for me? Please excuse my forwardness."

Geoffrey thought he could excuse her anything.

Geoffrey: "If you don't mind an amateur, you are welcome Margaret. Now can I help you with anything?"

Margaret: "You can ask Mrs Mc to put these sandwiches in the refrigerator and we can have them with something cold on the terrace around 1:00 , if that is OK with both of you. Meanwhile, Mr Mc and I will survey the damage and remove some of the debris. I have called our insurance agent who will be here later today to assess the damage and once approval has been given, which should only be in a day or two, we can arrange for the removal of the fallen branches and damaged bushes. Over lunch we can discuss your Lease."

For Geoffrey, It was love at first sight. He took the bag of sandwiches into the kitchen where Mrs Mc stood with a grin, noting how he blushed when he offered to play for her.

Mrs Mc: "Quite the girl, our Miss Margaret."

Geoffrey: "She reminds me of Katherine Hepburn in one of her early movies all full steam ahead and get out of the way."

Mrs Mc: "Funny you should say that, they both went to the same school. But, if you want to see a steamroller wait until you meet her college roommate – Robyn Coleman."

Geoffrey: "She asked me to give these to you and we ….."

Mrs Mc: "will have them with something cold on the terrace about 1."

Geoffrey: "You heard!"

Mrs Mc: "Of course, that is part of my charm. I hear and I anticipate."

That afternoon, as they waited for the insurance appraiser, they talked about the books they liked, the poetry they read, the music they played and their view on life.

He sensed she would have stayed longer, but she left with the McMillans with the promise that she would return the following day. When she left, Geoffrey knew that he had found his soul mate. She returned the following day and the conversation flowed easily.

It was several months later that she told him about her MRKH and that she could not bear children. Her telling him only strengthened his feelings for her. He had not thought of marriage for several years, let alone children. He only knew that he could not think of his future life without her being part of it.

He told her about his childhood, lonely and formal. How, after the death of his parents, he had lived with his paternal grandmother and her unmarried daughters, his great aunts, Alice and Estelle. He told her about his choice of St Xavier.

Margaret: "What were you like at Xavier? Were your nerdy or sporty or what?"

Geoffrey: "I was neither! I was needy. I wanted best friends and to be liked but I also wanted my independence and solitude.   I was on sports teams, I played chess, and I was on the school newspaper but did not want to be editor. I did not run for any class office. My self-esteem was low; however, I did have a best friend, Fred Russell. I see Fred and his wife and children once or twice a year and we write from time to time. He was my roommate at St Xavier and then at Melbourne University and we spent a year travelling through Europe."

Margaret: "What about your social life?"

Geoffrey: "As you may have heard and seen, I am a loner, I can be very focused and when I am in that mode I tend to lock everything and everyone out. This is especially true when I am practicing the piano or my harmonica or have a project.   Fred use to say to people "He's in his lock out mode." Some have said I have an inferiority complex, I would say that I am an introvert and a serial monogamist."

Margaret: "But I see you in a totally different way. I see you as an outgoing, funny and the handsome man that I have come to love."

Geoffrey: Laughingly "I am blessed by your discerning insight. When I was 16 years old, my grandmother and I had a bizarre discussion, which I thought would evolve into a discussion of my entering sexual maturity. To avoid this, I asked her if she thought I was good looking."

Margaret: "What did she say?"

Geoffrey: "She said the Hamilton men were never handsome when they were younger. They were passable. However, as they matured their natural instincts for fair play and their goodness were reflected in their faces and they became handsome men. That is what will happen to you. You will find someone who will appreciate your good points and will love you for them and you will become handsome, if not in your eyes in theirs."

Margaret: "She was right and I am that someone."

They had many such discussions, including Margaret's summer in Paris before she entered Bryn Mawr and her resolve not to marry until she found someone "exactly like you." They either saw each other daily or spoke on the telephone.

They were married in November, 8 months after they first met. Margaret insisted that the wedding would be simple with only a few close friends and family and held at North Grange. They enlisted the support of what Geoffrey called "The Wedding Team" – Tiffany Tyrell, Margaret's cousin's wife, Robyn, and the McMillans. Robyn, who arrived 4 weeks earlier, and Margaret sent out the invitations. Tiffany was responsible for the guests list and helped Mrs Mc with the seating at the wedding and the wedding reception. Margaret and Mr McMillan designed the garden, where the service would be held. Margaret and Mrs Mc worked with Steven and his partner, Mike, from Executive Catering on plans for the special lemon wedding cake, Geoffrey's favorite dessert, and the wedding luncheon.

Over tea, one afternoon 6 weeks before the wedding, Robyn, Mrs Mc and Margaret were discussing Margaret's wedding gown. Margaret wanted something simple but classic. Suddenly, Mrs Mc left and came back with a large box marked "Worth of Paris."

Mrs Mc: "Miss Margaret this was your great grandmother Maud's wedding dress. It has been sitting in the upstairs closet for years. She wanted you to wear it, when you married."

Margaret opened the box and unwrapped the tissue.

Margaret: "It is exquisite. Look Robyn, silk with seed pearls and a lovely seed pearl capped veil. I can't wait to try it on, although granny was smaller than I am."

Mrs Mc: "I think with a little needle work, it will fit. " They left to try on the dress.

Margaret: Viewing herself in the mirror. "I guess that I remember Granny Maud as a small woman. The dress fits perfectly and it is just what I wanted. What do you think?"

Mrs Mc: "It suits you. You will make a beautiful bride and Mrs Maud would have been so pleased."

Margaret: "I have something old, I have something new, the pearl earrings Geoffrey gave me. But I don't have something borrowed and something blue."

Robyn: "How about this? The blue garter that I wore at my wedding, which can be both something borrowed and something blue." Margaret: "I am ready. Now where's the bridegroom?" They laughed, as Tiffany Tyrell arrived.

Tiffany: "Margaret, it is beautiful and perfect for you. By the way, the Anglican Bishop's office called and said that he would be happy to officiate and Julian Day from the **Newcastle Herald** wanted exclusive pictures of the wedding."

Margaret: "No. Reverend Peters has been our pastor for the past 25 years. Please tell his eminence that we thank him for his offer but that we are keeping this a simple wedding. Julian Day is a real pest, but I suppose that we should allow the **Herald** to have exclusive rights, but for that, we will expect a donation to the Wilson Centre for the Children at Risk program. Robyn would you handle the **Herald?** How many people have accepted?"

Tiffany: "Fifty one accepted and 5 declined with regret. The ring bearer will be Quinton's son, James, the flower girl will be my daughter, Maud, and Mr Wooley said he would be delighted to give you away. There are only 16 people from Geoffrey's side, his best man, Fred Russell, his wife, Jane, and the boys and their families, Bradley Haines and his wife and Larry Abbott and his wife."

Margaret: "I know that we have left some people out, especially the American and English part of our family, but I have promised that we would see them during our honeymoon."

* * *

Mrs Mc: "Wasn't it a beautiful wedding" she said to Robyn

Robyn: "It was perfect. Geoffrey acted like a 20 year old groom and his face was beautiful to watch as he saw Margaret walk down the aisle with Mr Wooley. They are a lovely couple and very much in love."

Margaret and Geoffrey spent their first night in North Grange and left for Sydney by train from Newcastle. They stayed overnight at the Bigelow apartment on Macquarie Street and the next evening caught a Qantas flight to LA, where they visited relatives and several days later to New York City for a luncheon hosted by a very respectable Lady Rothschild and her two daughters and then on to Paris where the honeymoon would begin.

During their absence, Margaret and the McMillians had organised the much needed redecoration of the house. Margaret insisted that nearly 75 years of accumulated grime would be removed and that the outdoors would be let into the house. Geoffrey left these details to Margaret and David Leichhardt, an architect that Margaret had used for the Wilson Centre, since he knew that her tastes reflected his own.

He had brought very little with him, since he had sold the Toorak house and donated its contents to the National Gallery of Victoria and placed the remainder in storage.. When he moved to Morton, he had his books, record collection, two paintings – an early Stretton and a Brett Whitley – and a Frederic Remington bronze. These would be placed in his new office, which had been the library. Before they left, they had emptied the library and donated the books they did not want to Northup University Library and paintings by lesser known Hunter Valley and NSW artists to the Newcastle Art Gallery.

When they returned, the house had been painted, the floors sanded and polished, as were the shaker like styled wainscoting and wooden staircase. The new drapes were light and floral. Chairs were recovered and pictures transferred from storage and Margaret's house were hung according to the plan Margaret had drawn before she left. A picture by John Singer Sargent of Margaret's great grandmother, Maud, wearing a pale pink silk dress with pearls tied around her waist, similar to the painting of her friend Isabella Stewart Gardiner, was hung above the fireplace in the living room against a pale pink wall.

In their bedroom, which was painted pale rose, she had 2 small Renoir sketches and a large Monet watercolor. In addition to his artwork, in his new office she added 2 large Audubon prints and a cast iron bust of Rodin. In her study and office were 2 Margaret Preston prints and a Paul Klee 1914 watercolour 'In the House in St Germain', which reminded her of the time she spent in Paris studying art and drinking at the Café Les Deux Magots, while listening to outdoor concerts in the square opposite St Germain des Pres Church. The 2 additional bedrooms, while painted, remained in their original condition to be renovated later. Margaret retained the duplicate samplers in each bedroom that were created by Maud and read:

Margaret, Geoffrey and their guests found this amusing.

Mrs McMillan was delighted with the new kitchen, as was Geoffrey with Mr McMillan's outdoor barbecue and oven, the enlarged terrace off the lounge area and the new French doors.

Prior to their marriage, Margaret had met with Mr Woolley a Trustee of the Bigelow estate. He advised her to have Geoffrey sign a pre-nuptial agreement, which she refused. She argued that Geoffrey's personal assets were substantial and he had not thought of a pre-nuptial agreement. Instead, she asked him to meet with Geoffrey and explain the details of the Bigelow Family Trust and the restrictions that it imposed over North Grange, in the event that Margaret died before him.

As Geoffrey understood it, the property would never be his because of a clause in the Trust Deed that stipulated that the house remained the property of the Bigelow Trust. However, upon the death of the heir to the Bigelow estate, the next in line could occupy the house or rent it but not sell it or the land. It also stipulated that the spouse of a deceased descendant would have life tenancy at no cost. However, if they vacated the premises, married or died, the next descendant would be able to take possession. He often teased her by saying that he liked being a "kept man".

9.   MARGARET

* * *

Mr Mc Millan looked at the headstone and removed the dead leaves and flowers that had accumulated since their last visit.   Mrs McMillan arranged the camellias and white rosebuds picked from North Grange. She also placed flowers at the Bigelow Mausoleum, a simple replica of the stone cottages made by the same Italian stonemasons. It housed 3 generations of Bigelows. Margaret had joked that she did not want to share her eternity with her mother and father and grandparents, so she and Geoffrey had a double sided tombstone made from polished black onyx, which Margaret said possessed mystical qualities.

Mr Mc: "The sum of a person's life on a headstone. She was born, she died and she was loved."

Mrs Mc: "But there was so much more to our Margaret."

Margaret Adams Bigelow was the only child of Nathaniel Hawthorne Bigelow Junior and Lady Elizabeth Spencer Bigelow, a descendant of an old English aristocratic family. She was the great granddaughter of Nathaniel Hawthorne Bigelow and Maud Adams, a direct descendant of two American Presidents, and great great grandchild of David Kendall Bigelow. She was born into a family of wealth and social position. In the 1930s – 50s, the Bigelows were one of the leading families in New South Wales due to their wealth and ownership of the single largest manufacturing factory in the Hunter Valley and extensive coal interests..

As befitting the heiress to the Bigelow fortune and social position, Margaret was educated at home by a series of tutors in English, French, Latin, mathematics, geography and Australian and American world history. She took ballet and ballroom dance and piano and art lessons, in which she excelled, and, under the direction of her great grandmother and mother, deportment and etiquette sessions. Her father taught her to ride at an early age and she had her own horse by the time she was 10. She competed successfully in the local horse shows in the Hunter Valley and Newcastle area and later in Sydney at the annual Royal Easter Show.

At an early age, both her grandfather and father involved her in the family business and instilled in her the social responsibility of inherited wealth and the idea that giving was something that someone did without expectation of an acknowledgement or a reward but part of a social contract between those that had wealth and those that did not. Her grandfather explained that the term philanthropy was Greek and meant "love of mankind" and that the act of giving was a commitment to benefiting the needs of others through the gift of time, energy and money.

Her great grandfather had established the Bigelow Family Trust, in which in part her father, his brother and sister and their heirs were beneficiaries, as were a number of not-for-profit organisations like the Bigelow Rehabilitation Hospital. Her great grandmother had created the Margaret Bigelow Trust that provided funds for Margaret's social, medical, educational and cultural needs, as well as her personal needs. It was Maud's belief that every women had the right to an independent source of income and should not be dependent on their husband should they choose to marry and have an income should they choose not to marry.

At 12, she was a striking girl with long blond hair, blue grey eyes and an oval face. As a result of her ballet and her grandmother's training, she walked with grace and strength from years of riding, training and grooming horses. She was 168 cm and weighed 45 kg. It was at that age that her parents and her great grandmother decided that she should be sent to boarding school to meet other young ladies. They selected Fresham in Mittagong where her mother had boarded. Her great grandmother would have preferred a Swiss Finishing school for ladies, but after meeting with the Headmistress, Miss Bryant, she was confident that her great granddaughter would receive a solid education and the necessary social graces that would both prepare her for university and for her future role in society.

In preparation for her entry to Frensham, she underwent a complete physical at Women's Hospital in Paddington where it was discovered that she had MRKH, Mayer-Rokitansky-Kuster-Hauser syndrome, which meant she was born without a uterus. After exhaustve tests and consultations with Australian and overseas specialists, it was concluded that nothing could be done. It his was devastating to her family. Margaret accepted that she would bear no children. No member of the family ever spoke of it again.

Margaret attended Frensham and blossomed academically and socially. In 1969, she graduated second in her class of 100 and was valedictorian and head girl. She had won awards in dance, art and French and had even achieved some distinction in crafts. Upon graduation, she had her choice of scholarships to Sydney and Melbourne Universities. However, her great grandmother suggested that she delay further studies for a year and attend the L'Ecole Nationale Superiere des Beau-Arts in Paris and study dance and art while perfecting her French.

Although, in the previous year, she had inherited $50,000 from her great grandfather, her grandparents offered to pay the cost of her year in Paris, including tuition, room and board and give her a weekly allowance. Margaret decided to invest a portion of the $50,000 and on the advice of her father opened an account with Gallant & Associates and was assigned to Paul Gallant, the son of the principal, who would remain her broker and friend until her death. This was the beginning of Margaret's interest in investments and the development of her portfolio.

Her great grandmother decided to accompany Margaret to Paris. In July 1969, they flew by Qantas, to San Francisco, where they visited relatives, and then to New York, where they met Boston and Philadelphia relatives and a few of Maud's old college friends. As a surprise, Maud advised Margaret that one of her old friends' granddaughter would be travelling with them and would room with Margaret in Paris while attending the same school. Thus entered Morgan Fairchild into Margaret's life. Maud had booked two suites on one of the last voyages of the Queen Mary from New York to Southampton and they left two days later. The voyage was uneventful, although Morgan managed to attract the attention of a number of eligible bachelors. They docked at Southampton, where a member of the Spencer family met them. They stayed at the St James Hotel, which was Maud's favorite hotel whenever she was in London, owing to the fact that she met Princess

Elizabeth and Prince Philip there, shortly before their engagement in July 1947. Two days later, they caught the Night Ferry from Victoria station to Paris.

The Adams family had a long term lease on a 3 bedroom apartment on the Rue D'Anjou in the historic 6th Arrondissement, also known as St Germain de Pres. Over the past 20 years family and friends had used it and Maud visited it every two years. Margaret and her parents had stayed there several times. Madam Boucher, whose family owned the residence, had everything in order when they arrived. It was close to the Ecole Nationale Superieure des Beaux-Arts, where Margaret and Morgan would study. It was also close to the Jardins de Luxembourg and located next to the Latin Quarter, frequented by students from the art schools in the area and the Sorbonne, as well as young tourists.

The girls knew that once Maud left, they had opportunity to explore other areas of Paris and they did. People complimented Margaret on her French, while Morgan's French was passable, since she regarded anything remotely educational as a waste of time. Unbeknownst to Maud, Morgan was sent to Paris by her father to distance her from the "love of her life", an artist with little or no talent but, according to Morgan, "sexy as hell." Her father was certain he was interested in Morgan's inheritance and he was determined to thwart that ambition.

Margaret threw herself into her studies but decided that she would never be a ballerina nor a painter. What she enjoyed most were the social aspects of her trip, she enjoyed meeting people from different cultures and enjoyed reading and discussing art, books and music. She particularly enjoyed correcting images of Australia as a backwater country of Bogans, where sheep outnumbered people and kangaroos named Skippy were pets. She also enjoyed the anonymity, she was not one of the rich Bigelows but merely Margaret Bigelow taking a gap year between high school and whatever followed. Morgan surrounded herself with eligible bachelors and appeared to have forgotten her "sexy artist."   She certainly forgot that she was in Paris to study.

Morgan: "Margie, I can't decide between the future Duke or the Count. What do you think?"

Margaret: "Morgan are you going to marry for love or a title or money?"

Morgan: "What's wrong with all three? I haven't seen you putting a move on anyone. What about Sir Roderick, he seems smitten with you?"

Margaret: "First question first. There is nothing wrong with wanting all three but we seldom get everything we want. Maybe you have to settle for 2 out of 3 or just for love. Second, Roderick is delightful but he is more like Mr Elliot in E.M. Forster's "The Longest Journey" –"He passed for a cultured man because he knew how to select and he passed for an unconventional man because he did not select like other people. In reality, he never did or said or thought one single thing that had not the slightest beauty or value."

Morgan: "That is a bit harsh; he is handsome and rich and connected to the royals, so what if he's not an intellectual. How do you know when the right one comes along? My grandmother said that she didn't love my grandfather when they married. It was an arranged marriage based upon money and social status, her family had the social status and his family had the money.   However, he was besotted with her. She said, as they grew older, had children, shared many financial and health issues, she appreciated that he was a wonderful man, a gentle and thoughtful lover and a kind and caring husband and father. She said she always respected him but for a long time did not love him. She said it happened at a cocktail party. She looked across the room, they caught each other's eyes, and he smiled and mouthed the words "I love you." She said her heart stopped and she began to cry and he rushed to her side and she threw her arms around him and said, "I love you too". Isn't that the silliest thing you ever heard?"

Margaret: (With tears running down her cheeks) "Morgan that is the most beautiful love story I have ever heard.   I only hope that I can have that at both the beginning and the end of my married life. I do know that while it may not be the grand passion, it will be a meeting of mind and heart, something solid and fine and he will be my friend, as well as my lover. It may not happen immediately, but I will find him sometime and at an unexpected moment and it will take my breath away."

Morgan: "How very Jane Austen! Now is it the Duke or the Count? In either case, we have an invitation to this fabulous weekend party in Fontainebleau, or we can spend 5 days on a yacht cruising from Paris to Marseilles and take the Mistral back to Paris. No title there only a handsome hunk and some friends delivering a boat to another friend. You choose, but hurry since I have to organise my wardrobe."

Margaret chose the boat trip. The Captain was Alexander Reid, a Junior at Brown University in the USA. He was in Paris to improve his French and study at the Ecole Normale Superieure, which was located in the Latin Quarter. Margaret was impressed because the ENS was selective and one of the most prestigious institutions in France and well regarded internationally. Margaret and Alexander found much in common and to the annoyance of Morgan, who wiled away her time with two Spanish exchange students. They agreed to speak in French 3 hours each day. Margaret's French was the superior of the two and at the end of the 5th day, Alexander had to admit that his French and pronunciation had improved significantly.

Alexander: "I have always marveled at the French, they don't really mind what you say or do, as long as you pronounce it properly. "

Margaret: "It does seem so. Often the way in which you pronounce a word or use a word, seems to indicate a social class or educational level. There is a certain snob appeal in using a word or phrase in the correct context but this is not relegated to the French, it is the same in other countries, think of Spain's Castilian lisp. We have it in Australia and you certainly have it in America."

Alexander: "Let's eliminate all languages and all speak Esperanto, after all it was devised in the late 1800s as an international medium of communication."

Margaret: "Interesting idea, but the flaw in your Esperanto proposal is that it has its roots in European languages. What about Asian and African languages? In addition, would the French, Italians, Spanish, Germans and Russians give up their languages? I think not."

This continued through the trip, this intellectual tennis match between equally qualified individuals. On the last night of the trip, before the "crew" had their last dinner together, Margaret and Morgan were dressing.

Morgan: "You had the winner! Alexander was the 9, while Carlos is an 8, Enrique a 7, Warren and George 6s and Steven and Richard 0, since they are sleeping together. The 5 girls, Sarah, Olga, Monica, Susan and Domino were lovely girls but 6s or 7s, of course you and I were 9s."

Margaret: "Before you ask me, no, I did not sleep with Alexander, although I thought of it, if he were to ask me or the relationship had moved in that direction. However it has been the most intellectually satisfying relationship I have ever had."

Morgan: "So it was a good mind fuck? I can understand that, but it would do nothing for my libido. I need the physical contact, the give and take the ying and yang and then the bells and whistles."

Margaret: "And I can appreciate and understand that but that is not everything in life and it is not for me."

Morgan: "It damn well runs a close second. Let's both agree that we got something out of this trip and hopefully nothing but satisfaction." Margaret nodded and they left for dinner.

Margaret was back in Paris for over a week, when she received a telephone call from Alexander asking her if she could join him in a café near St Germain Des Pres where they had met previously. She did not know exactly why but she was excited by his call. She did not have time to return home and change, so she grab her Hermes scarf, Burberry coat and bag and arrived in her paint stained jeans and white silk blouse. Alexander was there with a much older woman, who he introduced as his mother. After ordering a cafe Noisette for Margaret and herself and pouring the hot milk, there was a pregnant pause. Margaret sensed that the reason for her being invited was about to be revealed.

Mrs Reid: "I am delighted to finally meet you Margaret. Alexander told us of your trip Marseilles and all about your discussions. You certainly had an impact on his French, it has improved. I am curious, are you related to Maude Adams?"

Margaret: "Yes, she is my great grandmother."

Mrs Reid: "I thought so; I met your grandmother socially in Newport."

Margaret wondered where this discussion was going.

Mrs Reid: "When I heard that Morgan Fairchild was one of the guests on the boat that Alexander delivered to Marseille, I was concerned, considering her and her father's reputation."

Alexander: "Mother is this really necessary?"

Mrs Reid: "Yes and I am certain that Margaret can understand what I am saying. Margaret, I don't want Alexander consorting with the wrong kind. If you were a mother you would feel the same way."

Margaret: "Mrs Reid, I am surprised by your insinuations.   Morgan is a perfectly lovely girl and my roommate. Granted, she is headstrong and overly romantic, but she is not a femme fatale. Besides, Alexander is not her type. Furthermore, I cannot believe that you would fly to Paris just to see if Alexander was consorting with the "wrong kind." (She looks directly at Alexander) I would have thought he would be able to sort this out for himself. Frankly, I really do not think we have anything more to say. Goodbye Mrs Reid, Alexander." Margaret stands up to leave.

Mrs Reid: "Well! I wonder what your great grandmother would say?"

Margaret: "Mrs Reid, if my great grandmother were here she would tell you to "Get Stuffed"". There was a look of shock on Mrs Reid's face.

As she was walking away, she heard Mrs Reid say, "That's what they teach young ladies at Bryn Mawr."

As she was walking home, she smiled to herself, wondering if that is what Granny Maud would have said. She also made up her mind that she would attend Bryn Mawr in the Fall.

She never heard from Alexander again.

The rest of the year passed quickly. Morgan Fairchild was engaged to a merchant banker, one of the titled English Rothchilds, much to her father's satisfaction and would be married in New York in early September. Margaret was accepted to Bryn Mawr and would enroll in September. She returned to Hawthorne Manor for the summer, where she socialised with some of the local teenagers, helped her father with the work of the Trust, reviewed her growing portfolio with Paul Gallant and worked at both the Wilson Centre and Bigelow Rehab.

She discussed her adventures in Paris with her mother and great grandmother, who agreed that it was a valuable experience and one that gave Margaret a new sense of maturity. She, also, related her encounter with Mrs Reid and her response. Her great grandmother was amused and said that while she would not have told Alice Reid to "Get Stuffed", she would have said something that implied the same thing. Margaret, her mother and her great grandmother attended Morgan's wedding in New York and spent 2 weeks shopping before they travelled to Bryn Mawr and the start of Margaret's Freshman Year.

The decision to send Margaret to Bryn Mawr was made by her great grandmother, Maud, who, in addition to her Adams ancestors was a descendant of Joseph Taylor whose bequest and encouragement resulted in the founding of the College in 1885. Maud graduated in 1929, the year after her friend Katherine Hepburn. While Margaret's mother and father preferred she attend Sydney University, Maud and Margaret's grandmother, preferred Bryn Mawr and their wishes prevailed, especially since they agreed to pay all fees associated with her schooling. They felt that Margaret's natural kindness and humanistic tendencies would be nurtured at Bryn Mawr but trampled by the male bullyboy dominated ethos at Sydney University, where women were often treated as inferior to men. They also were not pleased with some of the friends she had made during the previous summer in Morton, particularly with the Bower boys, despite their fondness for their mother, Mary.

Her time at Bryn Mawr went by quickly, enlivened by her friendship with Robyn Coleman. Upon graduation, she was accepted to Yale Business School. However, shortly after graduating, her father suffered a stroke and she felt obligated to return to Morton and assist him with his work and with his recuperation. For the next 7 years, Margaret and her father worked as a team. They complimented each other in so many ways and it was with pleasure that she took on his role of Trustee of the Bigelow Trust. She saw the Trust as a way of contributing to so many good projects in the Hunter Valley areas. In addition, she had her own portfolio and took pleasure in her quarterly meetings with Paul Gallant, who encouraged her to undertake a University course to broaden her understanding of the financial affairs of the Trust and her portfolio.

She enrolled in graduate courses at Sydney University under her mother's maiden name. She was Margaret Spencer from Newcastle.   She spent 2 days a week in Sydney attending to Trust business during the day and evenings at the

University.   She thrived on the course workload and because she was actually employing what she was learning, she had a better grasp of the subject matter than many of her classmates. As a result, she graduated with honors. She decided to use her real name on her Diploma and when the President read the name Margaret Spencer Bigelow, many of her classmates were surprised. Her father attended and they dined that evening at the Union Club, which was a comfortable walk from the Astoria where the Bigelow Trust had an apartment and where Margaret would stay when in Sydney. During an after dinner coffee, he gave her an envelope and asked her to read it. It was his resignation as a Trustee and the transfer of control over the Bigelow Family Trust to her. He explained that his doctors had advised him that he had only months to live and he wanted to put his affairs in order. Of course, she had expected the doctor's diagnosis but not the resignation. It seemed so final.

That evening they talked about many things. He expressed his concern that she had not found someone who would share her values and be a support to her and the Trust.

Margaret: "Father, I decided years ago that I would know when the right person came along. I have had offers from a number of eligible bachelors and God knows mother has had almost all the eligible bachelors in the Hunter Valley to dinner over the past 2-3 years. Most of them I already knew so that the dinners were never awkward. However, I know that it will happen and it may not be someone we know or it will not be a planned meeting. I know that you and Uncle David did not have your wives involved in the Trust's business, so why should you think that I would need my husband to help me with the Trust. I would rather that he not be involved and not know what I am doing."

Nathaniel knew that there was no way in which he would win this discussion with his daughter, after all he and his father had involved her in the work of the Trust, since she was a teenager, and encouraged her to express her opinion, so he changed the subject.

Within a year he, Elizabeth and Maud would be dead and Margaret would be he responsible for the Bigelow Trust and its assets.

10. GEOFFREY'S COMMITMENT

* * *

Geoffrey arrived early at the Wilson Centre on the 8th of March with his backpack filled with his ties and Margaret's scarfs and saw Robyn in the foyer.

Robyn: "What a pleasant surprise! I was just going to the Cafeteria for my morning coffee. Would you join me?

Geoffrey: "Delighted! Although, I had breakfast at home, Mrs McMillan comes 4 days a week, since she tells me I do not eat properly and at least she knows I will have a good breakfast on those days."

Robyn smiled and wondered if Margaret had also written a letter to Mrs McMillan to ask her to watch over Geoffrey. Robyn found a quiet table near the window where they discussed the quality of the muffins that Bryan had prepared. Reaching into his backpack, Geoffrey produced a shopping bag and placed it on the table.

Geoffrey: "Robyn, in this bag are some important memories of my life. I want to both retain the memories and move beyond them. Not wearing a tie is a symbolic gesture but creating something new and different, the quilt is a commitment to a new adventure. I am not usually an adventurous person, as you once told me or was it "Geoffrey take a risk, be adventuresome otherwise you will become a boring old fart." I feel the time is right for me, to quote from Star Track, "to boldly go where no one has gone before." To be a different Geoffrey and this would be a start."

Robyn   "Wow! Did I really say that? I might have thought that when you were courting Margaret. However, when you were married I knew that with Margaret, you would never be bored or boring, perhaps a little too staid for my liking but you have turned out OK.   However, I really am surprised but delighted that you came back and that you want to start a new phase in your life through the creation of the quilt."

He also knew that Margaret had been good for him. Although she had been 5 years younger when they met, she had maturity beyond her years. She was more social, more outgoing and more passionate about issues – global warming, good education for those less able to afford it and a supporter of cultural activities and a more passionate and inventive lover than he. He would have gladly continued living a quiet reclusive life, if she had not entered his life over 30 years ago. A life that was never boring and filled with love and happiness.

Geoffrey: "OK. When and !where do we begin. I need to give these to Maisie, who will review it and once she reviews it, she will decide what steps need to be taken and then allocate the space and time to produce the quilt. I will give her this bag today and we can meet with you tomorrow at 11 o'clock. Since you are here, why not explore the Centre and, perhaps drop in on one of the craft's projects. I have had a Guest Membership card prepared, so you can roam freely throughout the building. "

Geoffrey was on his own and decided to go to the music room/library and explore what they had there. The library was empty but from the music room came the sounds of a Chopin like piano sonata played with exceptional skill and sensitivity. He could not see who was playing, since the blinds were drawn. He resisted the temptation to enter the room, since he did not want to disturbed the pianist nor his appreciation. He sat in reverential silence relishing the moment. Suddenly, there was a bang and then he heard "Shit, I'll never get this fucking thing right". The door of the music room flew open and a person with purple hair emerged and was as startled to see Geoffrey, as he was to see him or her.

Barry: "Sorry about that mate but I can never get that phrase right. My name is Barry and I am one of the peculiar birds that inhabit this place."

Geoffrey: "I'm Geoffrey and new to the Centre. As someone who also plays the piano, I was sitting here appreciating the music and your sensitive interpretation. However, I did not recognise the piece. Was it Chopin or Schubert?"

Barry: "No Geoff, it was a Barry Oliver! Must go! See you around."

With a fling of a feather boa, he left, leaving Geoffrey stunned by the revelation that the music he had heard was written and performed by that eccentric fellow. He thought, "What other talents and characters did this place hold?"

On Tuesday, Robyn had delivered Geoffrey's bag to Maisie and they discussed how the project could unfold.

Maisie: "Robyn, there is not enough material for a full quilt, perhaps 2 panels of an 8 panel quilt. In addition, if this is to be truly meaningful, Geoffrey will have to create the panels himself. What do you think he would say to have other men join him in this project?"

Robyn: "I am not certain. He might prefer to have the 2 panels and then have them framed. Do you have anyone in mind? I have 3 people who could benefit from this type of project and you know them all – Barry, Bryan and Russell."

Maisie: "I would like to involve them in more activities but what a strange bunch to throw at Geoffrey. What would entice them to participate?"

Robyn: "Barry will not be a problem, he will like the idea of using his artistic talents and he really is supportive of others; Bryan and Russell have stories to tell and perhaps this is an outlet for them."

Maisie: "I agree about Barry but I am not so sure about Bryan and Russell. I am not certain about their reaction to Barry being part of the project."

Robyn: "Barry and Bryan are both in the DADs program, so they already have a relationship and both are under the influence of Mary Bowe. However, ultimately, it will be Geoffrey's call. How long do you think it will take, if we continue with a full quilt?"

Maisie: "This will be a special project. I would like to complete the Quilt by November and enter it in the Annual Regional NSW Quilt Show in December and our own Crafts weekend of the 10th of December. It would be good to have something representing the Centre and an all men's quilt would be something different. I can arrarge to devote one 3 hour session per week and allowing for holidays and other interruptions, we should be able to meet the November deadline. The two of us could meet with all 4 of them and we would discuss the plan. If they all agree, I would holc 2 sessions with each person in July-early August followed by weekly sessions with all 4. How does that sound?"

Robyn: "Daunting! Let's discuss this with Geoffrey. If he is agreeable, you can meet with Barry and then the two of us can meet with Bryan and Russell."

Geoffrey had a busy week. He organised to have dinner at home with Alice and Michael on Wednesday evening. On Thursday morning, he started a fitness program at the local gym with Euan a personal trainer, who George Henry, who had several challenging physical problems had, recommended. It would be a custom designed program that reflected Geoffrey' s age, weight and physical capabilities, as well as his goals– "a program for life" is how Euan described it. Although Geoffrey had continued his weekly running and occasional bike rides, he felt that he needed something more structured and Euan's twelve session program seemed to fill that need. It consisted of physical, mental and nutritional aspects – two 1 hour sessions – per week - I hour of cardio training and 1 hour of weight training.

11. THE SUPPER

* * *

All his life, someone else had cooked for Geoffrey, so his cooking abilities were minimal. For the past two months, he and Mrs Mc worked on the basics of cooking, starting with the "tools of the kitchen"– pots, pans, measuring equipment, how to read a cookbook and how to shop. Mrs McMillan was pleased with her apprentice's progress and Geoffrey was confident that he would have a healthy and tasty meal ready for Alice and Michael that evening. As Mrs McMillan said "Mr H buy good vegetables, good fruits and good meat, cook simply, have good friends and the rest will take care of itself. Oh. Do not forget the wine. Remember, no matter what you cook, Alice and Michael will appreciate it because it is done out of friendship and love."

He went down to the wine cellar, a place of many memories, and found the right wine for dinner. Before she had left for the evening, Mrs McMillan had set the table and laid out the dishes for dessert in the butler's pantry. He selected the music not too intrusive but calming. He walked on to the terrace, where he had set up the bar for pre-dinner drinks and paused to admire the garden that Margaret and Mr McMillan had created over several years.   He heard the footsteps and voices of Alice and Michael coming up the pebble drive and then the back gate opening and closing.

Alice: "Hello Geoffrey. We decided to walk over, since it was such a pleasant evening. I have never seen the garden looking so lovely. I love the smell of the jasmine."

Geoffrey   "Hello you two. I was just thinking the same thing.
Before you go, please let me cut some for you. I will explain to Mr McMillan, since he tends to treat each plant as one of his children."

Michael: "Tell Mr Mc that his children have been adopted and will have a good home. He can visit them the next time he comes to our house to do some gardening."

They laugh with the ease that friends with shared memories have.

Geoffrey: "What will you have to drink? I have been inventive and even made a new drink, which I call a Collada Daiquiri. However, Michael I have a Heineken for you, if you prefer."

Alice: "It sounds delicious. I will try one."

Michael: "I'll try one as well. What are the ingredients? Or is it a secret recipe that you will not divulge."

Geoffrey: "It was created out of necessity. Remember, "Necessity is the Mother of Invention." I wanted to make a Pina Collada but I was missing some ingredients, so I substituted other things and **voila** Collada Daiquiri a la Geoffrey made with rum, coconut milk, lime and a homemade sweet syrup made with raw sugar."

Alice: "Sounds easy to make. Bye the bye, if you want to keep your homemade sweet syrup put a spoonful of vodka into the syrup."

Geoffrey: "Here you are served in the glasses that you gave us on our 25th Wedding Anniversary. A toast to you."

Alice: "And to absent friends and loved ones."

Michael: "This is really good and it does have a punch."

Alice: "I agree. You must give me the recipe."

They sat talking for the next half hour during which Geoffrey rushed back and forth to the kitchen to finish his final preparations for dinner. In his absence, they comment on his general appearance.

Michael: "He looks relaxed and more like the old Geoffrey that I have not seen since Margaret died."

Alice: "It is more than that, he has a spark that he never had and seems much more adventuresome. Would Geoffrey ever have invented a new drink or cooked a meal or entertained without Margaret or Mrs Mc?"

Michael: "Well he said it: Necessity is the Mother of Invention."

Alice: "And often the Father of Experimentation."

Michael: "Nicely put.

Geoffrey: (Calling from the kitchen) "Once you finish your drinks, please come to the table."

They enter the dining room.

Alice: "Do I detect the hand of Mrs McMillan in the table setting and floral arrangements."

Geoffrey: "Yes, but I lit the candles."

Michael: "The artist assisted by the apprentice."

Geoffrey: "You mean the Sorceress's Apprentice?" They laugh.

Geoffrey served the entrée – avocado served on a bed of lettuce with lemon slices and served with a chilled white wine.

Alice: "I suspect that Mrs McMillan had a hand in the preparation of the meal."

Geoffrey: "Guilty. She has been giving me instructions on what to buy and what to eat – simple food, simple vegetables and quality meat and fish, good wine and understanding friends is what she prescribes. However, she left the preparation to me, so if the beef is overcooked it is my fault."

Michael: "That seems like a sensible recipe for good health and happiness. Speaking of good health I understand that you have joined a gym?"

Geoffrey: "I was given a life membership to the gym by Robo as a retirement present. I now have a personal trainer, Euan. We met and reviewed my medical records and general fitness.   Like Mrs Mc, who is also Scottish, he has a no nonsense approach to fitness, which he believes has 3 different aspects - physical, mental and nutritional.   I have my first session tomorrow and I have to prepare a self-assessment as part of my program."

Alice: "There is definitely a need for fitness awareness in people our age."

Michael: "Interesting enough, I have reviewed the statistics on aged care costs for a class I am teaching. Both the government and the medical health funds need to recognise medical services costs a billion dollar."

Alice: "And as the population is aging, this is increasing each year."

Geoffrey: "It doesn't have to be so. I think all those involved in representing those over 60s – the government, the healthcare companies, and the organisations representing the 60's + - are all missing the point."

Alice: "How so, they are committing more money to aged care programs."

Geoffrey: "That is just the point. A lot of money is spent on "case studies". In fact, one university recently received several million dollars to study a group of over 70s to find out what their needs are. We know what their needs are! The money might be better spent on pro-active programs."

Michael: "I agree! There is a lot of vested interest in health care, including the pharmaceutical companies." BUT what would you do?"

Geoffrey: "If I told you I could save $100 million dollars on the cost of aged care. What would be your reaction?"

Alice: "That would be an attractive incentive to all involved."

Michael: "Except for those who make money from the care and treatment of old people."

Alice: "You are a cynic Michael."

Geoffrey: "No Michael has a valid point. There are those elements within the healthcare system which benefit from people being ill or requiring care. There are others who can see that if we can keep people in their 60s and 70s physically and mentally healthy than the quality of their lives would be significantly better and the cost of their healthcare significantly lower personally and to the health care system."

Michael: "Extrapolating from what you're suggesting and using the figures that I have used with my statistics classes, roughly speaking $1 billion is spent annually on aged care for the 60s+. If you could improve the health of 10-15% of the 60s and 70s that could result in savings of $100-150 million dollars and provide a better quality of life for that group."

Geoffrey: "We are in that age pool and we are healthy. Why are we paying the same premiums and receiving the same benefits as someone who is in poor health? Why aren't we rewarded for good health?"

Alice: "Because we can afford to pay for gym and sports membership, we know the advantages of walking regularly, we have active lives and we eat well. We underwrite our own heath."

Michael: "And we have stimulating social contacts and we have jobs."

Alice: "I would like to see a reduction in our health insurance in the same way we receive a reduction in our car insurance for a good driving record."

Michael: "Or a lower interest rate for having a good credit rating?"

Geoffrey: "All that is true but aside from being from the right gene pool and having been kept healthy all our lives, we have the money!"

Michael: "Don't tell me that you're going to lecture us on our being the rich bastards who don't give a fig about the poor fat person who is on a pensioner's income and needs medical benefits. I don't buy that! Alice and I pay medical premiums, we pay taxes, we make donations to various charities and we donate our services."

Alice: "Relax Michael."

Geoffrey: "Michael, there are a lot of people who feel the way you do. In fact, to some extent I do. However, I believe that what we need is a paradigm shift in the way we look at aged care programs. A more proactive approach to better health. One that uses some of the money spent on studies and care programs to develop programs that assist people understand how to improve their nutritional , physical, mental and social health and then enacting programs that get them eating the right food, that get them moving on a regular basis, that stimulates their mind and provides opportunity for social interaction."

Alice: "Wow! You really have thought about this."

Michael: "You have my vote, if you are running for office."

Geoffrey: "I approached the General Manager of a major health fund, but was fobbed off to an assistant who said that they already thought of more proactive programs. She thanked me for my comments and that was it."

Michael: "Maybe you should have pulled the CEO of a major company card and used contacts through the Robo board."

Geoffrey: "I had thought of that but it was my hobby horse and I did not want to involve the company."

Alice: "Since you are not with the company, perhaps you should continue with your campaign."

Geoffrey: "Let's leave my soap box and get on with the main course."

Geoffrey removed the entrée plates and returned with the dinner plates, rib roast and roasted vegetables. When he left to fetch the wine, Alice turned to Michael.

Alice: "Is that a new Geoffrey?"

Michael: "I think so and I like him this way, much more assertive and committed."

Geoffrey returns with an open bottle of wine.

Geoffrey: "Michael would you carve the rib roast?"

Michael: "Happy to do so. What is the wine? I assume it is one of your cellar's best."

Geoffrey: "It is a Shiraz with a touch of Cabernet and it is one of 3 bottles left from the case that Margaret's father bought in the mid-50s."

Alice: "Then it must be a Penfold wine?"

Michael: "How did you know that?"

Alice: "Margaret and I would have our little wine tasting parties when Geoffrey was out of town and you were busy with some school athletic event. She walked me through the cellar and that was one of the wines we discussed and tasted."

Geoffrey: "Yes, that is it! A 1956 Penfold Grange Hermitage Bin 53."

Alice: "But Geoffrey that has to be at least $300 a bottle wine."

Geoffrey: "Probably more than that but it is a bottle of wine that I wish to share with my dearest friends. What would be the alternative? Not drink it and then die with it being left in the cellar and then distributed to friends as part of my estate."

Michael: "I like that alternative."

Alice: "Really Michael, be serious."

Geoffrey: "I don't like that alternative, since it would deny me the pleasure of drinking it and sharing it with you."

Michael carves the meat and passes the plates to Alice who serves the baked vegetables, while Geoffrey pours a small amount of the wine and tastes it.

He remembers the first time he tasted this particular wine. It was late in the afternoon of a rainy winter Saturday 4-5 years ago and he was dosing in his chair by the fireplace, when he felt a gentle tap on his arm.

Geoffrey: "If you are a beautiful princess, kiss this toad and he will turn into a handsome Prince."

Margaret: "Kiss the toad and get warts? I will accept my handsome husband without a kiss. But, I do have something for him."

She produced the open bottle of Penfold Grange and poured 2 glasses and then sat at his feet. They drank in silence with only the fire crackling and the patter of the rain on the windows for background music.

Michael: "Geoffrey are you going to share that drop with us, so that we can have the same idiotic grin that you have now."

Geoffrey: "Sorry, the taste of the wine brought back memories." He pours the wine.

Alice: "Were they memories of Margaret?"

Geoffrey: "Yes"

Alice looks at Michael.

Michael: "Good food, good wine, good friends. What more can someone have."

Geoffrey: "Good health and happiness. Now what are you two up to?"

Alice: "Aside from work, we are involved in the lives of 2 twenties daughters, Jane has announced she is a lesbian and Sue is engaged."

Michael: "I am more satisfied with the lesbian decision than I am with the engagement."

Alice: "Geoffrey, pay him no mind. He loves both of them."

Michael: "I do love them. I have a project! I have been coaching for 15 years and I have discovered a 12 year old boy named Billy who has speed, movement and brains. He is a natural in Rugby League. He can run, kick and his evasive tactics are inspiring, he is also a natural leader. I am going to work with him over the next 6 months and have him ready for the Australian Sports Academy."

Alice: "He has just discovered his surrogate son."

Geoffrey: "It sounds like you both are having a busy time full of excitement and challenges. I am also having my own adventure."

Alice and Michael looked at one another. Geoffrey smiled and took a sip of his wine waiting for the inevitable response.

Michael: "You're having an affair with Mrs McMillan"?

There was general laughter

Alice: "Michael be serious! Geoffrey tell all, remember you can do anything as long as you don't frighten the horses."

That odd expression reminded Geoffrey of his grandmother who said the same thing to him many years ago.

Geoffrey: "You know it bothered me that everyone kept on telling me to stop wearing a tie after I retired. I was attached to my ties, since many of them represented some event in my life for example, my prep school tie, the tie Margaret bought me in Scotland, the tie you gave me on my birthday, the Christian Dior tie I bought with my first pay. Every day I wore a tie there was an immediate and pleasant association with an event. Well, I have found a way of retaining those memories."

Michael: "You're going to bury them with military honors."

Alice: "Michael, you really are impossible! Continue Geoffrey and ignore this one."

Geoffrey: "I am going to incorporate them into a quilt."

Michael: "You're going to what?"

Alice: "He said he was going to make a quilt out of his ties.

Geoffrey I think that is lovely. What gave you the idea?"

Geoffrey described his visit to the Wilson Centre and his discussion with Robyn and Maisie and his commitment to the project.

Alice: "I don't think that you have enough material for an entire quilt, perhaps 2 panels of an 8 panel quilt."

Michael: "Geoffrey are you going to create the quilt yourself? I cannot see you sewing anything."

Geoffrey: "We are meeting next week to discuss the project and they will help me pull the quilt together. They suggested that I might have some help."

Alice: "I want to see you complete this project (looking at Michael) so Michael and I will help."

Michael: (Looking at Alice) "Of course we will! Is there a drop left of the wine?"

Michael and Alice regaled Geoffrey with the story of the visit of Michael's Mother, Olive, and her preparation of a meal for the family.

Alice: "It was the first time that Olive had ever volunteered to prepare a meal for us in our home."

Michael: "It was a great salad with 3 kinds of lettuce, capsicums, celery, onions, carrots, raisins, chicken and anchovies seasoned with basil oil dressing and garnished with herbs - Parsley and Oregano and feta cheese. The entire family was there, including the two girls and their partners. We had good wines and the conversation flowed easily. Even my jokes seemed to get a good laugh; in fact, everything seemed to be a joke. Toward the end of the meal, my mother said, "by the way Alice, you will need more Oregano, I used the last of it for the salad." The girls looked at one another and in one voice said "The Stash".   My mother had added all the marijuana the girls had hidden away in an empty Oregano can. Busted I said. They cried; we laughed."

Alice: "The next morning Olive said that she had had a wonderful sleep and she had none of her usual morning aches and pains. It was also the first time that we had such a pleasant visit from her. I am thinking of asking the girls to prepare another "Stash" for her next visit."

They all laughed. They declined Geoffrey's offer of a port or cognac.

Michael: "Thanks Geoffrey, but I have an early morning training session with Billy."

Alice: "No thank you Geoffrey, the wines with the entrée and the main were enough alcohol for me. It was a delicious meal and beautifully cooked. Congratulations to you and Mrs Mc on her training."

Geoffrey: "It has been wonderful sharing it with you."

Michael: "Follow up with the proactive care program and let me know, if I can help."

Geoffrey: "Oh! Don't forget the Jasmine. My secateurs are at the ready."

He proceeded to lop off a few Jasmine sprigs and wrapped them in an old newspaper and gave them to Alice.

Alice: "You are sweet Geoffrey." She kissed Geoffrey on the cheek and said, "Remember, we will help you with the quilt."

Geoffrey: "I will."

Savoring every drop, he finished his glass of wine. He felt that the evening went well, the guests well chosen, the food good, the wines a perfect complement to the meal and palate of the guests, the conversation challenging, amusing, stimulating and timely. It also had no reference to work and Robo, something that had not happened in over a year. Mrs Mc Millan will be pleased and so would Margaret.

He returned to the dining room and the kitchen and looked at the clutter. While he could have left it for Mrs McMillan, he decided to clear the table and rinse and stack the dishes and glasses in the dishwasher and turned it on. A half hour later he had finished and felt a great sense of accomplishment, one that only the novelty of the act can give a single person. "Perhaps, retirement is not such a bad word."

12. GEOFFREY'S ASSESSMENT

* * *

The night after the supper with Michael and Alice, Geoffrey awoke around 7 o'clock but lay in bed listening to the morning news on the radio and mentally checking off the things he had to do today. After over 20 years of the same morning routine, he still could not overcome the feeling that he should be up and dressed and ready for work. However, he quite enjoyed the leisure of these mornings.

He heard the back door open and close, which signaled Mrs McMillan's arrival. He had 30 minutes before she would have the breakfast table set and the coffee ready, and 15 minutes later his eggs, ham and toast would be ready. Mrs Mc would then join him for coffee and made certain that he ate every bite. Usually, they would discuss the day's activities but today she would want to know the details of last night's supper.

He jumped out of bed and performed his morning ablutions, including a shower and shave. Before dressing, he stood naked in front of the full length mirror to perform what Euan, his PT, called "Your Personal Assessment." It required him to honestly appraise himself physically and record details of how he saw himself and how he believed people saw him. He had avoided this as long as possible, for he neither liked looking into mirrors nor writing about himself. However, he had to have this completed today and submit it to Euan.

Euan,

I believe this is a fair and reasonably accurate assessment. My weight is 85kg. I am 173 cm tall and am 69 years old. I believe my body mass is 30% fat. I have a solid square shape body. I do not have much muscle definition but good legs. I am in good health and reasonably fit. I have an oval face and a square jaw, my eyes are hazel/green, my nose is long, my lips are full, and my hair is short and light brown with white streaks. My eyebrows are almost white. I have all my own teeth. I wear glasses for reading. People say it is a distinguished looking face. I have few signs of ageing but I do have laugh lines. I am soft spoken. I am reticent about demonstrating signs of affection. I seldom raise my voice in anger but my voice does command respect.

He remembered that when he was in his mid-teens, his grandmother told him that he was not a handsome man but was "passable" and if he looked after himself, would become more attractive as he grew older. Here he was 50 years later. "What would gran have said now? Probably, "presentable." Margaret always said that he was handsome and when they first met, he reminded her of Kirk Douglas without the dimple. He could never quite understand why she chose him. She always said that his inner beauty was what attracted him to her. Her support of his self-esteem all those years were the pillars upon which his life had been built, he thought when she died that the pillars would collapse and so would he, but this had not been the case.

He thought about his life. It had not been usual but he never wanted for anything and had more than most people, He was born into a family with wealth and social position on both his paternal and maternal side.

His father Augustus Terrick Hamilton, a descendant of Edward Terrick Hamilton, Governor of the Board of the Australian Agricultural Company, and after whom the suburb of Hamilton (Newcastle) New South Wales was named. After his father died Augustus inherited the family's shares in AAC and its coal mining interests in the Hunter Valley. This provided a steady income that, in addition to supporting his family, supported his mother and 2 unmarried sisters

Geoffrey's mother was Mary Piper the daughter of a High Court judge and a direct descendant of John Piper after whom Point Piper was named. His parent's marriage in 1944 was a major social event as was their tragic deaths, 2 years apart. She in 1947, from childbirth and his father in 1949 in an automobile accident in London.

Prior to Augustus's death, as the result of the impact of the Depression, he was forced to sell the family's shares in AAC. With the proceeds, he discharged all the family debts and established Trust funds for his mother, sisters and his son, Geoffrey.

After his father's death, his parent's home was sold and the proceeds of the sale and his estate placed in a Trust for Geoffrey and administered by their lawyer and his grandmother. At 4 years of age, he moved into his father's ancestral home, which was occupied by his grandmother and his two unmarried aunts. "Bonnygate" was a 16 room house in Toorak, Victoria that smelled of 150 years of ancestors. His room had been his father's, his grandfather's and his great grandfather's. It was filled with their toys and hobbies, including butterfly and stamp collections. It provided some sanctuary from an all female household, since no one was allowed to enter without knocking. The house was run in a Victorian manner. He had to dress for each meal and was expected to present himself to his grandmother before meals and his attire, his hands and fingernails were inspected. During meals, his grandmother or his aunts and occasionally a great uncle would correct his posture, his eating habits and inculcate the finer points of dining with adults. Until he was 12 he had piano lessons in the music room twice a week from 2-4. He attend a private academy that prepared students for entry into Trinity School. However, his mother's family were Catholic and requested that he be enrolled in St Xavier's College, a Jesuit run Boarding School in Kew Victoria. Geoffrey for the first time had a choice. "Which school did he wish to attend?" He chose St Xavier's, where he learned private boarding school survival skills. He befriended the biggest and strongest boy in his class, Fred Russell, who would become his lifelong friend and protector. He never tried to be the best and he participated in everything. He stayed in the middle of the pack. He excelled in his studies and at the end of 5 years he graduated with honors and he and, with his help, Fred passed the University of Sydney entrance exams.

In 1959, at the age of 17, he enrolled in the Faculty of Engineering and Technology at the University of Sydney and graduated 4 years later. At 21, he received $25,000, a part of the Trust left to him by his father. This allowed him and Fred to travel overseas with some degree of comfort for the better part of one year. He returned to Sydney and in 1965 and through his guardian's contacts, started work for NSW Department of Public Works as an electrical engineer and technical trainee.

His engagement to Alice Pendleton in 1968 ended tragically when a truck struck the car in which they were riding. Alice died and Geoffrey was hospitalized for 1 months with multiple injuries. At the suggestion of a great aunt, who still resided in the Hamilton area, he completed his 2 months of rehabilitation at Bigelow Rehabilitation Hospital near Morton NSW and, as a result decided to move to Newcastle. In 1972, he married Alice Higgerson, descendant of Mary Newbury convict, and daughter of prominent clergyman. She and their unborn son died in childbirth in 1974. He established his own electrical engineering practice and specialised in 3D and AI applications, while attending the University of Newcastle where he earned an accounting degree and a Master's Degree in Electrical Engineering.

He was engaged by Robotics Solutions to work on a number of special projects and was introduced to the CEO, David Smithe, who offered him a position as Director of Development. He moved to Morton, met, fell in love and married Margaret Bigelow in 1985. After 5 years at Robotics, he was appointed CFO, and 5 years later upon the death of David Smithe, he was appointed CEO. Margaret died in 2015 and now in 2017 at 69 he was retired. That was the quick sum of his life. He was still stark naked and starring into the mirror when he was startled by Mrs McMillan calling from the foot of the stairs.

Mrs Mc: "Mr H, you are dawdling, your coffee is ready and I am about to start your breakfast."

Geoffrey: "Be down in 10."

He folded the Assessment Report for Euan and proceeded to dress for the gym.

How is it Mrs Mc always made him feel like a schoolboy? He was positive that, like his grandmother, she would inspect his hands to see if he had scrub his fingernails and ask him if he had brushed his teeth. Geoffrey: "Good mornings Mrs Mc. It is a beautiful day."

Mrs Mc: "It is indeed. Here is your coffee, cream and sugar is on the tray. Thank you for cleaning up and washing last night's dishes. Why are you dressed in your sports clothes?"

Geoffrey: "I have my first session with Euan my new PT, that's personal trainer, at ten o'clock, so this is my gym outfit."

Mrs Mc: She placed her coffee cup down, pulled a chair to the table and said, "Tell me about last night. How was the dinner? How are Alice and Michael and the girls?"

Geoffrey: "First, the dinner was great. The rib roast was just pink and the vegetables al dente. They enjoyed the dessert. However, I could not pass the meal and the table decorations as my work. Alice immediately senses that it was your handiwork."

Mrs Mc: "You could never put anything over on Alice."

Geoffrey: "Second, they and the girls are both fine." (He decided to leave out the lesbian discussion) "Michael has taken on a project with a 12 year old boy named Billy, who he thinks he can turn into a Rugby star."

Mrs Mc: "I think Mr Michael still regrets that a broken leg stopped his Rugby League career. That is probably why he became a physical education teacher. He still is a big kid. The stories I could tell!!"

Mrs Mc: "Would you like your breakfast now?"

Geoffrey: "Yes, this morning I really feel hungry."

Mrs Mc Millan went into the kitchen and started preparing the eggs. Geoffrey continued to talk to her:

Geoffrey: "Mrs M I have a project as well."

Mrs Mc: "Hmmmm"

Geoffrey: "You know we discussed the ties and the scarfs that I had in the bag that you suggested I throw away or donate them to Vinnies. I told you I couldn't because they held important memories."

Mrs Mc: "Yes, I am listening."

Geoffrey: "Well, I am going to cut them into pieces and put them into a quilt."

Mrs McMillan returns with the plate of eggs and a plate of toast.

Mrs Mc: "Why do you feel guilty about cutting up the ties? It was the right thing to do."

Geoffrey: "No. You misunderstood me, I said I am going cut the ties into pieces and put them into a quilt."

Mrs McMillan looked at Geoffrey quizzically.

Mrs Mc: "When and how did this happen."

Geoffrey: "I went to the Wilson Senior Centre to see Robyn Coleman. She thought I might like something to do and we toured the Centre and during our tour we stopped in the Cafeteria and met someone named Maisie Cunningham, who is the Director of Crafts. During our discussion, I mentioned the ties and the scarf. She suggested that they might make an interesting quilt.. After thinking it over, I decided to commit to that project and produce my Retirement Quilt."

Mrs Mc: "I always liked Robyn. She was very attentive to Margaret during the last stages of her cancer and she was a loyal and true friend.   However, while you can do many things well, I cannot see you making a quilt. You can barely sew a button."

She could tell by his face and body language that this was not the support he wanted.

Mrs Mc: "Quilts are really difficult even for people like me who have made many quilts throughout my life – for weddings, birthdays, Christmas. If you want a quilt, I can make one for you."

Geoffrey: "Mrs Mc you don't understand! This is something that I need to do. Maisie is going to explain the process to me, she is going to devote time each week and she will help me design it."

Mrs Mc: "I know Maisie and she is the right person for this project. I would be happy to work with both of you when you are ready."' Mrs McMillan could see Geoffrey relax as he considered her offer.

Geoffrey: "That would be terrific. I will discuss it with you, after I see Robyn and Maisie later this week. Incidentally, Alice and Michael also volunteered to help."

Mrs McMillan removed the plates, as Geoffrey picked up his gym bag and waved goodbye as he headed for the gym. She watched him go and said to herself "This is going to be a very interesting adventure."

13. BRYAN

✳ ✳ ✳

ryan Bower was a larrikin, in the sense of noted historian, Manning Clark:

"… almost archly self-conscious- too smart for his own good, witty rather than humorous, exceeding limits, bending rules and sailing close to the wind, avoiding rather than evading responsibility, playing to an audience, mocking pomposity and smugness, taking the piss out of people, cutting down tall poppies, born of a Wednesday, looking both ways for a Sunday, larger than life, sceptical, iconoclastic, egalitarian yet suffering fools badly, and, above all, defiant."

He was a large man over 193 cm and 100 kg. He had a small round face, curly red hair with silver streaks and bright blue eyes. He had a scar on his right cheek that marred an otherwise handsome face. At 66, he was what some women would call a good catch, if there were not the drug history and the fact that he was an ex-convict. However, there were those rare few who saw through his larrikinism and found a fundamentally good person with a generous nature.

Three years ago, when she was 85, his mother had a stroke and Bryan became her sole carer. At least once a week he would bring her to the Centre to play bingo or attend a crafts class. She would then have lunch with Maisie Cunningham and one or two of her friends. Even in her 80s, Mary Kelly Bower had a sharp wit and sharper tongue.

Mary's father, Patrick was always quick to point out that his branch of the Kelly family were not the Victorian Kellys, whose most famous member was Ned, but directly related to the Kellys of Tasmania, a far more respectable branch of the Kellys in Australia.

His great grandfather, Casey Kelly had left Tasmania to seek his fortune in the Hunter Valley as a miner in the coalfields in the late 1800s. He found that he could make more money from selling alcohol than from mining and opened a small pub in Hamilton and invested in farm land in the Hunter Valley. Upon the death of his father in 1925, Patrick, his only son, sold the pub. He, his wife, Katherine Ryan Kelly, and infant daughter, Mary, relocated to Morton and bought a house on the hill and a building on Colliery Road, later named Elizabeth Street. They renovated the building as a hotel and pub and named it "Kelly's Paddock." This paid tribute to his's ancestors and to the Scottish/ Irish coal miners, who in 1884 formed the Minmi Rangers, the first soccer club in the Hunter Valley area, and chose Kelly's Paddock as their home ground. It appears that the Paddock was part of a grant to the Kellys by the Governor of New South Wales, Lord Augustus Loftus in the early 1880's.

Kelly's Paddock was a pub in the traditional sense as describe by George Orwell in "Moon Under Water" as having "draft stout, open fires, a garden and where the barmaids knew most of the customers and took a personal interest in everyone." Even now, over 90 years later and under new management, it had retained some of that old pub tradition, although the clientele had changed and there was live entertainment.

Mary Kelly was a legend in Morton. She had raised two boys and two girls, after their father, Dr Bryan Bower died during the WWII aboard the medical ship **Centaur.** She ran the family hotel she inherited from her father, and her household with the same military style that she had acquired as a nurse in the 2 years she spent in training in Ireland.

The children were always a part of the hotel. After their father's death, she sold their house and moved the family into the 3rd floor of the hotel. Each child had a bedroom. Her bedroom was both a sitting room and a bedroom and was between the boy's and the girl's rooms. There were 2 large bathrooms, one for boys and one for girls. All of the bedrooms opened to a balcony that wrapped around the hotel. In addition, there was a large parlor, a separate dining room, a classroom/playroom, and a commercial size kitchen. At various times, the children worked at the hotel. Bryan, always known by the family as Junior, used to refer to himself and his brother the "Bowery Boys", a name they heard from an American sailor, who described the New York City social scene of the early 1900s. Under the watchful eye of their mother, the boys began by sweeping the bar, laying the sawdust, washing glasses, eventually tending bar. At 17 Bryan, already over 180 cm, was the hotel's bouncer, when they opened a disco; the girls served as barmaids and cashiers and were responsible for the weekly inventory. All the children received a weekly allowance based upon the work they had done during the preceding week, 45%, they could spend, 45% was deposited into a bank account, and the remaining 10% went to some charitable cause. In that way, Mary provided her children with a good solid work ethic, an appreciation of the value of money and the obligation to contribute to the well being of others.

All the children attended local Catholic schools and all achieved good grades. Their homework was supervised by a series of overseas university students who traded their supervision of homework and tutelage in several foreign languages for room and board. Consequently, the children had a smattering of Italian, French, Spanish and Chinese, and Bryan could claim he could swear in 5 languages. The students earned extra money by working in the bar and cafe. Each night Mrs Bower had a report from the tutors and checked the homework and once a week she would sit down with each child and discuss their progress. Later, Bryan would refer to it as the Bower Boarding School and his mother as the Headmistress.

The boys, Bryan in particular, needed a firm hand, which was often provided by Sam Kelly, Mrs Bower's cousin, a constable and Bryan's godfather. Too often, he and James would find themselves delivered to the hotel by Sam. While it was never a serious offence, their mother would treat it as something that questioned the way she was raising her children.

Mrs B: "Boys, how could you do this again? You keep this up and you will never amount to anything."

Both the boys and the girls had the opportunity to go to university. Junior and James won scholarships to Newcastle University. Alice went to nursing school. May the youngest, married her high school sweetheart and the high school principal's son, George, when she was 18 and he had graduated from University and been hired to teach history and coach the soccer team at a high school in Newcastle.

Bryan never completed university, although he achieved a gentlemen's C and was the star of the University's Rugby Team. He never explained why he left. He travelled overseas and subsequently joined the Australian Navy where he served for the next 25 years, leaving as a Warrant Officer and a cook. He married and was divorced after 3 years of marriage. He had a married son, with whom he communicated but had not seen in 8 years.   He wrote regularly to his mother and returned home from time to time. After his retirement from the Navy and 5 years in Michelin hatted restaurants in Melbourne and Sydney, he returned to Morton to help his mother run the pub. In his 50s he was considered the most eligible bachelor in town. He had good looks, money, a vocation. a considerable amount of Irish Blarney and endless stories of visits to foreign countries. However, his life changed dramatically 3 years later when he was involved in an automobile accident, as a result of a drag race on the outskirt of Newcastle. The accident resulted in two deaths, the driver and passenger in the competing car. Bryan had facial lacerations, which would leave him permanently scarred, a broken arm, a broken leg, and some damage to his spinal cord. He would forever walk with a decided limp.

Upon his release from the hospital, he was charged with dangerous and reckless driving that resulted in the death of 2 people. At his committal, the judge noted that the accident was the result of two mature men behaving in an immature and reckless manner under the influence of alcohol. Two had paid the ultimate penalty and lost their lives and the other would live with the physical and emotional scars for the rest of his life. He sentenced Bryan to 3 years imprisonment with a possible probation after 2 years. Bryan's mother felt that it was a just sentence.

In September 2014, after 2 years in prison he was released on good behaviour and started his 1 year of Probation. As part of his probation, he needed a permanent residence and a job. His brother, James, and sister, Alice, had moved interstate, so they could not help. As for his sister May, she told her mother

May: "Mum, we can't take Junior! George has said no! He is now Vice Principal of the High School and he is running for mayor. How could he explain that he had an ex-con brother-in-law living in his house."

Mrs Bower: "May, he is family and you have an obligation to support your family."

May: "Mum, I do love Junior, but I will not go against George. I have a new family and I must support George in this, although it does hurt me to do so. Please understand!"

Mary never told Bryan about this discussion and Bryan never asked. Mary agreed that he could move into the one bedroom self-contained unit on the property she bought with the proceeds from the sale of the pub in January 2014. Bryan insisted that he pay his mother for food and lodging and she finally agreed to accept $500 per month. His Navy pension and his investment dividends and any money he might earn from any employment, would have provided him with a comfortable life, had he not become addicted to the opioids he took for his back pain, the result of the accident. One evening his mother discovered him in a drug induced coma and contacted her cousin, now Detective Tom Kelly. Together with his Parole Officer, Sam Ryan, a distant relative, and Dr Bruce Sullivan, the family's doctor, they arranged for him to enter the Morton Rehabilitation Hospital, where he remained for 2 months.

Following his discharge, he underwent back surgery. The surgery was successful and resulted in Bryan having almost no pain and greater mobility, although he still walked with a limp. At his mother's suggestion and with his Parole Officer's agreement, he joined a drug support group, "DADs Group", Drug and Alcoholic Dependency Group, at the Wilson Centre. His parole officer approved of his doing 25 hours per week of community service at the Centre. In exchange for this service, he could take any course it offered. He worked in the kitchen and created healthy and tasteful meals.   This led to his interest in sourcing local vegetables, fruit and meats and in his work with local farmers and vintners and helping develop organic farming in the Hunter Valley.

He also drove the Centre's Service Bus, which collected and delivered those who might not be able to reach the Centre on their own. This often included his mother. He enjoyed driving the bus and he greeted each passenger by name and with some complimentary remark that kept him or her laughing and sometimes singing all the way to the Centre.

Bryan: "Where is Mrs Davis? You must be her younger sister."

Mrs Davis: "Of course it's me Bryan."

Bryan: "You'll have to show me your ID before I believe it"

The other passengers would laugh. Mrs Davis, obviously enjoying the attention, would take a seat and say something humorous to one of the other ladies."

Bryan: "What Music today ladies. Old or New?"

Bryan knew that they would prefer the old, but he always asked.

Bryan at the next stop, "Hello Mrs Ramirez. That is a beautiful dress; it really suits you and makes you look 10 years younger. Is it a Dior?"

Mrs Ramirez: "You are a real charmer Bryan. You can call me Monica"

Bryan: "If I call you Monica people will think we are going steady and what would the other ladies think?"

So it went for the next 8-9 stops and then to the Centre. He would help them off the bus, since exiting was always more difficult than getting on. When they arrived, they were already in a good mood and ready for the activities for which they were scheduled.

Bryan enrolled in the woodworking courses because he enjoyed working with his hands and had done well in in high school and in prison.

Maisie, one of those who felt that she understood Bryan, was impressed with his furniture design and encouraged him to show a small brass and teak inlaid collapsible wood table at the 2014 Annual Crafts Fair. It won first prize, much to the delight of his mother and was bought my Margaret Hamilton for $350 at the auction held at the end the Fair. The proceeds from the sale of articles produced by the Centre members or donated by supporters of the Fair were deposited in the Crafts Program account

When Bryan's probation ended, in September 2015, he was offered a permanent position as chef with the Centre. He also volunteered to continue to drive the Centre bus. In addition, his enthusiasm for producing superior quality food resulted in his forming The Hunter Valley Organic Producers Association. With the assistance of graduate students from Northup University, the Association, he conducted seminars, developed guidelines for organic farming, and established a hydroponic facility that served as a laboratory for the University students but also produced fruit and vegetables that sold at local markets.

At the Annual Wilson Fair, the Association displayed their fruits and vegetables. This year their display would be in the form in a large cornucopia as the centerpiece of the Fair entitled "Fruit as Art."

Bryan would spend the early part of the mornings meeting with farmers and buying locally sourced products. He would then return to the centre to prepare lunch.   He still found time for his woodworking projects and sold 2-3 pieces a year to private collectors. Maisie felt that his new interest in jewelry showed that he had both good design sense and technique. He planned to show his first pieces at the 2016 December Fair.

Maisie felt that Bryan was in a good place in his life and thought that it might not be too difficult to convince him to participate in the Quilt project. Little did she know from where the catalyst for his participation would come?

14. BARRY

* * *

Few at Wilson knew Barry's story. However, no matter what it was, he was an unusual character. As he had said to Geoffrey when they first met, he was "one of those peculiar birds that inhabit this place." One could add a very colorful one. He was in his early 50s. He was small of stature, 166cm and slightly built weighing only 50kg.   He was a recovering alcoholic, who had spent 1 month in the Morton Rehabilitation Centre and now attended, "Leave It Behind", part of the DADs program at the Wilson Centre. He often dyed his hair blond with streaks; he had painted blue finger and toenails. He often wore makeup that made him look like Joan Crawford. He was always well dressed and once said to Robyn that he "would not think of going out in public without my makeup and my hair properly groomed." However, his general dress was more like Albert from the movie "Bird Cage" than Joan. He had exaggerated mannerisms, some would call this "camp" but kinder people would say it was a theatrical conceit. He was the star of the musical life of Kelly's Paddock and to a large measure Morton.

He was an American born in Fayetteville, North Carolina in the USA on 4 July 1967 and named Ulysses Barry Oliver, first son of George and Martha, who already had 4 daughters. The arrival of a boy after 4 girls filled his father with visions of teaching him baseball, going hunting and other manly pursuits; his sisters, the oldest 14 and the youngest 9, saw him as another doll that they could dress and bathe;

while his mother saw him as another person to take care of. His grandmother felt he could no wrong.

As a result, his father was disappointed, his sisters dressed him in dolls clothing, more Barbie than Ken, and his mother allowed her mother and daughters to assume her role in his upbringing. By the time, he was ready for school, his father had dubbed him his 5th daughter, his sisters were more interested in real boys, his mother had died and his grandmother assumed even a greater role in his life and indulged his every whim. He was a born entertainer and could sing, dance and tell funny stories.

Until he was able to find his theatrical voice, his early school days at a mixed sex public school were filled with bullying from his classmates and punishment from his father when he would not fight back. However, he was a good student and a talented entertainer, which made him even more a target of ridicule and abuse. Based upon his academic performance and through a well-connected teacher who recognised his talents he was accepted at Fieldstone Academy as a scholarship day student.

Fieldstone students came from upper middleclass families whose aspiration level was that their sons would make it into University, pledge the right fraternity, play sports and graduate and then enter the family business or profession and marry and have 2-3 children and that their daughters would make it into University, pledge the right sorority, become a cheer leader, find a suitable husband with money or potential, i.e. doctor or law student, marry and have 2-3 children. Barry did not fit into that mold. He wanted to be a star, he wanted recognition, he wanted love and he was willing to do anything for this but he would wait for his opportunity.

He was the outsider and had not had the advantages of most of his fellow students. Fortunately, Fieldstone required students to wear uniforms. Thus, the outward signs of the distinctions between those who had money and those who did not was not immediately obvious. However, the accessories did. The campus was an advertisement for the most expensive designer brands – Prada, Armani, Gucci, Boss, Fendi, Lanvin, Hermes, Valentino, McQueen However, Barry was smart enough to find a way to distinguish himself among his classmates and avoid any question of his financial position by asserting that he was a "minimalist" and "rejected all signs of material wealth". Meanwhile, he was in the library researching designers and fashion trends. He made it through his first term with little effort but a lot of luck and sheer bravado.

His home life was far from happy, his father, whose drinking had increased, did not like the fancy way his son talked and how he was dressed. If it were not for his grandmother and his eldest sister, he would have had no pocket money. They saw that he had found a way of shaping his world to fit his needs and they wanted to help.

His world came crashing down at the beginning of the term following the Christmas break when his classmates returned to regale each other with stories of Christmas spent overseas or in California or New York. He could contribute nothing to these discussions. Then his father was arrested after crashing his truck into a police car while drunk. This made the front page of the *Fayetteville Observer.* Finally, he arrived at school with painted nails, make up and blond hair.

While he received a warning from an understanding Headmaster about his physical appearance, he was shunned by most of his classmates and physically harassed by the jocks. The abuse continued during the next term and reached its climax with the sexual assault by two footballers, who said that he was a willing participant and available to anyone.   While he reported this to his teachers and headmaster, they ignored his complaints. His father felt he deserved what had happened. He thought of suicide but felt that that was the coward's way out. As a result, the assaults and slurs continued and he felt that he had no alternative but to leave Fayetteville.

Therefore, at the age of 16 and with $350 in his pocket and a bus ticket to Atlanta from his grandmother and oldest sister, he left home. He knew that he wanted to be involved in the theatre. He had talent. He had been in every school production as an actor, make up assistant, stage design and he did not mind hard work. He had seen a notice for auditions in the **Atlanta Constitution** for parts in a production of "Oliver". He knew every part, had a good singing voice, looked 12 or 13 and moved well. He went to the audition and was hired on a "run of the play" contract. He signed his mother's name on the permission form and changed his name from Ulysses Barry Oliver to Barry Oliver. He already had a social security number, owing to his work at MacDonalds in Fayetteville and a bank account at Wells Fargo, which had a branch in Atlanta. What he needed next was a place live. This came unexpectantly.

At the audition, he had met Alice Johnson, who also was selected for a role, and her mother. When Mrs Johnson found out he would be in Atlanta on his own she offered him a room in their house that had been her son's bedroom before he joined the Army. He offered to pay room and board but Mrs Johnson, a widow and a nurse with 2 daughters, Alice 13 and Taylor 10, said that she would provide room and board in exchange for his mowing the lawn, washing the car and taking out the trash and other chores. Barry, as he now liked to be known, agreed.

The night he moved into the Johnson's, he lay in his bed and reflected on the past 2 weeks and for the first time he was pleased with himself, he had a job at the theatre that included a Teacher for the school aged actors and a place to stay with food. He suddenly started to cry and was surprised to find Mrs Johnson standing at the foot of his bed.

Mrs Johnson: "Now don't you worry about anything, because you are now part of our family and we will take care of you."

She left and in the dark of his room he continued to cry and the tears were for the happiness he felt. They were 5 happy years with the Johnson's before he left for tours to Miami, Philadelphia, Greenwich Village in New York, Boston, San Francisco and in 1997 at the age of 30 he became a headliner at Le Faux Productions, Seattle Washington's longest- running continuous drag show, part burlesque, part celebrity impersonations, part disco-drag.

How did such a strange bird like Barry decide to build his nest in Morton? It started with his being part of the Australian tour of "The Bird Cage ". During its June 2005 run in Melbourne, Barry was fired for his drinking and his off stage antics. Stranded in Melbourne, which he called "a city with pretentions of being a great city but having no soul", he contacted a designer who he had met in Seattle and, as a result, he was invited to Sydney to work on a new burlesque show. This led to work on a new production of "Priscilla", a musical in which he had been involved in 2006, and invitations to provide costumes and set designs for various amateur and university productions. In May 2015, while at the Northup University 50 kms outside of Newcastle, New South Wales working on a production of "Cabaret", he collapsed and was admitted to the University's hospital with suspected kidney failure and for a week, he was in intensive care. Once out of danger, he had a meeting with Dr Simon Singh, who had been treating him and who had no illusions as to the cause of his kidney problem.

Dr Singh: "Barry you have a drinking problem! Unless you stop now, in 4-6 months, your liver will shut down and you will be in serious trouble. You need to take control of your life and give up drinking. You were fortunate this time but may not be so fortunate in the future."

Barry: "I know I have a problem but I have never been able to stop."

Dr Singh: "Did you really want to stop or did you like the high that drinking gave you? Did you try to stop for yourself? Did you ever commit yourself to a rehab centre?"

Barry: "The answer to all three questions is No, No NO."

Dr Singh: "What are you going to do about it?"

Barry: "What do you suggest?"

Dr Singh: "No, this has to come from you. I can arrange for one of our I counsellors to meet with you. I can provide her with your hospital records and my recommendations but you must decide what to do. Is that OK?"

Barry: "Yes. But Doc, why do I feel so awful! I am nauseous and feel like vomiting and light headed."

Dr Singh: "You are experiencing Stage 2 withdrawal symptoms. We have put you on medication to reduce the effects of withdrawal. If you decide to enter a detox program, you will be gradually weaned off all medication."

Barry: "When can I meet with the counsellor?"

Dr Singh: "I will meet with her today and give her details of your medical history. In a day or so, she will be in touch with you. Until then, we need to build up your strength. You also need more rest."

Barry: "Thanks Doc. I do appreciate what you have said."

Dr Singh: "I hope the appreciation will result in action on your part."

The next day Ava McManus met with Barry and they discussed the issues raised by Dr Singh and Barry's options. During the hour long discussion, Ava addressed Barry's questions regarding the treatment.

Ava "Yes, you will feel like shit. Because of the length of time you have been consuming large quantities of alcohol, you might hallucinate. However, the medication you will be given should help you to control the physical symptoms."

Barry: "When I finish rehab will I be cured?"

Ava:			"Unfortunately NO. Alcoholism is not a bug that you can cure. It is the inability to control drinking due to both physical and emotional dependence. It is not like getting over a cold or the flu. You will always be an alcoholic, so you must forever be vigilant; I suppose we can say that the "cure" is ultimately dependent on you. You, in fact are the cure."

Barry:			"Do I have to stop drinking altogether or can I have a glass or two?"

Ava:			"Barry, every person is different but with your track record and your age, and the state of your liver, I would counsel you against taking any alcohol for at least 2 years."

Barry:			"OK. What happens, if I have a relapse?"

Ava:			"Statistics indicate that 40% of recovering alcoholics have a relapse. As part of your program you will be taught to recognize what triggers the relapse and how to handle it."

Barry agreed to commit himself to a 2-4 week program at Morton Rehabilitation and then attend the Drug and Alcohol Dependency program (DADs) that Ava ran at the Wilson Community Centre in Morton.

Ava:			"I will make the arrangements with Morton Rehab and have Dr Singh sign the necessary papers. You will need to sign them as well. I will be back in an hour."

Ava left and Barry reflected on what had transpired over the course of the week. He recognised that this was a chance to overcome his drinking problem and, perhaps, find a new direction to his life. This wakeup call might very well be the catalyst for a change and Morton might be the place where he could start a new life.

Later that day Ava returned.

Ava:　　　　　"The next session of the Rehab program at Morton starts on the Saturday the 18th of June, which fits into your discharge from here. It also means that you can meet your new landlady, Mrs Bower before you enter Rehab."

Barry:　　　　　"Who is Mrs Bower"?

Ava:　　　　　"Mrs Bower runs a pub and hotel called Kelly's Paddock in Morton. It is across the street from the Wilson Community Centre, where you will be attending rehab sessions with me. She is willing to provide you with 2 rooms and 2 meals a day for 3 months for $2100.   This in itself will be a challenge, since you will be exposed to alcohol every day. However, she is a no nonsense women who you can depend on for support.   However, the decision to live there is up to both of you."

Barry:　　　　　"I really feel good about this! Doing rehab here is far better than returning to Sydney where the temptations would be greater. Morton reminds me of my own hometown in North Carolina, so I am comfortable with the choice."

Ava:　　　　　"I also want you to visit the Wilson Centre and sit in on one of my sessions and see what other programs at the Centre might be of interest.   Are you OK for money?"

Barry:　　　　　"I have regular income and I have transferred money from my account with Wells Fargo in the USA to CBA in Sydney and I know that there is a local CBA branch in Morton.   I am not certain that I will be able to obtain employment in the area, since I am not the usual person people would employ. However, I can turn my hand to much more than sewing and designing frocks."

Ava:　　　　　"Let's discuss this while you are at Morton Rehab. I will see you next week. If you have any questions I will give you my contact number. Please call me anytime."

They parted.   Ava wondered whether Barry's flamboyancy in person and dress would make it difficult both at Morton rehab and in the town. Certainly, it would make no difference at the Community Centre and she was certain that Mrs Bower would not allow Barry to be bothered. Meanwhile, Barry lay in his bed and experienced a feeling of quiet contentment something he had not experienced, since the days he was living with the Johnsons. He fell asleep.

The following week, Ava arrived to take Barry into Morton. He was dressed in a simple plaid shirt, jeans and mules and no or little makeup and he his hair was light brown with no streaks.

Ava: "Hi Barry, I almost did not recognize you, you look so rested"

Barry: He laughed, "Hi. You mean because I look so butch. I don't think Morton is ready for the full me, so I butched up a bit."

Ava: "I have good news. You can go on an outing with me.
First, to see Mrs Bowers., who will be waiting for us at Kelly's Paddock in 1 hour. Second, I will take you across the street and we can tour the Centre and have lunch there. I have to have you back here by 3 'clock."

Barry: "It will be good to get out of here and to have some real food."

Ava: "Is there anything you need to do before we leave"

Barry: "Let me just check my makeup and grab my handbag."

Ava laughed to herself. He checked his makeup and picked up a large handbag. Mrs Bowers was waiting for them at the pub. Since it was midmorning, there were no customers, so they had the place to themselves. There was an immediate rapport between Barry and Mrs Bowers, especially when he sat down at the upright piano and belted out a few tunes from the new musical Priscilla and gave a tender rendition of "Danny Boy." She showed him the two rooms at the end of the hall on the 2nd Floor, just below her rooms.   They were large airy bright rooms, one was a bedroom with a built in wardrobe and off to the side a bathroom with shower recess and toilet. There was a small pine desk with a chair, a double bed, a comfortable lounge chair and a covered pine storage bench at the foot of the bed. The other room had a television set, a couch and two comfortable chairs, a small oval pine dining table with 3 pine chairs and a small kitchen area with a microwave, fridge and sink and an assortment of crockery and pots and pans. The floors were polished pine. There were draw floral drapes, white wooden plantation shutters on each of the 4 French windows that overlooked the wrap around balcony.

Barry: "Mrs Bower these are lovely rooms and I feel I would be very comfortable here, if you accept me as a tenant."

Mrs Bower: "Anyone who can play and sing "Danny Boy" the way that you did is welcome and I would be pleased to have you here."

Barry: "May I have my things sent here?"

Mrs Bower: "Yes, and I will have them placed in your room and you can unpack them when you arrive. Any costumes that you have you can keep in the downstairs dressing room."

Ava: "Well I am glad that is settled."

Mrs Bower: "Not quite!

Barry and Ava looked at one another.

Mrs Bower: "Barry would you be prepared to perform once a week in our cabaret and wear whatever costume you want and maybe play the piano for the ladies more casually dressed one afternoon per week when we serve Devonshire tea? Of course, I would pay you or we you could do this in lieu of a portion of the rent."

Barry: Tears welled in Barry's eyes, "Mrs Bower that is the nicest thing anyone has ever done for me in a long time." His thoughts returned to Mrs Johnson.

Mrs Bower: "Let's consider this a trial. You can even design a poster to announce your arrival and we can have someone interview you for the **Morton Tribune** when you complete your Rehab."

Barry: "Thank you! Thank you."

He embraced Mrs Bower and kissed her on both cheeks. Mrs Bower was stunned, since it had been years since anyone had done that.
Ava smiled and Barry and Ava left.

They walked across the street to the Wilson Centre.

Ava: "Barry, that went well. It solves the problem of your having some income and something to do in Morton. People will accept you as having a role here as an entertainer, so that your concern about frightening anyone should be gone. In addition, Mrs Bower's endorsement will also count.

Barry: "She is a lovely person. I can't put words to my feelings."

Ava: "Barry this will be part of your home while you're in Morton."

As they entered the Centre, they were greeted by Robyn and Maisie,

Robyn: "You must be Barry, Ava told us you might drop by today to check us out. I am Robyn, the Centre Manager, and this is Maisie, who is responsible for the Crafts activities and a very good listener. We are a small Centre, only 6-7 staff members and 200 – 300 members, mostly in their 60s."

Maisie: "Welcome to Wilson. You might like to look through the attached list of programs we offer and a map of the centre."

Ava: "Barry is an entertainer and from what I have heard a good pianist."

Maisie: "Barry, those talents are in short supply here. When you are finally settled, please contact me."

Ava: "He already has accommodations at Kelly's and Mrs Bower has asked him to perform twice a week. He will be ready to start his sessions here in July."

Barry: "I am looking forward to being here and, if I can help, I am happy to do so."

Ava: "Robyn, Maisie I have to get Barry back to University Hospital in 2 hours and I want to take him on a tour of the Centre and then feed him."

Maisie: "I might see you in the Cafeteria. Bye."

Robyn: "Have a good tour."

Maisie and Robyn go into Robyn's office and Ava and Barry take the stairs to the 3rd floor. The music room empty, Barry sees the grand piano. Barry: "Can anyone use the piano?"

Ava: "Yes, you need to book the room or you can just come up here and use the room and vacate it if someone has a booking." Barry sits at the piano and starts playing.

Barry: "It is well tuned"

Ava: "There are some very fussy players, so I think that it is tuned on a regular basis. What is that you are playing?"

Barry: "It is only something that I have been working on for years and never seem to finish."

Ava: "Perhaps now is the time."

"Perhaps", Barry mumbles as they leave the room.

They finish the tour, have lunch in the cafeteria, and then head back to University Hospital.

Ava: "I think this was a very productive day. Don't you?"

Barry: "Yes! Everyone has been so pleasant and you have been extraordinary. Thank you. It has been a tiring day. I look forward to my afternoon rest."

When they arrive at University Hospital, Barry jumps out of the car and leaning into the car says:

Barry: "You need not come in. Thank you again for what you have done."

Ava: "OK, I look forward to seeing you at Morton Rehab in 2 weeks. There is transportation provided between University Hospital and Morton Rehab. You have my mobile number, if you need to contact me. Bye."

Barry checked into Admissions and went to his room, where he threw himself down on the bed and softly cried into his pillow before falling asleep.

15. THE CAINES

*** * ***

Russell Caine's permanent return to Morton after a 35 year absence was a surprise to all who knew the Caine family and Russell. In 1966 Russell graduated from Morton Regional High School, with reasonably good grades and several sports awards including the New South Wales Junior Boxing Trophy and other lesser boxing and wrestling awards. Within a month he left for Melbourne and a job as an apprentice tailor with his a distant uncle, Jack Canistesto. He convinced his father, Frank Caines, that the experience in Melbourne with Jack would give him the training he needed to obtain a trade and eventually return to Morton to run the family leather and tailoring business. Russell knew that if he told his father the real reason he wanted to go to Melbourne, his father would not approve. It was a half-truth. He would work for his uncle Jack and learn tailoring and leather work, while preparing for a boxing career. From previous visits, he knew that his uncle had contacts at the Star Athletic Club, which Russell learned was one of the best training centers for young boxers. Russell wanted the chance to train there.

His uncle introduced him to Pat O'Brien, one of Melbourne's leading coaches and former world and Australian Heavy Weight title holder. After he had demonstrated his abilities, O'Brien accepted him into the Level 1 training program. While he worked with his uncle Monday to Friday from 8 o'clock until 5 o'clock, 3 nights a week he was at the Star and 3 hours each Saturday and Sunday, unless he had a fight scheduled. For two years he trained at the Star and progressed up the amateur ranks and gaining experience under O'Brien. By the time he was 21, he had won the Amateur Light Middle Weight title for Australia and in 1990 was included in the Summer Olympics Boxing Team and went to Barcelona Spain. By that time, his father and mother had accepted that Russell would not be returning to Morton as a tailor. While they were proud of their son, his father was concerned for his future and his mother for the possibility of damage from repeated punches to his head and his handsome face.

In 1997, Russell's big chance for a major title fight became a reality as a result of an injury to one of O'Brien's fighters. Russell was asked to fight in his place against, Danny Calasoro, the 35 year old Light Middle Weight title holder. With ring experience and significantly more power and height and weight than Russell, he was favored to win. The press said so, the promoters said so, the book makers said so, but O'Brien and Russell believed Russell could win. He did, a lucky knockout punch in the 6th round. Overnight, at 28, he was a celebrity. Three years later, he had successfully defended his title 5 times.

Becoming a celebrity had been difficult for Russell. He was not prepared for it. He still was a kid from Morton, who, for the past 10 years spent all his extra time in a gym. Suddenly, he was courted by people who would not have paid attention to him in the past. He was able to enter clubs without waiting in line and found he did not lack for female companionship. Friends and even strangers wanted to share the limelight that was being focused on him and those around him and to use his new celebrity status to promote their own agendas. In retrospect, he did not know how to handle money and people. He was a trusting soul without guile. However, each month he sent money to his father, who deposited in an account for him. For over 8 years, he held his title. During that time, whenever he returned to Morton, he enjoyed his celebrity status, more so for his father's sake than his own.

During those visits to Morton, his parents reminded him of his family's history and the success they had made in their adopted country. The Caines were part of the 163 Italians, representing 12 families from Modena Italy who arrived in 1917 by steamer to Newcastle to seek their fortune in Australia, although several older members of the group thought it was Austria. Only a few spoke English and very few had ever travelled outside their home region.   Franco Canistesto, Russell's great grandfather, was 18 years old and his brother, Marco, was 16.   They chose Newcastle as an arrival destination and not Sydney, since more than half the families were farmers and had learned that the Hunter Valley had good weather, fertile soil and water. This was ideal soil to for growing fruit and vegetables and starting vineyards from the roots they had brought with them. The other half heard that there were opportunities for stone masons and other artisan jobs and work in the coal mines.

Russell's great grandmother, Carmelita, had been a teacher in Modena and started teaching herself English two years before they arrived in Australia. On the 5 week voyage to Newcastle she conducted daily English classes on 3 levels – children, young men and women and married men and women. She met the Canistesto brothers in one of her classes. Marco had an ear for languages and rapidly learned everything Carmelita could teach him and was soon conducting classes for the children; Franco, though not as quick, was far more studious and determined and achieved a far richer vocabulary than his younger brother. He also knew that when he had established himself, he would marry Carmelita.

 In Newcastle, they were met by members of the local Catholic Church and several Italian families, who arranged for temporary accommodations in Newcastle. Marco and Franco left immediately with a small group of farmers and labourers to explore the Hunter Valley, to acquire land and to build temporary accommodations. A year later Franco returned and 6 months later, he and

Carmelita were married and they and other farmers moved into the Hunter Valley with the farming families. Like many immigrants, they changed their names and became Frank and Carmen Caine and when their twin sons were born two years later they named them Anthony and Alfred. The farmland was as rich as they had hoped and the vegetables and fruit grew well and the Caine's farm prospered. Carmen completed a teacher training course and establish a school for the farming community. In addition to running their farm, Frank became an apprentice to a saddle maker.

While the rest of Australia was suffering during the 1930s Depression, the farming families in the Hunter appeared to have been more self-sufficient than their counterparts in Sydney where unemployment reached 30-40 % of the population. Along with a significant number of men and some women from the Hunter Valley and Newcastle area, Anthony and Alfred enlisted in World War II, Alfred would die in France and Anthony would come back to a hero's welcome.

A year or so after his return, Frank and Carmen decided that Anthony should take over the farm. They moved to Morton and bought a vacant 3 story building on Colliery Street, which had been built by the Italian stone masons who had arrived with Frank and Carman and first used as a post office. . They opened a saddlery and leather goods business. They lived on the third level and rented the 2nd level to Mrs Petraca, a war widow and a dressmaker, and her 1 year old daughter, Sarah. The front of the Petraca's space was devoted to her work room and the 3 rooms in the back to their living area. Frank and Carmen's grandchildren, Giovani and Estelle, were playmates of Sarah.

Giovani would come to work for his grandfather when he was 16. When he was 18, his father died and his mother died the following year. He and his sister, Estelle, sold the farm. Giovani moved into Morton staying at Kelly's Paddock, across from his grandfather's building, and continued to work with his grandfather until he acquired his grandfather's business in 1952. The following year, he married Sarah Petraca and they moved into the third floor with their 2 year old son, Russell, when his grandparents decided that they would move to a stone cottage they had bought at the base of Morton Hill.   Two years later, Giovani bought the building from his grandmother on the death of his grandfather. Giovani expanded the business to include leather goods and accessories and Sarah continued working with her mother as a seamstress. When her mother died, she moved her dress making to the ground floor and they rented the 2nd floor to teachers from the local public school, while continuing to live on the 3rd floor.

Every time Russell heard about his family, he wondered what life would have been like had he stayed in Morton.

He was married when he was 31 and a year later his son Giovani was born. His wife, MJ (Mary Jane) was 8 years younger but many years older in experience and more PR oriented. She knew that Russell's celebrity status would disappear once he lost his title and she was determined to maximize this status while it had cache. Having been a fitness instructor and fitness model, MJ knew how a centre should be run and how the trainers should look. It wasn't difficult for her to convince Russell to open a fitness centre near Fitzroy Gardens in Melbourne. It was called **Star Power** and it was designed to attract people who were young, good looking and had money. Russell's new found friends, the press, B List socialites and politicians, including the Premier of Victoria attended the gala opening. The Centre was a roaring success. Russell would make regular appearances and pose for pictures with members.   And MJ insured that celebrity members were photographed at the centre. However, its success was its downfall, since MJ and several of Russell's friends decided to build on the success of the Melbourne centre and opened another centre in South Yarra near Como Park and shortly thereafter one in Docklands Melbourne.

Neither MJ nor Russell had either organisational or financial skills, let alone the time, to manage a multimillion dollar business. Russell continued with his boxing career and his endorsement commitments and was involved in the training of several fighters; while MJ was busy running the Fitzroy Garden operation at a profit. Both neglected the other 2 centers. MJ's selection of centre manager and trainers for looks rather than business acumen resulted in the Centers not meeting the high expectations of their members. The result was inevitable. Three years later, Russell had lost his title and in 2010, was forced to sell the business at a considerable discount to its value and MJ left him for a younger and richer man. The divorce was lengthy and costly and resulted in his losing the custody of his teenage son, Giovani, and denied visiting rights.

Now he was back in Morton, one year after the death of his mother. He decided it was a time for him to take an inventory of his finances, his health and his future goals and options. He had moved into the stone cottage, since the tenants had moved out the previous month. He sat with a cup of coffee, an A-4 pad of paper, and a pencil and a rubber. He had never been good at planning, which was partly the reason for the failure of his business, however he was determined to get it right.

Health – Age 62   Weight -98 kg Height – 172 cm

Health – Not good

High Blood pressure   and   Diabetes –low level

Partial blockage of right artery

Financial Position - @$1.5 million

Mother's saving account - $25000, Personal savings account - $16000

Investment Portfolio -$120000, Value of Stone cottage - $400000

Value of Store - $650000

Income – Total weekly - $1500 per week

Dividends - $150 per week , Store - $800 per week

Pension - $550 per week,

He had outgoings of around $1000 per month, which covered his food, utilities, gasoline and miscellaneous other general expenses. His savings would provide a cushion for any emergencies.

Well that wasn't too difficult!" he said to himself. He looked at the pad again and silently thanked his father for investing the money he sent each week in a joint account which was not included in his assets at the time of his divorce. This left him with several options: (1) remain in Morton, live in the house and sell or rent the building, (2) sell the house, move to the third floor of the building and rent the 2nd and ground floors., (3) keep the cottage and the store and start a business and rent out the 2nd and 3rd floors or (4) sell everything and take $1.5 million and return to Melbourne and start again.

He needed fresh air and a drink, so he went to Kelly's Paddock. He had no real connection with any locals, except for Bryan Bower who he had run into at the bank the previous week and he did not expect to see Bryan there, since Bryan had told him about his addiction problems and the DAD's program over lunch at the Wilson Cafeteria.

Bryan: "It was a low point in my life when I was sentenced to jail and lower still when I overdosed. However, my mum never gave up on me and has been there ever since. I have had to rebuild my life and overcome the stigma of the drugs and excon label. It has not been easy and I am still a work in progress."

Russell: "Compared to what you have been through, what I went through was really nothing. Yes, I lost a lot of money, I lost my son and my livelihood, but not my self-respect. No one lost any money from the Centres, I am confident that I will re-establish contact with my son and his family and I am equally confident that I will find a new direction to my life."

Bryan: "I like your positive approach to life and I share your optimism about what lies ahead."

Russell: "I always wondered what you did in the Navy and I envied you the opportunity to travel to all those exotic places and have the leisure to play the role of the tourist. My overseas trips were orchestrated to maximize gate attendance, so there were the interviews, photo shoots, training, the fight, the post fight parties or post fight hospitalization or both and then the flight back home. Then, the homecoming and the preparation for the next bout. People think of my life as exciting. It was initially but after 10-15 years you envy the guy who leads a 9-5 work life, comes home to his wife and children and enjoys taking his kids to sports practice or ballet and going out to a simple dinner with his wife."

Bryan: "I know what you mean. We often wish for things and when we are granted our wish, we are disappointed. But, I would not swap my experiences for anything else. They have made me a better human being."

He did run into Bryan at Kelly's Paddock. Bryan was there to check on the menu for the following day and the provisions that he needed to supply for the next day's menu.   Russell had a stout and Bryan his usual lemonade, since he was still abstaining from alcohol'

Bryan: "Let's talk about you here and now! Mate you look like shit! You need to look after yourself. What are you doing about the weight? I always remember how the girls in school use to hang on you biceps for fun in high school. Now look at you!"

Russell: "I know what you mean but my medical problems have restricted my physical activity."

Bryan: "Bullshit! My PT would say that you are using this as an excuse. A three prong program can be designed to work around your medical problems – the right exercise, the right food and the right mental attitude. Why not meet with Euan and work out a program. Also, you should see Dr Bruce my family doctor for an assessment.

Russell: "When did you become a health consultant? "

Bryan: "The day I started my rehabilitation program. My mum made me read everything I could. I talked to the doctors and the counselling staff and I made a plan. I then met with Euan and he designed a program for me, as a result in a year I have lost 10kgs and feel better than I have in years."

Russell: "What about the Wilson

Bryan: "You should join and I would be happy to introduce you to Robyn Coleman. Now, let me call Mum and tell her I am bringing you home for a meal."

Russell enjoyed the evening and the meal with Bryan and Mrs B. When he was younger, he remembered her as "tough old bird" but now, although in her 80s, she was still a force of nature but generous and full of life. She still called him little Russell, she still called Bryan Junior. She still treated both of them as boys and wanted them to eat all their greens, if they wanted dessert.

The following day, he went to the Centre and joined. He was surprised to see so many very active men and women in their 60s and 70s, enjoying the activities. He learned that the Centre's cafeteria served the best and least expensive meals in Morton and catered for different diets – vegetarian, vegan, Mediterranean – and tastes.   What he did not know was that Bryan was the chef. He enrolled in the drawing and painting classes and within 9 months had perfected his technique and produced a number of acceptable water colors. He joined the chess club, which met every Friday morning. He had always been good at chess and felt that this would sharpen his mind and perhaps slow down the advancing symptoms of Alzheimer.

At the start of 2016, almost one year after returning, he was settled into a routine that was extremely satisfying, he had an interesting circle of friends and activities that he enjoyed. He had financial security. His health problems were stabilized and his weekly gym sessions had given him more flexibility and mobility and resulted in a loss of 7 kg. Although he had not decided to sell the store, he had determine its value and, since the current tenant's Lease expired at the end of December 2016, he had sufficient time to consider his options, including opening a business in that space and renting the 2nd and 3rd floors.

He felt better than he had for a number of years. He had re-established his relationship with his son, Giovanni, his son's wife, Belinda, and, his 2 year old grandson, Franco, named after his great grandfather. They were planning to visit in December.   He was also assisting with the training of some of Wilson's young boxers. He, like Bryan, felt he was ready for a challenge.

16. WILSON AND THE DADS

* * *

Since settlement, over 200 major floods have occurred in the Hunter Valley area. During the period 1970 – 2000 the occurrence of droughts and floods in the Hunter Valley resulted in a significant increase in mental health issues that led to suicides and depression. In April 2010, the Board of the Bigelow Rehabilitation Hospital (BRH), Chaired by Dr Globus Azzari, the Director of Community Medicine at Northup University, completed its discussion of a study it had funded on the impact of climate changes in the Hunter Valley on mental health issues. The findings were not surprising. The Study, known as the Northup/Bigelow Study, found that there was a direct correlation between mental health issues, including depression and suicide, educational performance and general health, during unusual weather patterns that led to drought and floods, especially in farming and coal mining families and especially in men and children.

In addition to the chairman the other participants in the discussion were Margaret Bigelow Hamilton representing the Bigelow Trust, Mary Kelly Bowers, representing the Kelly/Ryan Foundation, Hamilton Fish, representing the NSW Department of Health, George Madoo, representing the Wonnarua Nation, the Mayor of Morton, Steven Evans, Susan Johnson of the CWA (Country Women's Association), and Dr Franklin Burke, BRH's Director and representative of the RACGP. The Chairman presented a report from Margaret Bigelow. Mary Ryan and Susan Johnson that proposed that a community outreach program be implemented to address the issues raised by the Study. The report noted that the Bigelow Trust and the Kelly Foundation had secured a 5 year lease on a 4 story government derelict building on Elizabeth Street at a rental of $1 per year and with an option to buy. It was to be the site of a community centre that would provide programs that would address the mental health issues raised by the Northup/ Bigelow Study.

Goal of the Community and Senior Citizen Centre

The stated aim of the Centre is to provide women, children and men in Morton and the Hunter Valley area with a welcome respite from their daily lives, especially in times of flood, drought or natural disaster. It will have special programs for men, senior citizens, indigenous citizens and new migrants.

It is a Membership organisation but fees will be modest and can be waived by the administrator or paid for in kind. Funds for the renovation   of the Centre would come from the Bigelow Trust, Kelly Foundation and the CWA with matching funds from the City of Morton and the NSW Wales State Government. Its programs will be funded for 5 years from yearly grants of $50,000 each from the founders and it will seek funding from local, state and Federal bodies, individuals and corporation. It will assist the Bigelow Rehabilitation Hospital with post hospital support by providing a drug and alcohol dependency (DADs) program and a volunteer home visitation program for the depressed, sick and elderly. It will be supportive of but not replace traditional services provided by the police, hospitals, welfare agencies, schools and the Aboriginal community.

The Goals were accepted and all participants agreed to provide some form of funding by the end of the year. The Chairman said that the Committee had recommended a name for the Community Centre. The Committee chair, Susan

Johnson, said the Committee had considered many names, including Morgan, Bigelow and Kelly but felt that a name with a more symbolic meaning would be more appropriate.   She said the Committee had asked George Madoo to find out if the elders of the Wonnarua Nation would have any problems with the Centre being called the Wilson Community and Senior Citizen Centre, in recognition of Mary Wilson, the much loved nurse and elder, who had worked for over 60 years in the Hunter Valley.

Mr Madoo reported that the elders, after some deliberation, said that they had no objection. However, they had some conditions that reflect tribal law. There was to be no image of Mary Wilson, however a plaque with her name and accomplishments would be appropriate. The elders also wished that a plaque be erected on the outside of the building acknowledging that the building was built on the traditional land of the Wonnarua Nation and finally that a smoking ceremony be held when the Centre was ready for occupancy.   In response to the question regarding the "smoking ceremony", Mr Madoo said: "A smoking ceremony has many purposes but often it is used as a sign of welcoming and to show a sign of respect for people past and present."

Both Hamilton Fish and Steven Evans thought the Premier of NSW would be greatly interested in this, as well as local political representatives.

The Committee reported that it had raised an additional $150,000 from various businesses, including Robotic Solutions, Tyrells and other vintners, BHP, the coal miners association, the City of Morton, the CWA and several anonymous givers. The Newcastle Knights had agreed to hold an exhibition game to raise funds.

The Chairman closed the meeting by congratulating everyone on the work they had done.

"Now", Susan Johnson said, "the hard work begins. We need to select a Centre Executive Board, a Director, support staff, and engage an architect to design the various spaces and engineers to assess what is required to meet the Town Planning guidelines."

On the 15th of November 2011, with a large audience and the Premier of NSW and representatives of the Prime Minister's office, local community leaders and residents in attendance,   the Wilson Community and Senior Citizen Centre was opened. Its architect, David Leichhardt, had restored the exterior to its early 1900s designs by J W Pender, which followed his drawings of Maitland's Australian Joint Stock Bank building.   David maintained the integrity of the ornate Italianate staircase, flooring and windows while adding the rooms required by the Committee and adding a lift, new electrical cabling, heating and air conditioning and new water lines.

There were 210 new members 170 who paid $240 or $20 per month for a year and 40 who were allowed to join without fee or provided payment in-kind. This gave them full access to the full range of educational, social and crafts programs.

The initial clinical program would focus on mental health issues, such as Drug and Alcoholic Dependency (The DADs program).

The DADs program was a project developed and supported by Wilson Centre, Northup University and Bigelow Rehabilitation Hospital. It was housed at Wilson Centre. While it operated within Wilson Centre, it had an independent board of Directors of 5 representing the stake holders and the NSW State government and one independent community representative. They monitored the programs, raised funds and appointed the Director. The counselling staff were provided by the Rehab Hospital, the administrative support staff from Wilson and the University provided graduate students, who serve as part of their professional training.

Under the direction of Dr Ava McManus, the DADs Program Director, each session of the program, in addition to Ava or a member of the Bigelow Rehab staff, had 4-5 participants, who had previously undergone rehabilitation at Bigelow or other accepted program in the Hunter Valley area, and one graduate student from Northup Graduate program. They would meet 3 times a week for 3 hours per session for the 12 week period. At any one time Ava had 3 groups, in a program staggered at 4 week intervals. At the end of the 12th week, each participant would provide their own assessment of their progress and be assessed by the graduate student assigned to their group and Ava. Based upon the assessment, the participants could continue with another 12 week session or be transferred to a one week session or be released from regular sessions and report back each month. The goal was to slowly develop strategies that would allow participants to deal with any temptations that might result in their returning to their dependency on drugs or alcohol. There was also a buddy program that allowed participants to call each other, if they felt the need for support and a hot line to Bigelow Rehab for more serious interventions.

Ava met with the November 2015 Group at their first session in December 2015. She knew all the participants, two from a previous 12 weeks – Barry and Julia and two new members – Bryan and Helen. She was glad to have a gender balance, since this combination seemed to be the most successful. She reviewed her notes, Barry and Julia were both recovering alcoholics – Barry appeared to be more dependent than addicted and his heavy drinking only developed 10 years ago while Julia at 40 had been drinking all her life and was a product of a family of alcoholics. Bryan and Helen were drug dependent but had responded very well to rehab, since both became addicted to opiates while being treated for Depression in Helen's case and muscular pain in Bryan's case. The prognosis for all four was positive.

Ava:	"Welcome to this our first session of the November 2015 Group. My name is Ava McManus and I am a clinical psychologist at Bigelow Rehabilitation Hospital and Associate Professor at Northup University's Medical School and the

Director of the DADs. My associate is Daniel Elders, who is a Wiradjuri man and a graduate student in his last year at Northup Medical School."

Ava: "Daniel, do you have anything you wish to say."

Daniel: "Thank you Dr McManus for inviting me to work with this Group. I would like to tell you something about myself. I am proud to be a descendant of the Wiradjuri. For most of my 32 years, I have played an active part in tribal activities. However, my day-to-day life was as a middle class school boy from Collaroy, who did well in high school and received a scholarship to Newcastle University. I completed my medical degree and then interned at North Shore Hospital and went into a medical centre in Redfern, where I also lived. I worked in general practice for over 5 years in Redfern, which as you may know, has a large Aboriginal population. It was there that I saw the waste of talent and life that the use of drugs and alcohol brought to so many bright and gifted Aboriginal children. As a result, I decided to devote my professional life to doing something about it. That is why I am here! Through helping you, I can gain insight into the problems that you have faced; through helping me understand your problems, you will benefit many others.   I look forward to working with you."

There was clapping from all 4 participants.

Ava: "That was beautifully said Daniel and quite inspirational. Today is the first day of 12 weeks, 36 3 hour sessions. This means we will not end our 108 hours until the end of January 2016, unless we are able to add additional session during 10 week, then we could finish before the end of December.   The prognosis for all of you is positive. Some of you have had a long tough road to travel to reach this stage in your program. Together the 6 of us will discuss your problems and the way in which you can recognise the symptoms that led you to drugs or alcohol. The goal is to have you see yourself in a positive light and to accept that you are a person of worth and that alcohol and/or drugs is not the way to escape from your problems; facing them in a positive way is."

"Some of you already know each other but because we have a protocol to follow, I will ask each of you to state your first name, why you are here and why you were dependent on drugs and or alcohol."

She nods to Bryan.

Bryan: "My name is Bryan. I am here as a result of my taking prescription drugs and adding opioids to that cocktail and then overdosing.
I have been clean for 10 months."

Helen: "Hi, my name is Helen. For 10 years, I took drugs to overcome depression and like Bryan I overdosed and as a result, I loss custody of my daughter. I have been clean for 8 months."

Ava noticed that Barry had been less flamboyant about his appearance than when he first arrived in Morton. He had settled in at Kelly's Paddocks and was considered a welcome addition to the musical life of Morton. He had even directed some amateur musicals for Morton Academy and had formed a barbershop quartet. The support he received from Mary Bower, and Bryan insured his acceptance by more conservative Mortonians.

Barry: "My name is Barry. I am a homosexual. I am here because I almost died from drinking too much alcohol. I have been a heavy drinker for 12 years. I am ashamed to admit that I am an alcoholic but I am determined to eliminate alcohol as my choice to escape my problems. I have not had a drink for over 12 months."

Julia: "My name is Julia. I am a 40 year old alcoholic and have been drinking since I was 11 -12. I know that if I don't face my demons that I will be destroyed by them. I have not had a drink for 6 months."

Ava: "Thank you. You can see that you all have something in common - you all have addictions that you are determine to overcome. I am going to partner you with another person for the first half of this program. Barry your partner is Bryan and Helen your partner is Julia."

It was in this program that Bryan Bowers and Barry Oliver formed a closer friendship. They had already met through, Bryan's mother, Mary, who over a year earlier had provided room and board for Barry in exchange for his weekly cabaret performances at Kelly's Paddock, and who introduced them when Bryan returned from prison and was then admitted to Bigelow Rehab. Barry had already been in the program for 3 months, when Bryan joined. Although Barry was assigned as Bryan's partner, it was Bryan who largely played the role of big brother, since Bryan's mother had asked him to look out for Barry.

Ava: "Now Julia, in the last Group, you and Barry were partners what did you do and what did you learn?"

Julia: "First we got to better understand each other and I learned to trust Barry. For example, when I felt particularly depressed I was able to call Barry and he walked me through the reasons for my depression and I felt better and he once called me and said that he really felt wanted a drink, since working at Kelly's was a great temptation."

Barry: "It did help knowing that Julia was there and that I could tell her things that I could not tell anyone else. It was also good to have someone to work with on our assignments."

Ava: "Good. Bryan! Helen! Yes there are assignments and Barry and Julia will be able to walk you through them. Now today's lesson is 'Learning to Live with Dependency'."

The next hour past quickly as they interacted with one another and responded to questions of regaining their self-respect.

Ava: "Ok, good session. Let's take a 20 minute break and go to the cafeteria and then back up here for a new topic and an assignment."

As they were leaving Robin Coleman came to the door.

Robyn: "Ava, how is it going? Do you need anything?"

Ava: "No Robyn everything is fine and this particular Group is going to be the best that I have had since I started working at DADs and the graduate student, Daniel, is going to be a real asset to me and the Group. The vibes are good and the participants are open and receptive."

Robyn: "How are Barry and Bryan doing?

Ava: "They are very involved and they have a good relationship, more like brothers, which I suspect is due to Mary Bower. I can see that both have found a place at Wilson and in their own way found a place in Morton, Bryan through redemption and Barry through his warm and giving nature."

Robyn: "I am happy with that."

Ava: "Sorry to dash, but I promised to join the Group and share a coffee. See yeah."

Robyn was glad that the report to Bryan's Probation officer, Sam Ryan, would be positive. This would be the last report, since his probation ended at the end of the month.

17. MEETING OF THE QUILT TEAM

* * *

Wednesday, the 18th of May was the only time that all 6 could get together – Robyn, Maisie, Geoffrey, Bryan, Russell and Barry. Maisie had to admit that her approach to the boys – Barry, Bryan and Russell- had not been direct. She told them that the Centre was considering a project and wanted their comments and suggestions and possibly their participation. All three responded positively

The meeting was to be held in the room used for her quilt classes, where there were two quilts in progress - an Irish Chain Quilt and a Block Quilt. While she realised that the quilt the boys would undertake was far more complicated, Maisie felt that the opportunity to see 2 quilts in progress would help them understand what was involved. It might even evoke a spirit of competition. She had Geoffrey's bag of ties and scarfs and preliminary designs.

Geoffrey and Mrs McMillan arrived.

Robyn: "Mrs McMillan what a pleasure and surprise. It has been sometime, since you were here."

Geoffrey: "Robyn, Mrs McMillan insisted on coming. I have a feeling that she doesn't trust me on my own."

Robyn: (Smiling) "Don't be silly! We know that Mrs McMillan is a real quilter and I am certain that Maisie will welcome whatever help she can give. I suspect you boys could use the help." Bryan and Barry arrived together.

Maisie: "I didn't know you boys knew each other."

Bryan: "Mum introduced us and we both belong to the DADs' group. But we did not know we were both invited until today." Russell arrived.

Robyn: "Hello Russell. It looks like we are all here, Barry, Geoffrey this is Russell. Bryan you already know and Mrs McMillan I did not see you there. Have you met the boys?"

Mrs Mc: "Well Bryan and his brother were little terrors when they were younger and Russell might not remember but he once repaired my favorite leather hand bag."

Russell: "Yes I do. Mrs McMillan. You were my first real customer. Dad let me handle a repair for you. I remember he said, you have to treat her and this bag with respect because her endorsement will mean a great deal in Morton. It was a fawn colored deer skin bag that required a new leather strap and a new lining. I remember Dad saying "save the leather strap it's too good to throw away, we will work on that later. Give her a new blue silk lining.""

Mrs Mc: "I still have that bag."

Robyn: "Sorry to interrupt. You have 2 options would you like something to eat before the meeting or after?"

Bryan: "I would prefer to get started, since I am curious to find out about this special project."

There was general agreement.

Maisie: "Two months ago I met with Geoffrey Hamilton and during our discussion he said that he had retired. He also said that he had a bag filled with his old ties and scarfs of his late wife, Margaret, who some of you knew. He said that both the ties and the scarfs held special memories for him and he wanted to preserve those memories. I suggested that one way he could do this was to incorporate them into a quilt thus preserving the memories in a decorative piece of art. I will let Geoffrey continue."

Geoffrey: "When I was about to retire, someone made the comment "now you can stop wearing a tie". I had worn a tie all my life and not to wear one to school or work was like being naked. My ties had stories and when I thought of throwing them away I thought about all the memories I would be discarding. When I was sorting through Margaret's clothing, I could smell her on the scarfs and had the same feeling. The idea of a quilt appealed to me. When Maisie reviewed the bag I gave her, she said there would not be enough for a full quilt but there might be others in the Centre who might have memories that they would like to preserve. She thought that an all-male quilt team might be interesting and that the quilt could be entered into competition in the Centre's Annual Crafts Fair in December."

Bryan: "So we are here because you want us to help you create a quilt?"

Geoffrey: "Simple answer Yes. "

Bryan: "Even if the project interested me, I am not someone who can sew or wants to sew."

Geoffrey: "Neither can I but I am willing to work with Maisie and Mrs McMillan, who you know is willing to help us."

Barry: "I can sew and I like the idea of the project. I can help anyone who is having a problem. However, I need time to think about what I want to incorporate into the quilt."

Russell: "I am in! You all know that I can sew and listening to Geoffrey I have a design in mind."

Bryan: "I need time to think about this and I want to discuss this with my Mum. Can we meet next week?"

There was agreement that Wednesday the 26th at 1 o'clock was good.

Maisie: "Before you all tuck into the sandwiches and Mrs McMillan's brownies. I want to say a few words about what commitment you need to make."

Maisie outlined the timetable and what she wanted each of them to think about by the next meeting. She then removed the ties and scarfs from Geoffrey's bags and laid them on the empty quilting table along with the sketches she had made for them to review.

Maisie: "On the other two tables are 2 quilts in various stages of production, This Irish Chain Quilt is almost finished and just needs the backing added. The other is a simple Block quilt in the early stages with the blocks pinned in place. If you agree to continue, the goal would be to finish the quilt by Wilsons' Annual Crafts Fair in December and have it judged by the State Quilters Association. As far as I know, it will be the first Quilt created by an all-male quilting team in the Hunter Valley area."

Geoffrey: "Boys we could be breaking through the quilting glass ceiling."

There was laughter and general conversation around the quilt tables. Robyn noted with some pleasure that Barry had fitted in with the rest of the boys. He certainly was more comfortable owing to his relationship with Mrs Bower and Bryan, who was acting as an older brother. It helped that he and Bryan were both in DADs.

While Geoffrey, Barry and Russell were committed to the project Bryan was ambivalent. As with other things, he decided to talk to his mother and that evening after dinner, he discussed the meeting and his reservations.

Bryan: "Mum. I know nothing about sewing. And basting to me is what I do to a chook."

Mrs Bower: (With a laugh and smile) "Junior, please go into the closet in the spare room and pull out the 2 boxes on the floor and bring them in here."

Bryan left and returned with two large boxes.

Bryan: "Here you are!"

Mrs Bower: "Open the boxes and tip the contents on the floor over here by me."

Bryan followed her directions and saw that there were blocks of fabric squares each with a small piece of paper with some notes.

Mrs Bower: "Junior! Here is your project!"

Bryan: "What is it?"

Mrs Bower: "Many years ago, your Kelly and Ryan grandmothers, your sister and I sorted through trunks that contained cloth from christening gowns and remnants of fabric used for patches and quilts made by both your great grandmothers, grandmothers and me. Among them was your great grandmother's wedding dress that your sister wore when she was married. Your sister, aside from the wedding dress, did not want "that old stuff." However, even she recognised that it represented over 130 years of the Kelly/Bower/Ryan family. We decided to organise them into squares and attach little notes to them to indicate their significance. We even organised them by decades."

Bryan: "Why did you stop?"

Mrs Bower: "Many things. Your grandmothers died, I was busy with the pub and raising a family and your sister lost interest and then was married and moved away. Now there is a possibility of completing what we started."

Bryan: "You want me to take these scraps and tell our family's story?"

Mrs Bower: "It is your story and it is the Morton story too. It would make me happy to see it completed. I would help, if it were not for my arthritic hands. However, I can guide you with the design and the sewing, since I have made baby quilts for both your sister's and brother's children."

Bryan realised that he was committed. He knew he couldn't say no to his mother, when it obviously meant so much.

On the last Wednesday in April, Robyn and Maisie were in the Quilt Room awaiting the arrival of Geoffrey, Bryan, Russell and Barry and their decisions on their participation.

Maisie: "What are your thoughts on the boys? Are they IN or OUT?"

Robyn: "I think the only question mark is Bryan? If it is a GO what is the timetable."

Maisie: "Assuming that we proceed with all 4 boys, we can finish the planning and design stages by the Queen's Birthday in June. This will allow me two or three sessions with each of them and that would be completed by the end of July. We would then start with the cutting and pinning and be finished by the end of August. We need to break from the end of August until the 1st of October, since Geoffrey will be overseas, Barry needs to return to the USA to wind up his affairs there and then apply for permanent residency, Russell would like to spend time with his son, and grandson and I am conducting a workshop in Sydney. We should have everything ready before the end of November. What about you?"

Robyn: "I am glad that Russell has been able to re-establish his relationship with Giovani and his daughter-in-law and grandson, Franco. I have to be in Sydney to meet with the Directors of the Bigelow Trust in August and then there is the Commonwealth Conference for NFP executives in late August. In late September there is the reading of Margaret's Will."

Maisie: "What does the Bigelow Trust want with you?"

Before Robyn had time to answer Geoffrey and Barry entered the room laughing. Barry had a large bag overflowing with material. Russell arrived, also with a bag of materials. He was followed by Mrs McMillan, Bryan and Mary Bower in a wheelchair, since she had not recuperated from the stroke she had earlier in the year. Mary Bower was the centre of attention, since she regularly played hostess to

Barry and Russell and knew everyone else. She was a special favorite of both Robyn and Maisie.

Mrs B: "Well girls, Bryan and I will be working on his part of the quilt, for which I understand we owe a thanks to Geoffrey."

Maisie: "So you all are in?" There was chorus of "YES."

Maisie   "Here is my plan…"

Maisie outlined her goals and asked each to check their diaries for any conflicts.

Robyn: "I am intrigued as to what each of you plan, since you obviously had time to think about your project. Can you each give us a 25 words or less summary of what you want to express through the Quilt.

Let's begin with you Geoffrey, since you started this project."

Geoffrey: "I am still committed to using my ties and Margaret's scarf, but after talking to Maisie, I may have a different approach to the design. So my "grand design" is not clear but it will geometric in design."

Bryan: "As you know, I was not too keen on participating, but Mum made me see that the Quilt was unfinished Kelly/Ryan/Bower business and that it would please her to have it finished and no one wants to disappoint their Mum."

Barry: "I know from experience that you never want to disappoint Mrs B." They all laugh.

Mrs B: "Bryan's section will pay tribute to the women of the Hunter Valley over the past 150 years. The coal miners' the grape growers and farm families and …"

Bryan: "The footie and the war heroes. That part of the quilt really captured my imagination, so expect to see something commemorating the Minmi Rangers and lots of cinnamon and green."

Mrs B: "My dad named the pub the "Kelly's Paddock" as a reminder that in 1884 Scottish and some Irish coal miners formed the Minmi Rangers on land owned by the Ryan family. As you know the walls of the pub are covered with football memorabilia from the Hunter region. Bryan mentioned the colours cinnamon and green. This represents the uniforms worn during WW1 by the men in the 35th Battalion, which were mostly Hunter valley footballers. Like Bryan's father and Russell's great uncle, many never returned from the wars."

Barry: "I wanted my section to pay tribute to Morton and yet stay within my comfort zone. I learned that Sarah Bernhardt performed in Morton on her way to Newcastle and that she stayed and sang at Kellys. Other national and international actors and musicians performed here. So I thought I would incorporate this into my section of the Quilt.

Russell: "With scraps my father left, I want to celebrate those Italians like my father and others from Scotland and Ireland who worked with their hands to create useful things in a beautiful way with fabric and , leather. "

Mrs M: "What a wonderful imaginative quilt and I am delighted to be able to assist in whatever way I can."

Robyn: "What can I say? This is a quilt created with love that tells a story to which we and the community can all relate. My congratulations! "

She applauds them.

Bryan: "And created by men,"

They all laugh.

Mrs B: "Who will join me in the cafeteria for an afternoon tea and one of my son's new creations?"

Robyn: "Thank you Mrs B, Maisie and I will join you in a few minutes. Please order 1 for each of us." All but Robyn and Maisie leave.

Maisie: "I think we have something very special in this quilt. It has done everything you thought it would and it has already brought people together in ways that we could not have expected. Now, tell me about this invitation by the Bigelow Trust."

Robyn: "There is not much to tell. It has something to do with a letter that Margaret wrote before she died. Margaret always had secrets and perhaps this is just one of them."

Maisie: "Well I will be waiting for the next instalment. I cannot wait to start on the quilt. It's interesting how Bryan, Russell and Barry have become friends. That leaves Geoffrey as the odd one out."

Robyn: "That's not quite true. This is his quilt project and the boys seem to look to him as a leader, even though Bryan considers himself the Alpha male. Bryan, Russell and Barry have Mrs B and the Centre as their focal point and Bryan and Barry have the DADs and there is something between Barry and Geoffrey.

Maisie: "And now they all have the quilt."

Robyn: "Right! Let's join the others."

18. MARGARET'S WILL

* * *

It was late afternoon in early July and Geoffrey was working in his new office, which had previously been Margaret's sitting room, office and work space. It gave him more space than in the library and allowed him to have a large work bench and 2 file cabinets and floor to ceiling library shelves. New wiring for his computer and internet and broadband connection had been installed under the direction of Kathy Solovenic, his computer and internet trainer. The room had a fireplace, 2 large windows and French doors that led to the terrace, so that it always had natural lighting. He retained Margaret's floral covered divan and the matching chair and drapes.. The contents of Margaret's file cabinets had been given to her executor, George Wooley, prior to her death, since most of the contents related to the Bigelow Trust. Her office in the Bigelow Trust apartment in Sydney also contained documents and were reviewed by Mr Wooley. The documents relating to their shared interests were always kept in Geoffrey's file cabinet. He had made copies of these documents and given them to George. The life insurance payments had been made and Geoffrey had clearance to access the contents of their joint bank account. Only the probate of Margaret's Will was pending.

Mrs McMillan knocked on the door.

Geoffrey: "Yes Mrs Mc?'

Mrs Mc: "Mr Wooley is here. Would you like tea on the terrace or in here?"

Geoffrey: "Considering that it is a bit cool, why not in here, it might be more comfortable for him.

Mr Wooley: "Geoffrey, so good of you to find the time to see me."

Mr Wooley was in his late 60s and the son of the principal of Wooley and Associates, a Sydney based firm, which had represented the Bigelow family and half the other prominent families, including the Kellys, Ryans and Bowers for the past 60 years. When Geoffrey married Margaret, she suggested that he change to Wooley but he had a certain loyalty to Hunt and Peck, a name that always made Geoffrey smile and Margaret laugh, and to Adam Hunt with whom he occasionally played tennis.

Geoffrey: "George, it is always good to see you.   How are your father and mother?"

George: "They both send their regards. They are as well as you can be in your 80s. They both still play tennis once a week, Dad still plays golf and they are still spending 3 months at their place in Salon de Provence. "

Geoffrey: "I am glad to hear that. I saw them a month ago and they invited me to spend time with them when I go to France at the end of August. I assume you are here to discuss Margaret's Will"

George: "Yes, everything should be finalized in Late July – early August and I want your assistance to help to organise a time for the reading of the Will. I apologize for the time it has taken, while Margaret's Will was simply written, Margaret estate was complicated by the 2 trusts, the Bigelow Family Trust and the Margaret Bigelow Trust that controlled her assets and income. We believe that all issues have been resolved with the other Trustees and that with the Court's approval, we will be able to advise the beneficiaries of her bequests."

Geoffrey: "I was not aware that Margaret had her own Trust. I always thought that they were all Bigelow family trusts."

George:	"No there were the family trusts and Margaret's personal trust."

Geoffrey:	"When are you thinking about holding the meeting?"

George:	"It's on the court calendar for early August, allowing for any delays, I suggest we plan for early September. I was hoping that we could hold the meeting here? There will be 12 parties representing the major bequests represented by you, Mr and Mrs McMillan, Quinton Bigelow and his wife, Audrey, Alice and Michael Saas, Robyn Coleman, representatives of Northup University, representatives of the Wilson Centre. There are a number of smaller bequests and these people will be advised my mail."

Geoffrey:	"Of course you can have the meeting here, but I would prefer late September, since I plan to be in Paris for 3 weeks from the 27th of August to the 17th of September. What about the 20th of September?"

George:	"Then let's plan for the 20th of September at 2 o'clock. I will check with the others and get back to you, if there are any conflicts."

Geoffrey:	"I will confirm with Mrs McMillan who will arrange for refreshments."

George:	"Geoffrey, I believe that you are aware that under the terms of the Bigelow Trust, Quinton Bigelow is entitled to take up residence at North Grange. However, you are entitled to remain here until you die, vacate or remarry. If you do leave, the contents are yours, including Margaret's grand piano and the contents of the wine cellar."

Geoffrey:	"George when I married Margaret, she asked your father to explain the Bigelow Trust and the ownership of North Grange. I have not considered my options, since I love the house and the gardens, which Margaret and Mr McMillan designed and tended. Is there a provision for the sale of the house? "

George: "I will have to ask the Trust executors and my father, although I would have thought someone would have mentioned this previously but then there was never a male spouse who survived his wife."

Geoffrey: "Let me know, if you do find that this is the case, since it might be my preferred option."

George: "Or you can stay here till you die."

George gets up to leave, as they both laugh. George leaves through the French doors via the terrace as Mrs McMillan entered.

Mrs Mc: "Oh! Young Mr Wooley has left? Is everything OK Mr Geoffrey?"

Geoffrey: "Yes Mrs Mc. Margaret's Will will be read on the 20th of September at 2 'clock in the afternoon. I have agreed to host the meeting here. There may be 10-15 people. I suggest that we have some light refreshments. I will be back from France by 17th of September, so we will have a couple of days to prepare. Is that OK with you?"

Mrs Mc: "Yes, we will be away the first two weeks in August but return before you leave for Paris."

Geoffrey: "Oh! You should plan to have your niece and nephew help you that day, since you and Mr McMillan have been invited to attend, since you are mentioned in the Will."

Mrs Mc: "I never expected this. We already received money from the Bigelow estate when Margaret's father died and we received shares in Robotic Solutions, when the Bigelow business was sold and still receive dividends twice a year."

❋ ❋ ❋

Geoffrey returned from his overseas trip on the 17th of September and   reviewed the final details with Mrs McMillan over breakfast the morning of the 20th.

Mrs Mc: "Alice has been so organised, she confirmed all those on Mr Wooley's list, she checked on any dietary requirements, she arranged for cushioned chairs. She prepared a list of all those attending and has made copies for each person. (She hands Geoffrey his copy) Alice also asked Stephen Bailey of Executive Caterers to supply table linen, luncheon plates, cutlery, stemware and cups and saucers. He said he would have a barista here for coffee. We agreed that if the weather was pleasant that we would have the meeting on the terrace. As you can see, Mr McMillan has already set up the chairs and a table for Mr Wooley and Ms Chung, his assistant.

They walked on to the terrace.

Geoffrey: "It looks like all I have to do is take my seat and wait with the rest for the reading of the Will."

Mrs Mc: "No, Alice said that you needed to review this list and decide where people will sit. She will be here an hour earlier to help with any last minute details and help seat the guests. You also need to choose the wine, brandy and scotch.

Geoffrey: "I can manage the seating arrangements and prepare the list. I will bring the scotch and maybe brandy from the cellar. "

Mrs Mc: "Since we will not be sitting at table, I have prepared finger sandwiches and a crudité and some assorted cheeses and crackers, so we will have a minimum of plates. As we agreed, my niece and nephew will assist with serving food and drinks and cleaning up afterward. We have a drinks bar and another table for the coffee, tea, water and soft drinks. We will have a carafe of water on Mr Wooley's table and 2 glasses.

Geoffrey: "Without you and Alice this would have been a mess. When I agreed to hold it here, I did not realise what a circus it would be. Thank you and Mr Mc for all your efforts."

Mrs Mc: "It was no effort. Having it here would have been what Miss Margaret would have wanted. "

Geoffrey: "Yes, she would have wanted it here. I will check the wine cellar and then review the guest list."

Mrs Mc: "And I will check on my niece's finger sandwich making ability."

Geoffrey returns with a basket of wines and Scotch and brandy and placed it on the drinks bar. He goes to his study to review the list and finds a pot of coffee on the inlaid table. He pours himself a cup of coffee and takes it to his desk where he opens the list and reads through.

Mr George Wooley, solicitor and assistant Ms. Fiona Chung

Bigelows – Quinton and wife Audrey

The Bigelow Trust, Solicitors – Albert and Lucas Grant

Alice and Michael Saas

Henry Tyrell Jr and his wife Tiffany

Prof Peter Emerson, President of Northup University

Dr Ernesto Kohl, Director Centre for Artificial Intelligence

Paul Gallant, Gallant & Wilson, stockbrokers

Robyn Coleman, Wilson Community and Crafts Centre

Mr and Mrs Warren McMillan

Mr Geoffrey Hamilton

The addition of Henry Tyrell, Margaret's cousin and owner of West Grange and well known vintner was a surprise addition, as was Dr Kohl and Paul Gallant, the others he recalled from his meeting with George in August. As he recalled, George said that "those attending would represent significant beneficiaries; the minor beneficiaries would receive their bequests by mail after the reading of the Will." He completed the seating arrangement and was opening mail when Alice arrived.

Alice: "Have you settled back into the routine of Morton or are you still in Paris mode?"

Geoffrey: "The jet lag lasted longer than usual, but of course I am older than I was 3 years ago."

Alice: "We all are, but you seem to be wearing it better than most."

Geoffrey: "There is something invigorating about Paris. I met friends from when Margaret and I visited 25 years ago and we would see them every 2-3 years. The St Germaine area, as you know when you stayed in our apartment, is full of surprises – always the same, but forever changing."

Alice: "What I loved most was going from shop to shop for special bread, cheeses, meats and vegetables and discovering those wonderful little specialty shops for chocolate or wine. If you ever decide to sell, let us know. We would love to spend at least 2-3 months a year in Paris."

Geoffrey: "You don't have to buy. You can have your 2-3 months a year, as long as it's not in August - September."

Alice: "Are you serious. If we do, you must let us pay rent."

Geoffrey: "I am serious about your having 2-3 months. While I appreciate your offer to pay rent, I cannot accept it. The two of you do enough for me here, for example all the arrangements for today. Speaking of which, here are the seating arrangements. I will sit in the 2nd row right with Mr and Mrs McMillan and Robyn. You and Michael can sit in 2nd row left."

Alice: "OK. Let me review the list, check with Mrs Mc to see if there is anything else I can do and I will let you know when the guests start to arrive."

As she was leaving, Mrs Mc opened the door.

Mrs Mc: "George Wooley and Ms Chung have arrived with a Paul Gallant and they would like a few minutes with you prior to the meeting. Geoffrey noted that it was over an hour before the meeting."

Geoffrey: "Thanks Mrs Mc, please show them in. Could we please have a carafe of water and 4 glasses?

George, Fiona Chung and Paul Gallant entered.

George: "Welcome back. Did you have a good break?

Geoffrey: "Wonderful. I am always invigorated by my trips to Paris. I am forgetting my manners, please take a seat. Incidentally, I did have a few days with your father and mother when they came to Paris. They asked me to send their regards and said they would see you when they return in December."

George: "I am glad you had a chance to see them.

Geoffrey, this is Fiona Chung, a new associate at the firm. Fiona has been responsible for a full review of the two Trusts – The Bigelow Family Trusts and Margaret's personal Trust – both the Trust Deeds and a forensic analysis of the Trust assets and distributions.

Geoffrey: "Although at our last meeting you mentioned the Margaret Bigelow Trust., I was not aware of her personal Trust. "

George: "Margaret's grandmother, Maud, established the Trust, since she believed that every woman should have money of her own and not have to rely on her husband, if she married. From your comments, I assume she did not mention her personal investment portfolio, thus the reason for the presence of Paul Gallant. He and Fiona have worked together on reconciling the portfolio assets."

Geoffrey and Paul Gallant exchanged greetings as Mrs Mc entered with a tray with Lemonade and 4 glasses.

George: "The Bigelows, for the past 4 generations have maintained an old fashion, almost Victorian approach to their philanthropic activities. They gave in many instances in anonymity, unless the use of the Bigelow name would assist with attracting donors or supporters. One of the conditions of the Bigelow Family Trust was that no Trustee could ever reveal the name of the Trust in any distribution it made, except for the distributions to members of the family. In this regard, Margaret inherited the traits of a philanthropic code that no longer exists but was part of her DNA. She lived by the Motto of Frensham, **"In Love serve one another."** What you will discover after today is that Margaret managed the Bigelow Family Trust and donations that the Trust made and her own Trust and a significant share portfolio. I will let Paul Gallant discuss her portfolio.

Paul :   "I am pleased to finally meet you Mr Hamilton, since Margaret talked about you so often. I first met Margaret the year she completed Frensham and before she left for Paris. It was my first year working in my father's brokerage firm, and my father asked me to take on a new client. I was introduced to Margaret Bigelow, who was from a family well known in the Sydney business and social circles. She said she had an inheritance and wanted to invest a portion in shares. Much to my surprise the amount was $30,000, which was more than I was making in a year. She said that she wanted to buy shares in coal and oil. I suggested a few shares and she said she would be back in a week. A week later she returned with a cheque for $30,000 and a list of 3 stocks. During the next 40 plus years she was an active trader and rarely lost on her trades and she always reinvested her dividends. Her largest share purchase occurred after her grandmother died when she purchased, at market the share portfolio of the Bigelow Family Trust, which was then administered by her father and uncle They had decided to invest in more real estate and vineyards without resorting to bank financing. She made regular yearly withdrawals and regular transfers to a number of charities and research foundations. She made a $50,000 withdrawal when she funded the renovation of North Grange. The value of her portfolio as of today is $26.5 million. Directly though her portfolio and indirectly through 2 companies of which she was the sole shareholder her estate is the 2nd largest shareholder of Robotics Solutions.   In addition, she and Mrs Mary Bower reached an agreement before she died that upon Mrs Bower's death her 2%

could be acquired by the Trust. That option still exists. With regard to her portfolio you are her sole beneficiary.   Mr Hamilton you are a very wealthy man."

Geoffrey: "I am not certain what to say. As the CEO of Robotic Solutions, I was not aware of the extent of the Bigelow holdings nor did Margaret ever indicate that she had bought the shares."

George: "Probably, because the shares were bought prior to your marriage. I will let Fiona report on her investigations, especially your question regarding the purchase of North Grange."

Fiona: "I will not bore you with the details of how I conducted my research and analysis of records dating to the early 1900s but it was thorough and aided by the meticulous way in which the Bigelows, and especially Mrs Hamilton, accounted for every transaction in the Bigelow Family Trust, and in her personal Trust. In addition the records of Gallant & Wilson and, in particular, those of Paul Gallant and his son Junior were well documented."

George: "Fiona get on with it!"

Fiona: "The research covered (1) the way in which the Trusts were constructed and any interpretations that would allow the present beneficiaries to change the Trust Deeds or to wind up the Trusts, (2) the conduct of the Trusts over the past 30 years, which cover the period Mrs Hamilton was co-Trustee or sole Trustee of the Bigelow Family Trust and (3) the financial way in which the Bigelow Family Trust was managed."

Geoffrey: "George, where is all of this leading?"

George: Jokingly "Geoffrey, you have to give us an opportunity to dazzle you with our brilliance."

Geoffrey: Annoyed "I am not dazzled only blinded and confused and if this was a play and I was in the audience I would walk out. To quote Charlton Heston, "You're not blowing anything up my skirt."

Fiona: "Mr Hamilton, forgive me for my pedantry and thank you for your patience. The result of my nearly 8 months of work on the Bigelow Family Trust:

(1)   The beneficiaries have the right by 2/3 vote to amend or wind up the Trust and sell its assets,

(2)   The Trust has been administered in an exemplary manner, especially during the time when Mrs Hamilton was a Trustee and

(3)   The distributions from the Trust accounts and the sale and purchase of assets are consistent with the Trust Deed and the accepted guidelines for such Trusts.

With respect to the Margaret Hamilton Trust, you as the sole beneficiary have the power to wind up the Trust, which has been managed with " great sensitivity" and to paraphrase Paul Gallant, "astute investment acumen.""

Paul: "You wondered why you did not know that the Bigelow family and Margaret were one of the major shareholders. The original shareholding was acquired as part of the Bigelow's sale of their factory and business more than 25 years ago, at that time everyone involved knew of the shareholding but at that time it was less than 10%. At that time, the rules on shareholding notifications were far more relaxed then currently. Prior to your marriage and as a result of her father's and uncle's decision to sell the shares the Bigelow Trust held in Robotic Solutions, they offered them to Margaret and she bought them off market at a fair and reasonable price.

Subsequently, Mrs Hamilton through various companies, continued to buy shares and took advantage of share entitlements adding to her holdings."

George: "Geoffrey! Among Margaret's documents, we found a letter to me, which specifically asked me to meet with you before the reading of the Will, so that you would not be surprised by what it contained."

Geoffrey: "You mean there is more?"

George:	"The influence of The Bigelow Trust and Margaret's personal philanthropy is staggering and it touches almost every corner of the Hunter Valley and Morton. Most of it was done without anyone knowing the name of the donor."

Geoffrey:	"This is almost too much to take in. A person I have known, loved and with whom I have shared so much, has another personae. "

Alice walks into the room.

Geoffrey:	"Did you know about Margaret's' other life?"

Alice:	"You mean her philanthropic activities and her share portfolio! Yes, she told me and worried about your reaction and asked me to tell you that no matter what she loved you and hoped that you would forgive her."

Geoffrey:	"I need a breath of fresh air."

Geoffrey leaves through the French doors to the terrace.

Fiona:	"It would have been worse, if all this came out at the reading or worse once the **SMH** and **Newcastle Chronicle** published the story.

George:	"Ah the bloody press! The press was so much nicer 20 years ago. Now, they have to have some sensation to sell newspapers or increase TV ratings."

Mrs Mc Millan enters

Mrs Mc:	"Mr Wooley, I just wanted to let you know that some of the guests have arrived."

George:	"Paul, Fiona thank you for your presentations and the perspective you gave to Margaret's role. Each of you will be surprised by the Codicil to Margaret's Will only signed 10 days before her death." Fiona: "Could it be contested?"

George:	"Possibly, but I and Dr Peterson, her GP, witnessed it and neither of us had anything to gain from it."

Alice:	"Why not join the others and perhaps have a drink."

George:	"After this session, I need a Scotch."

They leave by the door to the living area, as Geoffrey re-entered the room. He pours himself a lemonade from the carafe and sits down.

Geoffrey: He looks at Margaret's picture on his desk and speaks directly to the picture. "Margaret, I should have understood what you were doing. I could have helped." Mrs McMillan re-enters.

Mrs Mc: "Mr Geoffrey are you OK."

Geoffrey: "Yes, I just needed some fresh air. Have the guests arrived?"

Mrs Mc: "Yes, Alice and Michael are making them feel at home and have directed them to their seats."

Geoffrey: "Mrs Mc did you know about Margaret's philanthropic activities?"

Mrs Mc: "I always knew that the Bigelow family made donations and contributed to the arts, education and medical causes. They and the Ryans/Bower/Kelly families supported the rehabilitation hospital and the Wilson Centre."

Geoffrey: "Did you know of their investment in Robotic Solutions?

Mrs Mc: "I knew the Bigelows had some investment in Robo. However half of Morton and even Mr McMillan and I have shares in Robo."

Michael enters.

Michael: "Sorry to interrupt but Alice sent me to tell you that Mr Wooley is ready to start whenever you are."

Geoffrey: "I am as ready as I can be under the circumstances." Geoffrey, Michael and Mrs McMillan leave the room.

Geoffrey's entrance prompted everyone to turn around.

He took his seat in the 2nd row, next to Robyn and Mr and Mrs McMillan. With a nod to Geoffrey, Mr Wooley took a sip of water and cleared his throat.

Mr Wooley: "Ladies and Gentlemen I am here as a representative of the estate of Margaret Bigelow Hamilton, who died in August 2014   The delay in reaching this stage of the presentation of her wishes was unavoidable. My assistant Fiona spent the better part of 6 months conducting a forensic analysis of the Will, the Trust Deeds associated with estate and considering any impediments to the bequests. No person has come forward with any claims against the estate that have not or will not be met. Court documents have been filed and I, as the Executor, can distribute the proceeds of Margaret Hamilton's estate as detailed in her Will. Unless there are any objections from the Bigelow Trust Solicitors, the Bigelow Family Members and any beneficiaries represented here today, I will proceed." He looks at Lucas and Albert Grant, Quinton Bigelow and Henry Tyrell Jr., who nod.

"I will forego the usual legalese and move directly to the bequests. Copies of the Will may be obtained directly from my office, although we have" He looks at Fiona who holds up 5 fingers. "five copies with us today."

"The bequests are as follows and only come from Margaret's estate and not the Bigelow Trust, which do not form a part of her estate, since it continues in accordance with the Trust Deed. Twenty recipients of bequests of less than $100,000 will be notified by registered mail later this week. There are certain stipulations attached to the gifts to the University and Dr Ernesto, which I will discuss with them next week."

"To the University of Northup - $800,000 toward the construction of a building to house the Department of Artificial Intelligence and 3D Education."

"To Dr Ernesto - $250,000 per annum for 5 years to support Artificial Intelligence research."

"To Wilson Community Centre - $450,000 for general support, $150,000 for the Students at Risk Program and $125,000 for the DADs program."

"To Wilson Crafts Centre - $100,000 as a matching grant to the Australian Government's Indigenous Arts Grant for the development of an Indigenous Crafts Centre."

"To Hunter Valley Farmer's Drought Fund - $250,000 donation and $1 million as a Loan."

"Now to the personal gifts:"

"To Mr and Mrs Warren McMillan - $200,000, To Alice and Michael Saas - $150,000 and the right to purchase East Grange from Quinton Bigelow at a price agreed. To Robyn Coleman - $150,000, and to my darling husband and soulmate for life Geoffrey Hamilton – my undying love, my thinking seat, the balance of my estate, including my investment portfolio and the right to acquire North Grange from the Bigelow trust, including all its fixtures, furnishings and artwork at a fair market price."

"Margaret left a letter for Mr and Mrs McMillan, Alice and Michael Saas, Robyn Coleman and her husband, Geoffrey."

"Ladies and gentlemen that concludes the reading of the Will. Geoffrey has invited you to enjoy Mrs Mc Millan's excellent finger sandwiches and the wine from his well-known cellar."

Paul: "Geoffrey. If I can be of any assistance, please contact me."

Geoffrey: "Thank you Paul. I need to process everything that has happened. I will be in touch to discuss the portfolio."

Alice: "I am floored by Margaret's generosity. She has given us a home that we have always wanted but could never afford. How are you coping?"

Geoffrey: "As I said to Paul Gallant, I am still processing all this but what I could use is a glass of wine." They walk to the bar and the waiter pours a glass of wine for both of them.

Alice: "Are you certain that Michael and I can't help? Would you like to join us for a light supper? It won't be as good as the one you prepared."

Geoffrey: "Thank you but I want to be... No, I need to be alone to read Margaret's letter. Thank you for your help with the arrangements."

Mrs Mc: (With tears in her eyes and a tremble in her voice.) "Mr Geoffrey, Miss Margaret was generous throughout her life, as were her mother, father and grandparents."

Robyn: "Geoffrey, what can I say? She is someone we will always remember. I need to go off and have a good cry. I will call you tomorrow." She kisses him on the cheek and leaves with tears streaming down her face.

Quinton: "Geoffrey, I am glad that Margaret, Henry and I were able to resolve the future of the Bigelow Trust and that you will be able remain in North Grange and that Alice and Michael can acquire East Grange. Once you have recuperated from the shock of all this, we can talk. I would like to have everything settled by the end of the year, if that is possible. I have asked the Bigelow Trust solicitors to draw up the documentation. Audrey and I will leave for Melbourne next week. "

Geoffrey: "Thank you Quinton and thank you and thank Audrey for coming."

Mr Wooley: "Geoffrey, I think that this went well. Fiona and Paul will be in touch with you regarding her Trust. Here is your letter from Margaret, I would suggest you read it someplace quiet."

Geoffrey: "George, I apologize for my reaction earlier, I over reacted. I thank you for your efforts to make this as easy as possible. Please thank Fiona as well."

Finally the last guest left and there was only Mr and Mrs Mc Millan, Mrs McMillan's niece and nephew and the staff from Executive Caterers. Geoffrey sat at a small table on the terrace with a half empty glass of wine and an unopened letter. He was startled by Mrs Mc,

Mrs Mc: "Mr McMillan and I are leaving, do you need anything before we go?"

Geoffrey: "Yes, could you drop me off at our special tree in Sumner Park. I feel I need to be there when I read this letter. Have you opened yours?"

Mrs Mc: "We would be happy to take you. We decided to wait until we were home to open the letter, since I am certain that I will cry when I read it and I would rather do so in the comfort of our home."

Geoffrey: "I can appreciate that!"

When they arrived at Summer Park, Mr McMillan offered to return and drive him home.

Geoffrey: "I am not certain how long I will be. Since it is a pleasant afternoon, I will take the shortcut through the woods."

They watched until he sat on the Thinking Seat and, as previously, he seemed to be having a conversation with another person.

Mr Mc: "Do you think he will be OK? Should we wait?"

Mrs Mc: "Geoffrey will be fine. Margaret has made certain of it." They left as Geoffrey opened the letter from Margaret.

* * *

My darling,

I know that you are reading this letter sitting on your Thinking Seat, that very special place where we shared so many secrets and where we first made love.

The fact that you are reading this means that you have been presented with the terms of my Will and the obligations that that entails. Knowing you, I assume that you have gone through various stages of emotion, which probably range from betrayal to understanding. There have been times when I wanted to share what I was doing with you but the way in which I handled the Trusts was part of the Bigelow DNA, so forgive this genetic imperfection.

I have been blessed by having you in my life and my only regret is that we did not have children. I believe that we came into each other's lives at a time when we each needed that special someone. I am glad that I waited to find you, since you are my soulmate as well as my lover. How do I love you? I love you when you are gentle, caring and creative and when you see life through a poet's eyes. I love you when you are in your organizing, articulating and doing wonderful things mode. I even love you, thou often through clenched teeth, when you are being manipulative, pompous, dictatorial and self-righteous, since I know this will pass quickly. There has not been a moment in the past 30 years that I have not rejoiced in our relationship. I believe I am a better person for sharing my life with you and seeing life through your eyes.

I regret that you did not die first, since I believe that I would have handled your death better than I suspect you handled mine. In fact, most women handle death better than men and, in many ways, women handle many things better than men, given the opportunity to be placed in a position of responsibility. However, I believe that given the right circumstances that you will achieve greater things after you leave Robotics and I believe that your use of my Trust funds and investments will provide you with the means to further your goals.

As Mr Wooley or Quinton may have advise you, Quinton, Henry Tyrell and I resolved the issue of the future of the Bigelow Trust. We agreed to wind it up, since neither Quinton nor Henry intend to live in Morton and, I gather, that they both have financial needs. They have agreed that you may buy North Grange with all its fixtures and furnishings. We had an assessment of all the Bigelow assets, so the price has been agreed. I could not think of you living anywhere else, except in your apartment in Paris, which holds so many memories. I would not like to see you parted from the artwork nor the garden that has become so much a part of our life at North Grange.

I do not believe that my Trust and investment portfolio could be in better hands than yours. You will understand what I supported and why and continue the work of the Trust. I have added some codicils to my Will, which stipulates that you should be involved in the legacies to the University and the AI program, the extent of your involvement will depend upon you. The surprise will be the size of my investment in Robotics, again, as you will inherit all my investment portfolio, you must decide the extent of your future involvement in the company. I never told you about my investments in Robotics, because I did not want you to be accused of having a conflict of interests. The holding will entitle you to a seat on the Board of a company that you helped grow and from which you will derive good dividend income.

We were lucky to have such wonderful friends. Mr and Mrs McMillan, Alice and Michael and Robyn will continue to be there for you, since they love you. You will discover new friends as your new responsibilities take you in a new direction. I found this so when I first met Mary Ryan Bowers. She and I made and executed many plans over the years. If it were not for her encouragement, I would not have been active in the Wilson Centre. We met at least once a quarter for lunch and discussed our latest projects. We both supported and served on the Board of Bigelow Rehab and the Wilson Centre. She was a wonderful friend.

I worry that you will retreat into yourself and shut the door on so many opportunities that await you in and beyond Morton. My legacy to you is the opportunities that my estate offer to you to do all the wonderful things of which you are capable. My last reading of poetry was from the well-worn book of Emily Dickenson poetry that you gave me years ago. It provides me with my closing thoughts. I will always be with you, since a portion of us resides in our loved one. Emily said it more poetically: "Unable are the loved to die . For love is immortality".

With everlasting love

Margaret

He lay back against the trunk of the tree and felt the warmth of the late afternoon sun, heard the lapping of water at the base of the tree and listened to the calling of the lorikeets. He felt as if he was watching himself from above and removed from all worldly cares.

* * *

Mrs Mc: "And that is how we found him. So peaceful and with a smile on his face."

This was addressed to Alice and Michael, who had arrived within 10 minutes of having received a call from Mr McMillan.

Alice: "Tell us everything."

Mrs Mc: "After you left, he asked us to drive him to Summer Park and the tree that he and Miss Margaret called Geoffrey's "Thinking Tree".
We left him alone."

Mr Mc: "We drove home, where we opened Margaret's wonderful letter. An hour later, Mrs McMillan had this feeling that we should return to see if Geoffrey was OK. We did. We saw him on the branch where we had left him. We watched for about 10-15 minutes and he did not move."

Mrs Mc: "I had this feeling that something was seriously wrong, so we got out of the car and walked quietly toward the tree. Still he did not move. I called to him, Mr McMillan called to him and there was no answer and no movement."

Mr Mc: "We moved closer and we could see that he was breathing. Mrs McMillan called his name again. Still, no answer ...."

Mrs Mc: "He had the most beautiful expression on his face...

Mr Mc: "I then shook him..."

Mrs Mc: "He sat up and looked at us and said "I had the most wonderful discussion with Margaret. I must have fallen asleep".

Mr Mc: "We helped him off the branch. He was very unsteady, so we walked him to the car and drove him home. He said he was tired and would like to rest. We helped him to his bed and as soon as he lay down, he fell asleep. I removed his shoes and covered him and called Dr Bruce and then you. Dr Bruce was on his way home, so he was here within 10 minutes. He is with Geoffrey now."

Alice: "I am glad you called. We were concerned, when he was given Margaret's letter, I could see that he was holding back his emotions. If the letter to Geoffrey was anywhere near the letter we received from Margaret, it would have been very emotional.

Mrs Mc: "We also received a letter. We both cried, since it thanked us for all the years of friendship and her appreciation of all the things we did for her,

Geoffrey, her grandmother and the Bigelow family. I could almost hear her reading the letter to us."

Alice: "We arrived home still in shock over Margaret's arrangement for us to buy West Grange and her generosity. We opened her letter with mixed emotions, - the reality of her death and the last communication we would have from a dear friend. We also had the feeling that Margaret was reading it to us. It was full of humor, wisdom and love and we both cried as we read it."

Geoffrey coming down the stairs with Dr Sullivan.

Geoffrey: "I had the same feeling that Margaret was reading the letter to me. When I finished a wonderful feeling of wellbeing swept over me. The same feeling you have when someone you love embraces you. That was the last thing I remember, until Mr and Mrs Mc woke me."

Alice: "How do you feel? Are you OK?"

Geoffrey: "To quote Mark Twain "The rumors of my death are greatly exaggerated."

Michael: "You gave us quite the fright, although I did think about your wine cellar."

Alice: "Michael that was not funny. Ignore him Geoffrey

Geoffrey: "Let Dr Sullivan share the news."

Dr S: "Geoffrey is fine. His blood pressure was elevated but all his other vital signs are good. From what he told me, it was a stressful day. The reading of the Will and Margaret's letter opened unhealed emotional wounds but also provided the salve to heal them. I believe the healing process has started and that Geoffrey will be OK. However, I am recommending a full physical later this week. Aside from that, I see no reason why he cannot continue with his regular activities. Mrs McMillan I am leaving these tablets for you to give him twice daily for the next week."

Geoffrey: "What about a glass of wine or scotch for everyone, including you and Mr McMillan."

Mrs Mc: "Should you be drinking?"

Geoffrey: Looking at Dr Sullivan who shakes his head positively "Absobloodylutely"

Geoffrey: "Then it's settled. Drinks for all."

They move to the drinks trolley and Geoffrey pours the 6 glasses and raises his glass.

Geoffrey: "To Margaret who always has been and always will be there for us. May we live up to the faith she had in us and may we use the gifts and opportunities she has given us to make decisions that would justify that faith. "

All: "To Margaret."

19. THE QUILT PROJECT AND DEATH

* * *

Masie had not seen Robyn for over 3 weeks, so she was looking forward to Robyn's report this morning on her meeting with the Bigelow Trustees and the Australian National Non-Profit Conference. She had her own status report on the Craft's Program and the good news that the Quilters Guild had decided to hold their Regional Quilters Awards in Morton and at the Wilson Centre. In local quilting circles, this was a significant decision, since in the past 10 years, the Hunter Regionals were held in Newcastle. Maisie had a friend in the Guild head office, when Morton was announced as the venue, one director said; "Where the hell is Morton?" While it would require some expenditure by the Centre, she was confident that the discretionary funds she and Robyn control would cover this. Since the sporting rivalry between Newcastle and Morton was legendary, she knew that the Mayor and Town Council would contribute funds and host the formal dinner for the adjudicators.

Robyn arrived breathless.

Robyn:	"So much for walking up the stairs. I definitely must enroll in Yung Ok Oh's Pilates class."

Maisie:	"It has done wonders for me. I started with private sessions and after 3 months moved to a matt class with 4 others. My goal was to touch my toes. Yung OK laughed and said while that was a laudable goal, more than half the population cannot touch their toes and never will. But, I am still trying."

Robyn: "What is the procedure?"

Maisie: "Yung OK will do a physical assessment and find out what you want to accomplish. She will then design a program for you. I would recommend the private sessions for at least 2-3 months.

Robyn: "I will see her right after our meeting. I brought some samples of Bryan's new "Healthy Eats" and a large café latte for each of us."

Maisie: "Bryan is a changed person; he seems to have found a focus to his life with "Healthy Eats." He tells me that he has taken over the kitchen at Kelly's Paddock and has been providing food to Executive Caterers as well. Yet, he has found time for the quilt project, is involved in the organic food group and still drives the bus."

Robyn: "I think his mother has something to do with his commitment to the Quilt Project."

Maisie: "First, how was the conference? Second, what did the Bigelow Trustees want with you? "

Robyn: "The best part of the conference was the opportunity to discuss what programs others are doing and make comparisons and share resources. Most of the Australian centers in the CBD areas are struggling and are quite envious of our resources. None of them have any discretionary funds and most are heavily dependent on government subsidies, which means that the focus of their programs are reflected by what the government will fund. Several people expressed their appreciation for Margaret's input in past discussions. They missed her and Mary Bower's commitment and their ability to deal with government policy makers and hoped that I would be a fitting replacement for them.

I came away knowing that I had made the right choice coming here. Margaret was right when she said "Even a small centre like ours can serve as a beacon for others."

Maisie: "It seems that Margaret's influence was everywhere and that you have large high heel shoes to fill. Now, about the Bigelow Trust meeting."

Robyn: "The meeting was about Margaret's personal trust, which has considerable assets. Before her death, she gave Mr Wooley, her solicitor and the Trust's solicitor, a letter requesting him to meet with me and offer me a position as a Trustee, subject to Geoffrey's approval. He said he had met with Geoffrey and Geoffrey had been enthusiastic."

Robyn did not share the contents of the letter that Mr Wooley had given her from Margaret after the Will was read. She waited until she was home to read it, since she knew that she would cry. Aside from Margaret's thanks for being a good friend and for her loyalty, there was her comments about Geoffrey that startled Robyn:

Robyn, I always knew that you loved Geoffrey and now that I am dead I trust that you will share your feelings with him. He is a passionate man, but not always the most forward when it comes to expressing his emotions nor the most observant. I trust you to find a way to initiate this and do so with my love and blessing."

Maisie"   "And then what happened?"

Robyn: "I am now a Trustee, with a stipend for my services.
Geoffrey arrived an hour after I did and we discussed the Trust's shareholding in Robotics, which was reported in some detail in the media. We agreed on a number of grants and donations. While I am not at liberty to say what Geoffrey wants to do, I believe it will be a surprise to the Directors of Robotics, with whom he will meet sometime before the December AGM."

Maisie: "Interesting and congratulations. My news is not as exciting as yours. Our simple Quilt Awards program has been escalated in focus by the decision of the Quilters Guild to hold the Regional Quilt Awards in Morton and at the Wilson Centre."

Robyn: "How exciting for you, Morton and the Centre. Obviously, this is going to cost us! What is the figure we need to allocate?"

Maisie: "The total cost of previous Awards Programs was $10,000, however, if we involve the Mayor and Morten Town Council, Robotics and the CWS, the costs to Wilson would be considerably less and perhaps, if we generate increased income from the Festival, nothing."

Robyn: "So my job is PR. fundraising and politicking. All the fun things!"

Maisie: "That's it and you are good at it!"

Robyn: "Now about the boys."

Maisie: "They have been busy! In the last 2 months. I organized individual meetings before Geoffrey and Barry left for overseas. Geoffrey from the end of August until early September and then the week of Margaret's Will reading. OH! Margaret left the staff at the Centre $5000 to $10,000 each. Barry was overseas about the same time. They were also the easiest of the four to organise, since Geoffrey only had to decide on the pattern, although he personally cut the ties and arranged them. Barry knew exactly what he wanted to do and had already cut the patterns and sewed them together. It took two individual sessions and then I had them work together, which really worked, since Barry is very helpful. Mrs McMillan contributed her expertise and before they left, we had the general outline of the blocks. When they returned and reviewed what they had done, they made some changes.

Bryan started with an advantage, since Mary Bower and her mother and daughter had cut blocks and labelled them ,but it was Bryan who found soccer material and pieces of WWI uniform material and buttons and medals and those were incorporated into his section. Mary Bower and Barry helped Bryan, since he had to squeeze the work on his panel into his busy work schedule, including trips to farmers to discuss organic farming.

Russell designed his section to represent the major industries in the area and to acknowledge the Wonnarua nation as the traditional owners. His previous experience as a tailor made it easy for him to shape the blocks to fit his design and sew them in place.

We had the first full meeting this past week. It was the first time that all the pieces were brought together. They were pleased with the results. We agreed on the design of the border, which incorporated the V ends of the Geoffrey's ties. He found more ties to provide the border. We still need to submit a design for the space between the sections and I am responsible for the batting. Since this will be a hanging quilt rather than a bedcovering, we need something stronger. We will require tabs to hang the Quilt. This can be made from more ties, which Geoffrey may not know he has to supply. Providing there are no major surprises, sewing is scheduled for the first week in November

Robyn: "Your boys have been busy. Any issues?"

Maisie: "None, but some surprises. They are going to produce a booklet of the story of the Quilt. Geoffrey offered to give up the title, "The Retirement Quilt", since he felt that the quilt represented more than his retirement and his memories but the memories of Mortan and its history, traditions and values. However, they all submitted names and then voted on them, and this resulted in "The Retirement Quilt" being the name of the booklet, while the Quilt would be called the "The Morton Heritage Quilt." They also offered to pay for the booklet from their own funds. However Geoffrey said that Margaret's Trust would pay the cost. They agreed that it would be dedicated to Margaret Bigelow Hamilton, Mary Ryan Bower, Franco Canistesto, the Wonnarua Nation, the traditional land owners in the Hunter Valley, and the people of Morton."

Robyn: "What a wonderful idea. If they sell the booklet, it can raise additional funds for the Centre. In fact, if the Mayor agrees the Morton Town Council could buy 1000 copies to give to VIP visitors. I can think of other ideas."

Maisie: "You need to run this by the boys, since I don't think that it was their intention to sell them. However, a larger print run could reduce the costs. "

Robyn's mobile telephone rang. Seeing it was Barry, she answered it. "Hi Barry. What? Slow down and start from the beginning. Oh No! When? Does Bryan know? I think he is in the building, I will check. What have you done? I think that was the best thing to do? You might also call her cousin, Sam Ryan, he will know how to handle the police. I will find Bryan and drive him home."

Robyn was in tears when she finished.

Maisie: "What's wrong?

Robyn: "Barry called to tell me that when he went to have coffee with Mary Bower, he found her dead on the floor of her kitchen. He has called Dr Bruce Sullivan, her physician, but he could not locate Bryan, who he thought was either at the farmer's market or here. ."

Maisie: "He is here. I saw his van in the parking lot."

Robyn: "I have to find him and tell him. It was not unexpected, since she had the stroke a few years ago."

Maisie: "She looked fine when she was here with the boys to view the quilt and pleased with the results. It will be a great loss to Morton, the Centre and to the boys"

Robyn: "I must find Bryan. I don't want to call him on his mobile. I need to do this face to face."

Robyn found Bryan in the kitchen of the Centre talking to his staff. She motioned for him to join her.

Bryan: "Morning Robyn. Can I interest you in a coffee and a new tart that we have just baked? " He sees tears running down her cheeks. "What's wrong?"

Robyn: "Barry called and he found your mother dead on the kitchen floor. He has called Dr Sullivan and is calling Sam Ryan who I believe can deal with the police."

Bryan: "Oh, No" Bryan starts to cry and Robyn puts her arms around him.

Robyn: "Let me drive you home and don't worry about lunch, George and Pepi will be able to handle things. Is there anything I can do for you? Can I contact anyone?"

Bryan: "Thanks Robyn. I would like you to drive me. You know, it's the shock of her death and the fact that I was not able to say goodbye that has upset me. It was only a few hours ago that I saw her and she seemed fine."

Robyn: "You were fortunate to have her for so many years. I know that she was happy that your life was back on track and that you were involved in something you truly love."

Bryan: With a sob "I will miss her."

Robyn: "We all will."

Robyn went into the kitchen and told the staff and returned to Bryan and they leave.

When they arrive at the Bower house, Dr Sullivan was there with Sam Ryan, Barry and Detective Capalino.

Dr Sullivan: "She died of natural causes. The bruise on her head was caused by the fall. Her death was not unexpected, since she had a stoke three years ago. At that time she was given 12 months to live but she was a fighter."

Sam: "Capalino, I see nothing suspicious about her death. Just an old women dying at home while making a cup of coffee."

Capalino: "Agreed. I see no reason to involve the coroner, so you can call White's and have her body taken to the funeral home."

They lifted her body from the floor and placed it on the living room couch.

Bryan: "I will make the arrangements. Can I have a moment alone?"

They leave Bryan with his mother.

Bryan: He knelt next to her body and took her hand. "Mum, we did not have the opportunity to say goodbye to one another, if I had I would have told you I loved you and how much you have meant to me, especially your support over the past 6 years when I needed it the most. We did become closer and as a result of your encouragement you gave me a new direction to my life. I hope I have made you proud. I will miss you."

As Bryan leaves to make the telephone call to White's, Barry came into the room in tears.

Barry: "I cannot believe she is gone. She was like the mother I never had. She gave me confidence in myself and made me feel part of your family. I will miss her."

He throws his arms around Bryan sobbing and Bryan kisses him on the top of his head and returns the hug.

Bryan: "You still have a place in the Bower family bro, as she would have wanted."

As Mary had directed, there was only a church service at St Patricks for the family and a few close friends, including Geoffrey, Barry, Russell, Alice and Michael Saas and Robyn and Maisie, followed by the burial in the Kelly family plot and a memorial reception at the Wilson Centre. Robyn and Barry organised the lunch and the printed booklet that commented on Mary's life. Robyn read the expressions of condolences from the Prime Minister, the Governor General on behalf of the Queen, the Cardinal and other political, social, cultural and religious figures. But it was the

100s of ordinary people of Morton and the Hunter Valley who had signed the condolence book as they came to pay their respects to "Dear Mary or Mrs B" that impressed Robyn and surprised Bryan.

Robyn: "You can see how much your mother was regarded and loved."

Bryan: "It is funny; you see only a small portion of a person's life without realising the impact that they can have on others."

Robyn: "Often a small gesture can have a surprising impact on people and events"

Little did either of them know what additional surprises Mary Kelly Bower had for them and for Morton?

The quilt team met in late October. They would have understood, if Bryan had decided not to continue but they were surprised at his positive approach to the project.

Bryan: "I want to thank all of you, especially Robyn and Barry for your comments and support over the past 2 weeks. I know that you may have suspected that I would not continue with the Quilt project. This is not the case. I promised Mum that I would complete it and I will. So let's get on with it. "

Maisie: "We are still on target for completion. I have bought the batting and thanks to Geoffrey, I have enough ties for the border and the loops. Russell has found 2 antique wooden rods with brass ends – one for the top and one for the bottom of the quilt – and he has polished the brass. Over the next 2 weeks we will complete the sewing of the blocks. Today, you have the final opportunity to review your designs. If you have any questions, please let me know."

It wasn't until the middle of November that Bryan learned of the contents of his mother's Will. He knew he, his sister and brother and their children were beneficiaries of the Trusts she had created several years previously. However, it was the codicil to her Will that surprised Bryan and his siblings.

To Bryan, my eldest son, in recognition of his support these past few years, I leave my house and its contents and my shares in Robotic Solutions and the option to acquire Kelly Paddock on the right of first refusal.   I also leave the sum of $50,000 to Barry Oliver and $200,000 to the Farmers Drought Relief Fund.

Geoffrey's sisters and brother accepted the codicil with some reluctance after it was noted that they had declined to accept the responsibility for their mother when Bryan originally raised the question with them after her stroke.

Bryan knew that the Chinese company who purchased the pub were not satisfied with the profits it generated and that they wanted to sell. He thought that a quick sale without the usual costs of advertisement and promotion might appeal to them. He contacted Geoffrey, who agreed to acquire Bryan's shares in Robotic Solutions, so he was able to approach Mr Kook, who represented the owners, and they agreed on a sale price of $2.5 million. Bryan had budgeted for $3 million, which included $500,000 for much needed renovation. He had the $2.5 million, so he was short $500,000. He could not borrow more from the bank, since he had borrowed to fund "healthy Eats". He had over a month to find the money and he was confident that he would find the money but what he didn't know that it would come from an unlikely source.

20. THE ROBO BOARD MEETING

* * *

Bradley Haines was reading the *Financial Review* when Alice arrived with his morning coffee and the draft of the Notice of the Board meeting which would be held 2 weeks before the AGM in December.

Bradley: "I suppose you knew that Geoffrey Hamilton is now the 2nd largest shareholder in Robotic Solutions"

Alice: "It was as much a surprise to Geoffrey as were the other items in Margaret Hamilton's Will. We were surprised that Margaret had offered us the options to buy East Grange at a below market price and even more surprised that she left us $100,000. There were many surprises: her donation of $500,000 to Northrup University for the funding of an AI Centre and $100,000 per year for running costs and matching funds to Wilson Centre for an Aboriginal Crafts Centre."

Bradley: "Certainly Geoffrey must have known the extent of Margaret's investment in Robotic Solutions"

Alice: "Geoffrey did not know or even have an inkling of the extent of Margaret's investments. When he was told by Mr Wooley, the Executor of Margaret's Estate, shortly before the meeting, he was visibly upset that after nearly 30 years of marriage she had not told him. Mr Wooley, a long-time Bigelow family solicitor, explained that the Bigelows always adhered to a strict code of silence with respect to their donations and financial position. In addition, I think Margaret did not want to compromise his position, if people knew the extent of her investment in the company in which her husband was CEO."

Bradley:	"I suppose she felt it would be a conflict of interest but I find it a very strange way to treat your husband. Certainly, my wife wouldn't do that!"

"You would find it strange!" Alice thought.

Alice:	"Strange or not that was the Bigelow way and it was also the Kelly way."

Bradley:	"What does that mean?"

Alice:	"Mary Kelly Bower's Will was read last week and, among other things, Bryan inherited 2% of the shares in Robotic."

Bradley:	"Bloody Hell! Between the two of them they control 20% of this company. That is enough to demand a seat on the board and voting rights that could result in a new Board. Has Geoffrey said anything about his intentions?"

Alice:	"There is another 3% controlled by the Bigelow Super Fund, which had an initial injection of stock when old Mr Bigelow formed it. There is also another 1% owed by key executives. With regard to Geoffrey, he is still in a state of shock and trying to grasp the impact of suddenly being the Director of a trust with significant financial muscle, including controlling a large block of Robo stock and financing the acquisition of North Grange from the Bigelow Trust. In addition, he has been trying to keep his distance from the media."

If Alice had wanted to give Bradley an epileptic fit, she could have told him that Geoffrey was arranging the finance to buy the Bower shares. She resisted this temptation.

Bradley:	"I thought that North Grange was inherited by Quinton." Alice: "Not really, Quinton had life tenancy. It was owned by the Trust. However, it was discovered that there was a clause in the original Trust Deed that if 2/3 of the beneficiaries agreed, the Trust could be wound up and the proceeds distributed to the beneficiaries. Prior to her death, Margaret and Quinton, who does not want to live in Morton and did not want to wait until Geoffrey died to take possession of North Grange, met with representatives representing over 75% of the beneficiaries, and they agreed that the Trust should be wound up. Geoffrey is allowed to acquire North Grange at a fair market price. The appropriate legal documents were signed before Margaret died. A distribution of the Trust assets will be within six months from the date of the Courts approval. Quinton hopes to expedite the wind up, since he has certain obligations. The target date is the end of the year. "

Bradley: "I have to say that Margaret was an extraordinary woman. She actually organised everything to provide for the personal and professional life of those she loved, after she died."

Alice: "Mr Haines, women are extraordinary and I am always amazed when men are surprised by what we can do. We give birth to men, we wipe their bums when they are babies, we cuddle them when they are sick, we walk them to their first school day, we drive them to sports or music lessons, we help them with their homework, we prepare meals, we monitor their health, we counsel them when they have relationship problems. We are there at their wedding, the birth of their children, their divorce and the death of their spouse. We wipe their bums in their old age and we bury them. We do this not because we have an obligation, but because we care about our men. Of course, we also are lovers, homemakers and wives, some of us work, thus contributing financially to the relationship. And..."

Bradley: "Alice, please enough. Accept that I do respect and appreciate women. At home I am surrounded with them, my wife, my wife's mother, 2 daughters and a dog who is a bitch. So I understand the female mystique."

Alice thought for a moment and decided that there was no longer any value in continuing this discussion with him.

Alice:	"Mr Haines, I appreciate you sharing that with me. Now what do you want to do about the Board meeting? All the documents are here including Geoffrey's termination package."

Bradley:	"In light of recent events, I need to meet with the executive board ASAP and meet with Geoffrey this coming week to assess his plans. Could you please arrange this?"

Alice:	"Where would you like to hold the Board meeting? I would suggest that it be held in Melbourne, since it is more convenient for most of the Directors and, frankly less costly, than having them come here. You could also meet with two of the stock brokers who have been calling to get your assessment of the impact of Geoffrey acquiring a major stake in the company and accept the invitation from Melbourne University to address MBA students. Your meeting with Geoffrey, I should be over dinner but not the club, at your home."

Bradley:	"Splendid. Yes, dinner at my home would be the right touch, a friendly dinner between two old friends. Make the arrangements for Melbourne on Monday the 10th, at the RACV, since I can stay there the weekend before. Please make dinner, arrangements with Geoffrey on the 6th or 7th. Check my calendar and change any commitments on those days."

Alice:	"I will let you know."

What a change from the way Geoffrey would have handled this, he would have personally invite them to dinner.

Bradley:	"Alice, what do you think Geoffrey wants to do?"

Alice:	"I have no idea, his last words to us was "perhaps I will spend a month or two in Paris"".

Bradley:	"That's interesting?

* * *

The meeting of the Executive Board of Robotics was held on Monday the 11th in a private conference room of the RACV. It was one of Bradly's favorite clubs. He had been a member for 23 years, first as a regular member when he was working in Melbourne and now as an interstate member. It was convenient to have both accommodations and the meeting at the RACV, which was centrally located and had excellent facilities and good food. He checked the room prior to the meeting, which would last for 2 hours and include lunch.

At the last minute, he had decided to invite Alice to accompany him, and extended the invitation to her husband, Michael. They would stay for the weekend in Melbourne at the company's expense. He had discussed the costs with Larry Abbott, Robotics CFO and acting CEO and they both agreed that having Alice attend with her husband was less expensive than hiring a temporary secretary in Melbourne. It had the additional value of retaining the confidentiality of the discussion, which at this time was crucial.

When he entered he saw that Alice had already laid out the Board papers and had arranged coffee and tea on the sideboard.

Bradley: "Good morning Alice. I trust that you and Michael had a good night's sleep?"

Alice: "We did and we thank you for arranging tickets to the Victorian Opera. The production of "Voyage to the Moon" was something unexpected and we both enjoyed it...."

Charles Wilson and Sir Humphrey Warren arrived together interrupting Alice's comments about the opera.

Wilson: "Hello Brad, Alice. We saw James in the lobby with Simon. They will be up directly. I gather that this will be a very interesting meeting. Not one of our usual ones. Incidentally Brad, thank you for having the meeting in Melbourne, it is appreciated. While Morton or Newcastle are not the ends of the earth, it does require a 2-3 day commitment and, frankly, I have too much on my plate at the moment to spare that amount of time."

Both James Globus and Simon Cheng joined the group. They were only awaiting Connors O'Loughlan, Vice Chairman. There was a comradery among the Board members that reflected the long standing relationship among them. Collectively, they had served an average of 10 years, they were all men, they had similar interests, belonged to the same clubs went to the same universities, either Melbourne or Sydney, and were part of the same social set.

The Vice Chairman's arrival signaled the start of the meeting.

Bradley:	"Alice, could you give us 30 minutes before you return to the meeting."

Alice leaves.

Bradley:	"Gentlemen. Thank you for your attendance on such short notice. You have all read the articles concerning the Will of Margaret Bigelow Hamilton and Geoffrey Hamilton's inheritance and his control of what amounts to 20% of the shares in Robotic. The extent of Margaret Hamilton's shareholding was not directly obvious, since her interests were held in 3 separate entities – her personal Trust and 2 separate companies. However, Geoffrey's holdings leave us vulnerable to a potential takeover should one of the merchant banks acquire his shares or he decides to launch a takeover. Alice has prepared a spreadsheet of the top 10 shareholders, who collectively represent approximately 68% of the shares in the company – Geoffrey with 20%, Kensei Industries with 16%, the Coal Miner's Superannuation with 10% and then Northrup University and Montreal Super with 6% each and 10 shareholders holding 2%."

Connors:	"With the exception of the Japanese, there has been no real change in the shareholding over the past 5-6 years."

Bradley: "That may be the case but there has been some creeping acquisitions over the past 2 years by Montreal Super, which as you know is a large Canadian superannuation funds with unlimited cash."

James: "All this discussion would be academic, if Geoffrey's plans were known. You met with him last week. What are his intentions?"

Bradley: "I did meet with him. Frankly, I am not certain what Geoffrey wants to do and I am not certain that he knows. However, he was quite candid about his reaction to being coerced into retirement."

Sir H: "I can understand that. We did take advantage of his vulnerability in the aftermath of Margaret's death."

James: "That may be true but we recognised that Geoffrey was a consolidator and the company needed a more marketing oriented individual with good contacts in the financial world and overseas experience."

Sir H: "Geoffrey allowed the retirement to proceed because he is a gentlemen and felt he had lost the support of the Board after the rejection of his suggestion that the company play a more active role in providing a hands on approach to training teachers to better utilize the3-D printing equipment and to exploring the opportunities offered by Artificial Intelligence ."

Connor: "But the cost of implementing a new division would have significantly depleted our reserves and resulted in a reduction in dividends over the next 2 years and the return on our investment would have been minimal."

Simon: "Yes but it would have resulted in our regaining our dominant position in what is cutting edge technology. The Directors have a dual obligation – the future growth of the company, as well as dividends."

James: "OK. Geoffrey is pissed off because we haven't treated him well. He is pissed off that we did not adopt his proposals. Is he pissed off enough to allow or participate in a takeover of the company?"

Connors: "I don't think so. Geoffrey is a pragmatist and he is weighing his options. Option 1, he remains a passive shareholder receiving good dividends; Option 2, he becomes an active shareholder and seeks a seat on the Board or Option 3, he sells his shares and allows someone to decide the fate of Robotic. However, Geoffrey is proud of what he has built over the past 12 years as CEO and I don't think he wants to see this given to some multinational or taken over and its assets sold. Brad am I right?"

Bradley: "Connor, I think you have summed up Geoffrey's options. However, I would add one other option that might appeal to Geoffrey. What if we offered him a Board position when John Gage retires at the next Board meeting and an opportunity to Chair a Future Development Committee?"

James: "Geoffrey is entitled to a Board seat, offering it to him avoids any unnecessary conflict at the Annual General Meeting. Offering him the Chairmanship of the Future Development Committee might be a first step but I have sensed, since he left in January, that a new Geoffrey has emerged, one that might want to play a more active role in the future growth of the company and who now has the power, the money and, perhaps, inclination to do so."

Connor: "Gentlemen, I propose that the Chairman continue his discussions with Geoffrey and offer him a Board seat and the chairmanship of the new committee."

The proposal was unanimously approved.

Bradley: "There is one other issue relating to Geoffrey. We approved a retirement package at our last meeting but we have not presented to him. The package included a lump sum payment of $1.5 million and a similar amount in shares. He is still receiving his regular salary until December. Do we approve of this package, in light of our current discussions?"

Sir H: "Gentlemen, it would be churlish of us to change the package we approved in July. It is based upon past performance and it is something he deserves, since he served with distinction for almost 30 years as CFO and CEO. It should not be amended because of circumstances which appear to be beyond Geoffrey's control. I recommend that we reaffirm our previous resolution. I also recommend that he be notified by an appropriately worded letter next week." This was unanimous approval.

Bradley: "Let's take a 15 minute coffee break during which you can scrutinize the Agenda for the meeting and the documents included."

Bradley left the room and returned with Alice. During the break, He briefed her on the two motions that were passed and asks her to include them in the Minutes of the Meeting and to arrange a meeting with Geoffrey on a date of his choice.

The meeting resumed and the first three items, concerning the previous Minutes of the last meeting, the Financial Report and recommended dividend and the date for the December AGM were unanimously approved. The 4th item on the Agenda was Gender Balance on the Board. The attachments were newspaper articles reflecting targets for women on the Boards of major companies.

Bradley: "We have no women on our Board. The details regarding women in the company prepared by Alice have been included in your Agenda documents. In summary, women in our company represent 55% of employees but only 15% are in management positions and only 5% in executive positions.

Sir H: "Between now and 2020, we have 6 retirements, including mine. With a 12 member board, excluding the CEO, we would only need to find 3 women to fill the vacancies. I don't think that this would be asking too much."

Simon: "I dislike quotas! I believe in merit not a reward because of someone's sex."

James: "Simon, we have never ever thought about who should be a candidate for a directorship, we have chosen from within a small circle of people with mixed results.   The proposal is to enlarge that circle so that the pool of people will be greater and may also include aboriginals, Indians, Chinese."

Bradley: "James has a point, we should not rule out the possibility of adding those not white and male as candidates in our consideration."

Sir H: "All this reminds me of the Equal Opportunity Programs in the 1970s, where those awarded government contracts had to submit Equal Opportunity reports monthly in order to meet specific guidelines.   The CEO of a company I was advising told me that his EOP Compliance Officer, Dave, told him that their quota had been met for the following month.   When he asked how this was possible, since they only had 2 new employees.   Dave said "On the form it didn't ask for numbers hired it asked what % of new employees were Caucasian, Aboriginal, Indians, Chinese and other.   He put 50% Caucasian, 0% Aboriginal, 50% Indian and 50% Chinese and 100% female. In further questioning, David said, "one was white Australian born and the other was Indian/Chinese and they were both females."

James: "So you want us to find Aboriginal/Chinese/Indian women."

There was general laughter

Connor: "Gentlemen, this is a very serious issue and I wish to avoid any negative publicity, if we do not have a policy in place.   I propose at the AGM in December that we propose a women candidate to fill one of the vacant positions and set a target of 10% women in executive positions by the AGM in 2017. Furthermore, that we enlarge our pool of candidates and to that extent create the position of Equal Opportunity Program Officer reporting directly to the CEO."

The motion was seconded and unanimously passed.

The meeting ended and the Chairman invited the Board to have drinks, while Alice cleared the table and advised the kitchen that the Board was ready for lunch.

Sir H: "Alice, how do you think that went?"

Alice: "I am not certain what reaction Geoffrey will have to the proposal. I will make the arrangement for the meeting with him as soon as we return on Monday. I will also draft a letter to accompany the Board's retirement package and have it on Braledy's desk by 1230 Monday. I am glad we included those articles on women on boards. At least the directors are thinking. The job will be to find women who will want to serve on boards and have the right credentials."

Sir H: "I have a challenge for you. Make a list of all prominent women in the Hunter Valley region. I will make some discrete inquiries in Sydney and Melbourne."

Lunch was served.

* * *

At a little before 7:30 PM on Friday the 11th, Geoffrey arrived at the Bradley's house, an old stone manse, with embellishment that lacked the simplicity of North Grange and Hawthorne Manor. It clearly reflected Bradley Haines, thought Geoffrey. The door was answered by George Burns, who greeted Geoffrey warmly and conveyed his condolences on the death of Margaret. He showed him into the library, which, unlike his own, showed no scholarly interests. Even though it was floor to ceiling with books, nothing after 1950, which suggested that the Haines family bought an existing library to fill their shelves and to show they were well read but never added to it.

The wall over the fireplace featured a painting of Bradley's great grandfather whose business acumen had been the foundation of the family's wealth, unlike the Bigelows, the Haines family were merchant bankers and made the family fortune from investments. Bradley resembled his great grandfather but he and his father never had his financial skills. Bradley lived largely on stock dividends and fees from serving on several public company boards.

The resurgence of the family fortune in recent years was the result of Bradley's son's investment in retirement villages and childcare centers.

Bradley arrived 10 minutes later.

Bradley: "Geoffrey delighted that you could take the time to meet with me and forgive the delay but I was discussing my tennis schedule, since we are in the finals. Would you care for a whisky or something else?"

Geoffrey: "A whisky would be fine."

Bradley: "I have an 18 year Aberlour Malt that you might find to your liking."

Geoffrey: "I do but what is the occasion for such a vintage?"

They were obviously sizing each other up, much like good boxers, which Bradley was and Geoffrey wasn't, although he did earn a boxing blue at University. Geoffrey decided to throw the first punch.

Geoffrey: "Bradley, I know that this invitation to dinner is not a social one. What you want to know, before the AGM, is what I plan to do with my control over almost 20% of the shares in Robotic Solutions. Is that it?"

Bradley: "Partially. I have been meaning to have you here for dinner since Margaret died but there always was something that prevented this. I also felt that the way in which you resigned could have been handled more diplomatically by the Board and thought that a quiet dinner might allow us to discuss your future value to the company."

Geoffrey: "Actually Bradley, since the day I left Robotics, I have felt that a weight was lifted from my shoulders. I see more clearly what Margaret saw and I am happy with the new Geoffrey. I also see more clearly what a real shit you are and how you are punching above your weight as Chairman of Robotics."

That one is for you Margaret, he thought.

Bradley: "Geoffrey, let's not get personal. I understand that you are under some personal stress and I appreciate that. However, I have always worked for the good of the company and have been diligent in my role as Chairman."

Geoffrey: "Why not just say that I do not see it this way."

Bradley: "What do you plan to do about it?"

Geoffrey: "I am going to exercise my rights over 20% of the shares and vote against you as Chairman."

Geoffrey saw that he had landed the sucker punch and saw Bradley reeling. Bradley took a gulp of his whiskey.

Bradley: "You are within your rights as a shareholder to do that! However, I asked you here to make an offer to you – a seat on the board and the Chairmanship of a new Committee that will consider the future of Robotics. How does that sound?"

Geoffrey: "Like a bribe and it will not work. Both of us know that I can have one, possibly two board seats, and I can vote against all 6 of the Directors up for election. If I were successful, I would control the Board and the Chairmanship and could implement whatever changes I wanted. What you don't want is a proxy fight at the AGM. Frankly, neither do I, since we both know that one of the merchant banks, possibly in association with your son's bank, is planning to launch an on market assault on the shares. I have already been contacted and they have made a generous offer with a premium of a $1 per share above the current market price."

To say Bradley Haines was stunned is an understatement. He had lost the advantage that he thought he had, he had underestimated his opponent and he was left with no fall-back position, except, perhaps, the Board.

Bradley: "I appreciate your thoughts and will need to discuss them with the Board. I don't suppose that you would still join me for dinner?"

Geoffrey:	"Bradley, you have obtained what you wanted. You now know my voting intentions, so I see nothing to be gained by having dinner with you. However, I thank you for the whiskey."

Bradley:	"You are probably right! May I see you to your car?"

Geoffrey:	"No thank you. I can find my way out. Please advise the Board of my position and my willingness to meet with them prior to the AGM, if there is a reason to do so."

Geoffrey drove through Summer Park and was tempted to stop at the Thinking Tree but felt that there was no reason. "Thank you Margaret", he said as he drove by.

21. THE MORTON SUITE

* * *

Four weeks before the Crafts Fair, Geoffrey and Barry were in the music room at the Wilson Centre that they had reserved for 3 hours.

Geoffrey: "Well Barry, we have this to ourselves. What do you want to do?"

Barry: "I am not happy with the middle section and I am not certain that the ending should be in a minor or major key."

Geoffrey: "I think it is fine the way it is, although I tend to agree that the middle section lacks something, perhaps a little more **forte** there followed by **decrescendo**."

Barry: "I think you are right about the middle and I think that the gradual decrease in volume until it is like a whisper at the end would do it. You know I never would have completed this, had you not encouraged me. For that and your friendship, I thank you."

Barry picked up the score and took it to the small table near the window and started to make corrections.

Geoffrey relaxed in an easy chair and watched him. How different he was from when they first met on my first day at the Centre, he thought. He recalled the music and then Barry's appearance and comments that the music was by Barry Oliver. At that time, he did not associate Barry with the entertainer from Kelly's Paddock or the Director of a children's production at the local Primary School. They did not meet again until 3 weeks later, when Geoffrey had made his commitment to the quilt. Having some free time, Geoffrey gravitated to the music room. It was empty. He sat at the piano and found an open sheet of music with annotations on the original scoring. He started playing the piece and recognised that this was the piece that he heard Barry play several weeks ago. There were no notations as to how it should be played, so Geoffrey decided to play it as if it was written by Mozart, the first six pages flowed smoothly, but the seventh page contained crosses and scribbles and the word *NO.* While Geoffrey was not a composer, he was a good enough musician to recognise that something was wrong and the composer had recognised this. . He skipped the portion of the page with the crosses and proceeded with the balance of the page and the next 3 pages.

He recognised that after page 7 the composer was telling another story totally different from the previous section but related, like another chapter in a book. He could see why Barry was frustrated.

Suddenly, he had an inspiration, what if there was a key change at the end of first section and a change of tempo and a repeat of a phrase from the first entwined with a phrase from the new section. He did not want to write on the music sheets, since he felt that it would be like adding notes to someone's diary. He grabbed a blank piece of sheet music and jotted down the bridging phrases he wanted, it came easily to Geoffrey, as if the music in his head were writing the notes. When he finished he started from the beginning reached the section that had given Barry problems and added the section that he had created and moved to the next section. From behind him he heard clapping.

Barry: "That was exactly what this piece needed. When I first saw you at the piano playing my music I was annoyed. Then I heard you play and I realised that you were a better pianist than I was. When you stopped at exactly the place that frustrated me, I thought how will he handle that? I was surprised that you did not even try to play that section and went on and finished the next section. I wondered what you would do next. I did not expect you create the bridge that connected the two sections."

Geoffrey: "Barry, you may have not remembered but I am Geoffrey."

Barry: "But I do remember. You asked me whether the piece was Mozart or Chopin. I think I was rude to you, as I often am when someone says something nice to me. I have a favor, since you play better than I do, would you play the last section, which leads into the next section that I have scored on these sheets? It will also give me an opportunity to concentrate on the music and not the notes."

Geoffrey: "Of course, I might suggest you indicate how you want your music to be played by someone reading the score, otherwise it will lose the meaning and feeling you intended."

Barry: "Play this next section **Adagio**, and at the bridge **Allegretto** and the last phrases **Andante** or slow, lively and then at a walking pace, The final section, which I have not completed is the resolution of the piece which is a melodic dreamy section."

Geoffrey: "Why don't I play the whole thing from the beginning and then add the new section."

Barry nods agreement and Geoffrey started playing with Barry acting as a conductor and setting the tempo. When Geoffrey had finished, they both were surprised at the results.

Barry: "What I heard is better than what I thought. Either you're a brilliant pianist or I am a brilliant composer."

Geoffrey: "What about a little of both."

And that was how the friendship began. They would meet for a few hours each week and occasionally at Geoffrey's home but never when others were around. It was their secret until the Fair. Geoffrey learned that Barry had taken composing classes at the Juilliard in New York City   and continued with classes in Oregon and had been working on this piece for nearly 10 years. .

A week later, at their regular meeting:

Geoffrey: "Barry, I have a surprise for you. I talked to the Director of The University Chamber Group, Kevin McNally. He has agreed to orchestrate and play your Suite as part of their program at the Fair. He would like to meet with you and discuss some ideas. Here is his number, call him to arrange a meeting."

Geoffrey was in Sydney for almost 3 weeks meeting with Paul Gallant, Mr Wooley and arranging finances for the purchase of North Grange and Bryan Bower's shares in Robotic Solutions.

When he returned he contacted Barry.

Geoffrey: "How are things going with the orchestration of the Suite?

Barry: "Kevin and I have completed the first draft. Here is a copy of the score."

Geoffrey took the music sheets and went to the piano and began to play the different parts, a smile slowly crept across his face and when he finished he looked up at Barry.

Geoffrey: "This is brilliant!"

Barry: "What do you think? I have decided to call it the **Morton Suite.** It is here that I found peace and a sense of place. It was you, Bryan, Mrs Bower, Maisie and even Russell, who gave me the opportunity to step outside the façade that I created to protect myself."

Geoffrey: "I will only agree to play the piano part, something I would not normally do, if you agree to conduct."

Barry nods in agreement.

Geoffrey: "Now let's get over to the University and start rehearsals."

22. THE QUILT AWARDS

* * *

t was after 11:30 PM on the Friday before the opening of the Wilson Annual Craft Festival on the 10th of December and Robyn and Maisie shared drinks with all those who helped arrange the exhibition in the large meeting room on the ground floor and in the lobby area. Over 150 pieces had been placed and labelled. The 500 programs had been designed by the art class and printed and folded in-house and were ready to be distributed.

The centrepiece was an artistically arranged cornucopia of Hunter Valley produce organised and designed by Bryan Bower with fruit and vegetables provided by the Hunter Valley Organic Produce Collective. The handicrafts – pottery, jewelry, lacework, scarfs and small woodworking items and small paintings were labelled and to the right of the centrepiece; large paintings and sculptures were to the rear of the centrepiece; large pieces of furniture were to the left and two bronze statues were to the right. Two small round tables were on either side of the centrepiece and held ornamental floral arrangements.

The 11 quilts had been suspended from the upper balcony and hung about 2 metres from the floor. The boys' Quilt, #7, **The Morton Heritage Quilt**, was the largest. It did not conform to the usual quilt protocol and it was the only quilt by men. Their names were listed in alphabetical order and indicated which panel was created by which quilter and the meaning behind the panel. On a table under the Quilt were the printed booklets – "**The Retirement Quilt**".

* * *

Robyn and Maisie arrived early the next day to review the program for the last time and made notes.

Robyn: "I am pleased with everything, although I am disappointed that the quilt awards will be this afternoon and not tomorrow."

Maisie: "There was really no choice, the Guild has commitments in Sydney tomorrow, so this is the best they could do. We and the boys are the only ones who realise that this was a change and they are just as happy not to postpone the decision."

Robyn: "How did the boys react to the other quilts?"

Maisie: "I think there were mixed emotions. Bryan said holy shit we have stiff competition". Barry said "I think ours is the most creative." Russell said "Ours says something, the rest are just patterns". Finally, Geoffrey said "We should be proud of what we've done and let what we did speak for us."

Robyn: "If they don't win a Quilting prize there is always the People's Choice tomorrow."

The day passed quickly, Bryan arrived with a bus load of members and checked his entries in the jewelry design and furniture section, Russell was there comparing his watercolors with others.

Bryan: "How does it look?"

Russell: "The quilt? My watercolors or your jewelry and furniture?"

Bryan: "All 4."

Russell: "The Quilt looks great, my watercolors won't win, your jewelry looks good and your inlaid table has already attracted a lot of attention, so it should win. Have you thought about selling through a shop or sending them on consignment to Sydney?"

Bryan: "I have but too many things have happened in the past year, my parole, Mum's dying, the Organic Producers Collective, the hydroponic unit at the University, Healthy Eats and the quilt. Perhaps after this is over we can talk. I would welcome your thoughts."

Russell: "I would like that. Have you seen Barry or Geoffrey?"

Bryan: "No, perhaps they came earlier! Perhaps they are writing their acceptance speeches." They both laugh.

Russell: To himself. "What acceptance speech?"

Bryan: "See you later. I have to look at the cakes and pastries, since I have entered them as well." Bryan to himself, "What acceptance speech?"

Geoffrey looked at his watch it was 15 minute to 4:00 PM and no sign of the other boys. Through the crowd, he could see the 3 judges fingering the quilts and making notes. They were lingering over the quilt #2 with a Chinese motif and sewed with what looked like gold threads, they turn around and walked back to Quilt #7 and examine the front and back, he could not see their faces but there was a lot of body language that suggested that there was some disagreement. The judges looked at the clock and must have realised that a decision had to be made in at least 15 minutes. They found Robyn and she escorted them to a small office off the hall.

The waiters offered glasses of wine donated by Hunter Valley's vintners when Barry, Russell and Bryan arrived. Only Russell and Geoffrey accepted a glass, while Bryan and Barry had a glass of Hunter Valley orange juice.

Bryan: "It is at times like this I could really use a real drink."

Barry: "Fortunately, you have me as your keeper." Bryan: "And vice versa!

They laugh

Geoffrey: "Boys, let's toast the completion of the quilt and the continuation of our friendship."

The Adjudicators appeared on the raised platform with both Robyn and Maisie.

Maisie: "Ladies and Gentlemen, I am pleased to welcome you to this special Quilt Awards ceremony. It is the first time that the Quilt Guild is in Morton, so it is a great honor to welcome them here. The Australian Quilters Association is the guardian of the quilt tradition, which In Australia arrived with the First Fleet. It presents awards for outstanding quilts and to quilt makers. Not only is there the prestige of being a winner but the Guild can invite those it deems worthy to compete in the Biennial Quilt Exhibition in Sydney in February 2017. I would like to present the adjudicators – The Chair of the Association, Mrs Louise Henson, the Victorian Chair, Ms Diane Cappuccino, Mrs Yung Lee, President of the Singapore Quilt Association and Ms Sara Singh a member of the Australian Indian Quilters Collective."

Mrs Henson: "Thank you Maisie and Robyn. First, we were impressed by the quality of the quilts presented today, second, we were impressed by the number of quilts for a very small town, third, we were impressed by the thought that went into the creation of these quilts. Finally, we were impressed with the gracious reception that we have received and the efforts the Mayor, the Morton Council and the Wilson staff, most notably Robyn and Maisie, have made to insure that this was a memorable event. I know you join me in applauding their efforts.

She applauds, as does the audience.

Mrs Henson: "My fellow adjudicators found ourselves in uncharted territory for one quilt, Quilt #7, which did not fit the traditional form for which we have been accustomed. However, that quilt was well designed and sewed and told a story that we can all appreciate. The quilters were all men. Yes men, breaking through the quilt ceiling."

There was laughter and applause. The boys looked at each other, not knowing what was coming next.

Mrs Henson: "Quilt #1 and Quilt #3 were examples of the very finest quilt techniques and traditions and merit the highest recognition. However, in this century the art of Quilting has moved from traditional techniques to more innovative approaches and from making beautiful patterns to telling a story. Today, we have decided that the story told by "The Morton Heritage Quilt" is worthy of a First Place Award and an invitation to show at the Biennial Quilt Exhibition. We award Second Prize to Quilt #1 and also invite them to the Exhibition in Sydney; and Third Prize is to Quilt #3."

"Would the recipients, please come to the stage." Quilters for Quilt # 1 and #3 received their awards to applause.

Mrs Henson: "I am pleased to present the First Place Award to Bryan Bowers, Russell Caines, Geoffrey Hamilton, and Barry Oliver and ask them to say a few words."

The boys look at one another and Bryan says, "Geoffrey you go first, since it was your baby."

Geoffrey: "Ladies and Gentlemen on behalf of my fellow quilters, I wish to thank you for the recognition of the uniqueness of what we have produced. This is not just a quilt, it is the contribution of so many people. What started as a way of holding on to my personal memories has resulted in a celebration of many memories and their use as the path to friendship and understanding. It has resulted in new friendships and a reinforcement of old ones and it has reaffirm my belief that we are never too old to learn and grow. Thank you." There was enthusiastic applause.

Geoffrey: "I would like to introduce the other members of our team each will say a few words. Bryan Bower."

Bryan: "When I was approach to be part of the quilting team, I thought, why does a bloke want to be involved? However, it was my mother and her encouragement and that of Margaret Hamilton that convinced me to be involved. Those who knew my mother, Mary Ryan Bower, know that when she made up her mind to do something, it got done. When she heard about the idea of the quilt, she showed me a box of scraps that she, her grandmothers, her mother and my sister had collected. They hoped to make a memory quilt. In the box, were neatly cut squares from wedding dresses, children's clothes, curtain fabrics, dresses and school uniforms and sports uniforms. Each square was labelled.

She said, Junior, it would make me happy, if you and I could do this. Over the next few months, she and I assembled the squares to the design of Maisie Cunningham, while my Mum explained to me the significance of each piece, which told the story of the Kelly, Bower and Ryan families over 125 years. A story I did not know. While she saw the final design, she died before she saw the finished quilt. About Margaret Hamilton, Geoffrey you may know that Margaret not only bought the first furniture piece I made but she gave me the design for the inlaid work. She also supplied the stones that I used in my first piece of jewelry and bought that piece. Both my mother and Margaret had faith in me and to them I dedicate my piece of this quilt with gratitude and love."

Again enthusiastic applause. A number of older members of those assembled had tears in their eyes.

Russell: "Most of the older residents of Morton will remember my dad, Geovanni Caine, whose great grandfather arrived from Italy in the 1800s.

When I returned after a 30 year absence, I thought that I would find it difficult to settle in Morton. This was not the case, I met old friends like Bryan and Mrs Bower and Michael and Alice Saas and through the Wilson Community Centre some wonderful new friends – Geoffrey, Barry, Robyn and Maisie.

I was like Bryan, blokes don't make quilts. Then I reminded myself that my father had been a tailor, my mother a seamstress and I had been a tailor's apprentice. So it in my blood, or as Bryan said "It's in your DNA mate." I also remembered that when I was cleaning out the storeroom of my father's shop, I found a large box of fabric samples that my father had saved. I remembered the fabrics and my Dad's comments regarding them and the linings of the suits and bags he had made from those fabrics for the Kellys, the Bigelows, and even you and your brother Bryan and for me.

Working with my Dad was one of my happiest memories. Being involved in the Quilt project recaptured some of that happiness, while paying tribute to my Dad. By using the fabrics I found, it was also a way of remembering the people for whom my father used his talents to create something beautiful, as well as useful. So Dad, I dedicate my contribution to you with love and thanks. To you Maisie, Bryan, Russell and Barry, thank you for sharing this experience with me."

Again, enthusiastic applause.

Geoffrey: "The final comments are from one of the newest members of our community, but one who has enlivened and brightened Morton, since his arrival, and who we are pleased to call a friend, Barry Oliver."

Again, enthusiastic applause.

Barry dressed in a white jacket, red shirt, blue pants, red suede shoes and multi colored socks, waved to the audience.

Barry: "I bet you are surprised to see me without feathers and glitter! (Laughter) This is not an occasion for me to perform but for all of us to reflect on what has been done by the creation of this quilt. The fact that I was accepted by Bryan, Russell and Geoffrey is a reflection of the way the people of Morton have made me feel welcomed from the first day that I was here. It was Mrs Bower who said to me "Barry be yourself and let people see who you are not what you wear, or what you do to your hair or that you use makeup and they will accept you."

My contribution recalls the show business life of Morton and joins those memories with those of Geoffrey and his wife Margaret, Bryan and his mother Mary, Russell and his Dad, Geovanni, and the people of Morton. This indeed is a Quilt celebrating the spirit of Morton. For this I thank you. Viva la Morton"

The audience is on its feet stamping and applauding, some with tears.

Robyn: "Thank you boys and thank you Maisie for your patience and inspiration.   Boys, your comments have been an inspiration to us all and a fitting close to today's Awards Ceremonies." There is more applause.

Robyn: "Thank you for your enthusiasm.   Please continue to view the crafts produced by our members. I invite all of you to tomorrow's closing ceremonies and the Annual Craft's Auction of all the crafts produced by and donated to the Wilson Community Centre. As part of this year's musical program we have the Northup University Chamber Group and, in addition to their published program, we have the World Premier of the 'Morton Suite'".

When she finished a number of people, including Julian Day, the local gossip columnist from the **Newcastle Chronicle,** wanted to know about the "Morton Suite" and its composer.

Robyn: "I have been asked not to disclose the name of the composer nor anything about the musical piece. Come tomorrow and all will be revealed."

Robyn knew that Julian Day would feature this mystery in his regular column in the **Newcastle Chronicle** and try to find out who the author was. Julian reminded Robyn of the character from "My Fair Lady" who exposed Eliza as having noble blood. Maybe she should plant some little hint to help him in his hunt. She did just that!

23. THE ROBO AGM

*   *   *

The Monday following his meeting with Geoffrey, Bradley received a telephone call from Sir Humphrey, while he was at the Racket Club.

Sir H: "Bradley would it be convenient for you to meet me at Northup University at 6 PM on Wednesday, November 16th?   I am here for the AGM of the Board of Trustees and I thought we could discuss the Geoffrey matter and the AGM."

Bradley: "I have been meaning to contact you to discuss my unpleasant discussion with Geoffrey and his position on his shareholding. Yes, Wednesday the 16th at 6PM would be fine. I will meet you in the Member's room."

When Bradley hung up, he said to himself "I wonder what the old fart wants?" After his tennis game, which he won, he tried to contact Alice but was advised that she had gone to lunch with Robyn and his wife at the Wilson Centre and would not be back until 2 o'clock. He emailed her a list of appointments he wanted to make for the next week and included Sir Humphrey's dinner invitation on his calendar and told her that the following day he would be playing golf with his son and several of his son's banking colleagues.

*   *   *

Sir Humphrey was waiting for him in the foyer of the Member's room. He had reserved a private room for their discussion and dinner. To Bradley's his surprise, Geoffrey and Connors O'Loughlan were already there.

Bradley: "Humphrey, you did not tell be that Geoffrey was going to be here."

Sir H: "Would it have made any difference?"

Bradley: Bradley was thrown off guard by this question, "I suppose not, but I wanted to share some thoughts with respect to my previous meeting with Geoffrey, who apparently has already told you."

Sir H: "On the contrary, Geoffrey has not shared any part of your discussion with me. You said that you had an "unpleasant discussion with Geoffrey." I wanted to see if we could resolve any difficulties before the AGM and avoid any signs of disharmony, which could only be taken as a sign of weakness. Gentlemen, please help yourselves to a drink."

Geoffrey: "I am happy to have your intervention Sir Humphrey and pleased to have the opportunity to discuss my thoughts on the company and my present plans for the AGM."

Sir H: "All in good time Geoffrey. Let's postpone any discussion of the company and the AGM until after our meal. Nothing is worse for my digestive system than to have what could be an unpleasant discussion during dinner. Now, what are your thoughts regarding the Newcastle Knights chances on Saturday?"

As the host, Sir Humphrey, commanded the table and as much respected business man and former Army General, he commanded the attention of his guests. The conversation flowed easily throughout the remainder of the meal.

Sir H: "Gentlemen, thank you for your avoidance of matters relating to Robotic Solutions, which we will discuss in due time.

I have some good news. You will recall that we discussed gender imbalance on the Board. I had an interesting discussion with Justice Helen Skeleton, who will be leaving the High Court this coming month, having reached the retirement age. She and her husband, James, the well-known thoracic surgeon, are moving to his family property in the Hunter Valley. She would be pleased to be considered for a position on the board of Robo, since she is also a shareholder, and a prominent Chinese Australian, born into the Chung family."

Bradley: "That is good news – 2 for one. Well done Humphrey! Alice has also come up with a list of 3 others in the area that would be good candidates and we could contact them?"

Connors: "I would suggest that we circulate the list and encourage the other Board members to submit names as well. I would not contact these individuals until we have a consensus of the Executive Committee."

Sir H: "I like the idea of circulating to all Board members not just the Executive Committee. Would you do this Bradley?" Bradley nods.
"Now to the issue of Geoffrey's shareholding and his plans.

Geoffrey, I understand as a result of the reading of your wife's Will, you own or control 20-22 % of Robotic Solution shares. In that regard, you should have a seat on the Board and I understand, Bradley, that you were empowered by the Board to offer Geoffrey a seat on the Board. Is that true?"

Geoffrey: "Yes."

Bradley: "Yes."

Connors: "Then what is the problem."

Bradley: Petulantly, "He believes that I should not be Chairman and will vote against me for re-election and threatened to vote against all Directors."

Connors: "As is his right, if he feels that we have not performed our duties in the best interest of the shareholders."

Geoffrey sat quietly considering his reply and looked at Sir Humphrey who had what Alice would call a Cheshire cat smile on his face. Sir Humphrey looked at him and nodded.

Bradley:		"But... I have been a good Chairman and shareholders have received increasingly greater dividends and there is a large surplus in the bank."

Geoffrey:	"I don't disagree with anything that Bradley has said. I do disagree that this is the best course of action for this company. We were at the forefront of technology when we changed from a manufacturing company to one that produced robotic solutions for 3D and other equipment. We are now losing our edge and we are not providing sufficient R&D funding and not applying our capital in the most productive way. Warren Buffet said that not investing in your own company is not the way to grow your company."

Bradley:	Petulantly, "You're just pissed off, because we did not support your proposal."

Sir H:		"Gentlemen. I have been sitting listening carefully to what has been said and what has not been said and believe that we will not resolve the differences between the two of you today. Perhaps, you should go away from this meeting, consider your positions and see if you can reach common ground before the AGM. I am available to you, if you need to discuss your positions. Thank you for joining me today."

With that, the meeting was over. Bradley left first and then Geoffrey.

Sir H:		"Connor, what do you make of this?"

Connor:	"Geoffrey is right, Bradley needs to go, perhaps not as a Director but as Chairman. Bradley was right for 10 years ago but not for now. He and I, and I suppose you, are dinosaurs. Directors now should have their finger on the pulse of their companies and on the marketplace in which their company operates to best serve their shareholders. Bradley likes being Chairman and likes the dividends but he has no "skin in the game", as you and I both have. I like the idea of Justice Skelton – Chinese and a women and a shareholder."

Sir H: "If it came to a vote, would you vote for Bradley as Chairman."

Connors: "No."

Sir H: "Neither would I. Perhaps, I should have a talk with Bradley. He may have reached the same conclusion and will contact me."

Connors: "I wouldn't bet on it! Bradley has a big ego and I believe that he thinks that Geoffrey will not carry out his threat. I saw a different Geoffrey today and I believe that he is up to his threat."

Sir H: "I agree but let's see if common sense prevails. Thank you Connors for being here and for your insight."

* * *

It was late the following week when Sir Humphrey received a call from the Chairman of Commonwealth Bank, Sandra Stedman, which prompted him to contact Bradley. He reached Alice, who said that she would contact him and yes, his schedule was clear for the afternoon of the 21st of November at the University Club. When Bradley arrived at 2 o'clock, Sir Humphrey was not there but he arrived a few minutes later.

Sir H: "Sorry for being late, but the Vice Chancellor wanted to discuss what to do with the money that Margaret Hamilton left to the University."

Bradley: "She did have her hands in everything."

Sir H: "The reason I called you on such short notice was that I received a call from the Sandra Stedman from CBA and she asked me if anything was happening in Robotics Solutions, since they received an offer from one of the Canadian Super Funds to buy their shares for $1 above current market. Do you know anything about this?"

Bradley: "Geoffrey mentioned that he had the same offer."

Sir H: "And you did not think that this was important enough to tell the Board?"

Bradley: "I thought it was another ploy by Geoffrey to scare me."

Sir H: "Bradley, I am glad we are having this discussion, since it reaffirms my decision not to support you for Chairman at the AGM."

Bradley: "You can't do this to me."

Sir H: "I can and I will. I will also not support you as a Director. Bradley you have two clear options and only one that will allow you to save face. You will resign and receive the kudos you so richly deserve plus a bonus for your over 10 years of service or you can fight and you will lose and receive nothing."

Bradley: "You leave me with little choice."

Sir H: "No, I leave you with 2 choices."

Bradley: "I reluctantly choose the retirement option."

Sir H: "Good , this conversation never happened. You can submit your resignation as if it was totally your own decision."

Bradley knew that Sir Humphrey would keep his word. He wondered about the bonus, $500,000 seemed like a realistic figure.

Sir Humphrey was relieved to have this matter settled. He wondered, if Geoffrey wanted the Chairmanship or should he support Connor O'Loughlan. He decided to let events unfold and then make his decision.

* * *

Bradley was not going to retire without fanfare. He knew that Mondays were a dull day for newspapers, so he waited until 10 o'clock on Monday morning, November the 21st. He told Julian Day that he could have exclusive rights to the story and he said that he had another story equally exciting attempted takeover of

Robotics Solution by a Canadian Super fund. Having arrange for his son to buy shares on margin in Robotic Solutions on the previous Thursday, he expected that the newspaper article would result in the share rising by 4-5 %, which would net him at least $20,000-$25000 profit in seven days. His son would then sell the stock, repay the margin loan and deposit the proceeds in a company bank account.

The announcement was made, the story was published and on Wednesday the 23rd, Robotic Solutions shares went up by 6%. Bradley's son sold the shares, repaid the Margin loan and collected the $26,500.

* * *

Connors and Sir Humphrey decided to meet with Geoffrey on the 23th to determine his true agenda, now that the matter of Bradley was out of the way. While the meeting with Sir Humphrey was scheduled for 2:00 o'clock in the executive conference room of Robotic Solutions, Geoffrey arrived early. He could not help but look into his old office. He had to admit that it did have a pristine look about it. All black and chrome. It did match the executive conference room. The paintings were postmodern - Andy Warhol, Jeff Koons and Michael Graves, not particularly to his liking but worked well with the décor.

Connors and Sir Humphrey arrived together. There was the usual exchange of pleasantries and then the meeting began in earnest.

Connors: "Geoffrey, we need to establish some ground rules, so that we are all on the same page regarding your position."

Geoffrey: "I agree. First, I am not selling my stock to the Canadians. Second, I do not want to be Chairman but I want to appoint the next Chairman. Three, I want to appoint an EEO Officer. I also want at least 2 women on the board.

Sir H: "That sounds reasonable, doesn't it Connor?"   Connor nods. "Who do you propose for Chairman?"

Geoffrey: "You Sir Humphrey."

Sir H: "While I am flattered, I am 74 years old and well past my prime. Besides, you said that we needed younger board members.

Geoffrey: "You would fill one of my Board seats and I would fill the other. You would make certain that I remain honest and I would back you up when you needed it. In addition, you have direct access to the University Board and, as a result of Margaret's legacy for the Robotics Centre, we will need that access to implement the arrangement between the University and Robotic Solutions. I see it as a Win Win solution to what could be a sticky problem."

Connor: "Sounds like a formidable team to me."

Sir H: "I accept on the basis that Connor accepts the Vice Chairman's position and becomes Chairman on my retirement in 2019. Geoffrey, I welcome the opportunity to work with you and the new CEO, who I understand you have briefed. I have to say that you have shown both skill and fortitude in reaching this point. However, I do not intend to move here, so I will not need the Chairman's office and staff. If so, what will you do about Alice?"

Geoffrey: "I have already thought about that. I propose her as the new EEO Officer reporting directly to James Hunter. She will also assist the Board with finding new Board members.

Larry Abbott, the acting CEO entered the Board Room.

Sir H: "Larry your timing is impeccable. Have you been in touch with James?"

Larry:	"I have been keeping him informed. He appreciated Geoffrey briefing him on his position and agrees with Geoffrey's proposals. He has spent 3 weeks with our new partners in China and 3 weeks with the Americans. He has signed Heads of Agreement with both. The Chinese will produce the components we need. They have also agreed that we will have an option to take a 50% stake in their computer division. The American's have been more difficult, largely because they are not certain about the political outcome of the Presidential election. "

Sir H:	"Bloody Americans. What's his reading on the Presidential race?"

Larry:	"While Hillary Clinton is currently the front runner, there is a feeling that she is too establishment and they need someone different. According to James, the people with whom he is in contact believe that Trump's speeches saying that he will drain the Washington swamp of those that are there just for the money and his 'Make America Great Again' comments has resonated with a large number of people. If he can take the mid West and the larger states, he could be the new President."

Geoffrey:	"When can we expect James back?"

Larry:	"He is expected back in time for the AGM."

✳ ✳ ✳

The AGM did not usually attract a large crowd. However, this one on Saturday the 3rd of December did, owing to the resignation of Geoffrey earlier in the year, the resignation of Bradley, the opportunity to see the new renovations, the changes in the Directors and other announcements not foretold in the Notice to Shareholders. The meeting would be a large one, perhaps at least 70-80 people. Instead of the Executive Board room, the meeting would be held in the lobby of the building.

Alice, who had been told of her new appointment, was busy directing staff with last Minute changes to the room arrangements, and did not see Geoffrey arrive. Her two daughters did and greeted him with a kiss on the cheek. It was their responsibility to escort the guests in groups of 5-10 through the building before and after the AGM.

Jane:　　　　　"Hello Uncle Geoffrey. You look snazzy, relaxed and no Preppy look. Very much like Rhett Butler. I like it"

Indeed, Geoffrey had taken considerable time deciding what he would wear. He wanted the old Geoffrey to emerge from his year long absence. Earlier in the month, he had persuaded Barry to accompany him to Sydney for a day of shopping.

Barry:　　　　　"How much of a difference do you want?"

Geoffrey:　　　"I want a costume that sends a message that the old Geoffrey is gone and the new one is here and also pays tribute to the 100th anniversary of the company."

Barry:　　　　　"You want the real you to come out of the closet and the new you to reveal all the things that you want to be. So we need to ditch Brooks Brothers and MJ Bale and go for something a little more unusual. I know just the place!"

And then they were in Oxford Street Vintage. While Barry explained the look he wanted to Peter, the owner, Geoffrey wandered through the store looking at clothing from all periods and in all sizes.

Barry:　　　　　"I think that I have found it, if you don't wear it I will. It was a black frock coat with matching fawn pants and a black silk waist coat."

Geoffrey:　　　"I have never worn anything like this in my life. Isn't it a little theatrical for an AGM?"

Barry:　　　　　"AGMs are theatre! Do you want to make a statement or not. This makes a statement! If it was good enough for Rhett Butler, it is good enough for the

AGM. That and a new ruffled shirt will complete the look and set you apart from everyone else."

Geoffrey: "I will humor you and try it on but don't get your hopes up, since I am not certain I can emerge as the butterfly that you envisage."

Geoffrey goes into the change room and emerges and stands in front of the mirror.

Barry: "Well, what do you think? I think you look hot! What do you think Peter?" Peter fans himself, indicating HOT.

Geoffrey: "Barry I am not going to the AGM as someone who is HOT. But it does fit well and the fact that I have been exercising has helped."

He was brought back to reality by Susan.

Susan: "Uncle Geoffrey, we are acting as hostesses. How do we look?"

They looked fine as young girls in their 20s looked. They had their mother's good looks and their father's height both over 173 cm. Which was the lesbian and which one was engaged to be married? Did it really matter?

Geoffrey: "You look like professional women here to do a job! Are you being paid or is your mother still keeping you in servitude."

Jane: "You can't say that any more now that she is the EEO officer."

Alice: "Geoffrey, that Rhett Butler look suits you."

Geoffrey: "You can say nothing else, since that would be in violation of the EEO Code of Ethics."

Alice: "You don't have to worry about me, see what Michael says."

Geoffrey turned and saw Michael approaching and waited for his reaction.

Michael: "I like it!"

Geoffrey: "You what?"

Michael: "I like your outfit. It is something I could never wear nor would I want to, but it is you. If you ever wanted to make a statement, you have. In any event, who is going to criticize you and do you care anyway."

Geoffrey: "I am not certain whether you are being facetious or not. However, I like the way it feels and I really don't give a "fuck" what people say."

Jane: "Go Uncle Geoffrey."

Alice: "Now that you have finished discussing Geoffrey's clothing choice, would you girls get back to your job.   Michael I need help with the seating. Geoffrey please talk to Stephen from Executive Catering about the display."

Geoffrey walked over to where Stephen was giving instructions to his staff.

Stephen: "If it isn't Rhett Butler himself! Mr H I think that it suits you. Can I take a selfie?" He moves next to Geoffrey and takes the photograph. "Mike will not believe it. Now what can I do for you?"

Geoffrey: "I am not certain whether Alice wanted me to help out with the catering or I was disturbing her "work crew"".

Stephen: "No, I think she wanted you to review the layout of the display. We went a little crazy with the theme, since it is the 100th anniversary of the company."

Something only Alice would remember, thought Geoffrey.

"The backdrop is a collage of pictures from the opening of the factory with the Governor General and one of the Bigelow's cutting the tape and then through the years and finally you standing before the newly restored façade. The centrepiece is a 3D carving of the latest model of the 3XR and other pieces are made from pastries. What do you think, since you're the man of the hour?"

Geoffrey: "I think it will be a big hit, but be certain to take pictures of it for the archives.

Stephen: "Murray from archives was here and brought the photos and took the pictures. He really should take a picture of you."

The shareholders began to arrive, including Mr and Mrs McMillan, whose comment on seeing Geoffrey when he came downstairs for breakfast in his Rhett Butler attire sealed the fate of his dress: "Mr Geoffrey you look just like the image of Miss Margaret's great grandfather, I remember seeing pictures of him. All you need is the top hat. I like it."

Julian Day arrived with his photographer and had Geoffrey pose in front of the display.

Julian: "Well Mr Hamilton is this the way you are paying tribute to the old? "

Geoffrey: "No, it is the new me paying tribute to the old me."   The look on Julian's face indicated that this did not register at all.

Bradley: "Sorry Geoffrey. Julian, could you take a photograph of me with the Lt Governor."

Geoffrey was glad to be rid of Julian Day. He did not like the press and felt that they currently were creating news not reporting news and most of what they reported was based upon conjecture and not real facts. He was certain that they would report on what they would like to see happen to Robotic Solutions and not what would happen. But, here is someone who knows how to handle the press.

It was Robyn who arrived with George Wooley.

Geoffrey: "Hello Robyn, George."

Robyn: "Well Geoffrey, you have done it.   You have completely undermined my total image of you and now here you are Rhett Butler. I like the image and I think you look very smart."

George: "Geoffrey it does suit you and fits in perfectly with the theme of 100 years of the company. Not every ex CEO would try this but you have pulled it off. Good on you!"

Geoffrey: "It looks like our esteemed leader wants to start. I will see you after the AGM, since I have a role to perform in this production."

Bradley: "Ladies and gentlemen and distinguished guests. I welcome you to the 100th anniversary of the company's AGM. A company founded by the Bigelow's, who built this factory on land they acquired from the representatives of the Wonnarua nation. A plaque in the foyer of this building acknowledges this. In keeping with past tradition, I am pleased to introduce the retiring CEO of Robotic Solutions. Geoffrey Hamilton, resplendent in his attire paying tribute to the 100th Anniversary."

Geoffrey: "Thank you Bradley, I must pay tribute also to our retiring Chairman and for the fine work that he has done during the past 10 years." He turns and applauds Bradley as do the shareholders. Out of the corner of his eye, he saw Sir Humphrey mouths the words "Nicely done".

"There has been much speculation about my future role and the fact that through my wife's legacy that I would have considerable influence over the future of Robotic Solutions. I am here to address those speculations." He pauses for dramatic effect. "Like you I am a shareholder and the largest shareholder. I intend to have exert some influence over the future direction of Robotic Solutions but not as CEO, since I believe that James Hunter the new CEO will do an excellent job and was the right choice for the job; not as Chairman, since the new Chairman will be elected today and I will not be offering my name for that position; but as a Board member with "skin in the game" and as a shareholder like you."

However, I do have some specific areas that I believe that Robotic Solutions should and will explore:

... We will propose a woman as a member of the Board for the first time and will seek the appointment of 2 additional women by 2020;

... We will review all of our packaging and attempt to reach 100% recycling materials by 2020

... We will assist in the development of a waste recycling plant, so that Morton will become totally waste free by 2025;

... In partnership with Northup University, we will continue and expand our work in 3D solutions in the area of training for teachers; and

...We will increase R&D spending by 25% and in partnership with Northup University, we will develop a better understanding of the potential of application of Artificial Intelligence and 3D applications in health.

We will need your cooperation, since these initiatives, while bringing long term future gains to the company are not without their costs."

Again, he paused for emphasis.

"A wise man, once said that a company that does not invest in itself, either has no confidence in itself or is signaling that it has run out of ideas. Robotic Solutions has rewarded its shareholders with capital increases of over 245% in the last 10 years and generous dividends but it has not invested in itself. This has to stop! The Board will take a 10% cut in remuneration, there will be a natural attrition in management staff of 10%, who will be replaced with women of comparable, if not better qualifications and toward that end, Robo Solutions has appointed Alice Sass to the new position of Equal Employment Officer. We are proposing that the next annual dividend be reduced by 10% and that a capital buy back of 10% be instituted effective April 2017.

Fellow shareholders, this is a watershed moment in the company's history and I ask you to support your new CEO and the Board in a new direction for the company that recognizes its place in Morton, in New South Wales, in Australia and the World."

"Thank you."

He had expected everything from boos to No's but did not expect a standing ovation.

Bradley Haines came forward and took his hand and squeezed it. "You rotten little shit, you pulled it off."

Bradley: "Thank you for those inspiring words. James Hunter, your new CEO, is delayed in New York as a result of a snow storm, so he will not be here in person but he is here via satellite to say a few words."

James: "Well Geoffrey, you're a hard act to follow. Thank you for the upbeat approach to the next 5 years. Your comments were received in New York by our new partners with enthusiasm and the feeling that you are setting an example for other companies in gender representation, in responsible waste reduction plans and for reminding them of the importance of redeploying their capital resources. I look forward to returning later in the month and meeting with shareholders in the New Year. Merry Christmas to all."

The formal part of the meeting continued. Bradley's resignation was accepted and new Board members, Helen Skelton and Geoffrey Hamilton were elected and Sir Humphrey and the other retiring Board members were re-elected. Sir Humphrey was elected Chairman.

The financial reports were approved and the Resolutions regarding the 10% reduction in the 2018 dividend and the buy-back were accepted.

Bradley: "Ladies and Gentlemen the meeting is concluded. On behalf of the Directors and myself, I wish you a very Merry Christmas and a prosperous new year."

Sir H: "Great look Geoffrey and right tone in your speech. I did not anticipate the reaction of the shareholders. Incidentally, Helen Skelton has agreed to help Alice with recruiting more women to the Board of Directors. She also has suggested that Alice join her at a week long seminar on EEO in Melbourne in February.

I thought there would be more grumbling among our fund shareholder. I have talked to Clive Matthews from the Coal Miners Superannuation Fund and he felt that you achieved the right balance between the reduction in the dividend and the capital return, so that the impact on shareholders will not be felt for another two years at which time the capital appreciation should be increased. He also liked the idea that the Board would take a 10% cut in its remuneration."

Geoffrey: "I still worry about the little investors, like Mr and Mrs McMillan. What do you think the **AFR** will report."

Sir H: "They will report positively. An increase in profits by 16%, forward looking forecast and some innovative approaches to capital retention and an investment in the company's future."

And that is exactly what was reported the following day by the **AFR** along with an article reporting that the outgoing Chairman and his son were being investigated by the ASIC. The **Newcastle Chronicle** had a picture of Geoffrey with a caption – "**Something Old /Something New**".

He left the meeting ahead of other shareholders and in his MG headed directly for Summer Park to report to Margaret on the success of the AGM. What he found was not what he expected. A large truck was parked directly in front of the Weeping Willow Tree, obscuring it from his view. He jumped from the car and went over to where 2 workers were standing talking.

Worker 1:   "Well it was to be expected, each year it kept on growing leaning further and further and finally the weight of the crown finally toppled it over."

Worker 2:   "What is to be done now?"

Worker 1:   "There is nothing we can do. Head office will send out a crew and they will cut the branches and feed it into a mulcher, since they don't want the tree breaking loose and floating down the river and ending up acting like a dam somewhere down stream."

The workers looked up and saw Geoffrey in his Rhett Butler outfit with tears streaming down his face, then looked at each other.

Worker 1:   "Mr Hamilton?"

Geoffrey: "Yes."

Worker 1:   "Are you alright?"

Geoffrey: "No, I have just lost my best friend."

Worker 1:   "Is there anything we can do to help?"

Geoffrey considered for a moment.

Geoffrey: "Do you have a saw?"

Worker 1:   "Yes, we have a cross cut."

Geoffrey: "I need to borrow it."

The worker handed Geoffrey the saw and Geoffrey stripped off his shoes and jacket and waded into the water.   They look at each other as he began to saw his branch, his gift from Margaret just above where he had carved their initials.

Worker 2:   "Mr Hamilton, they will be in tomorrow to do this."

Ignoring them, Geoffrey continued to saw until the branch was severed from the tree.

Geoffrey: "Will you give me a hand with this." Together they pulled the branch up on the bank.

Geoffrey: "Thank you. I have a favour. Could you load that branch on to your truck and follow me home? Of course, I will pay you."

Worker 1:   "We can do that Mr Hamilton but there will be no charge. That is the least we can do for you, since Mrs Hamilton had been so good to us at Christmas and special occasions."

Geoffrey to himself "You are always there, Margaret!"

They followed Geoffrey to North Grange and helped carry the branch to the back garden and then left.

When Mr and Mrs McMillan arrived later in the day, they saw Geoffrey sitting on the branch, his head in his hands weeping.

Mrs Mc:	"He has obviously discovered the Weeping Willow."

Mr Mc:	"I know exactly what to do with it. We will convert it into a bench and anytime that he needs to, he can come into the garden and visit her."

Mrs Mc:	"Shall we tell him now?"

Mr Mc:	"Let him be."

24. THE CRAFTS FAIR – FINALE

* * *

Geoffrey was running late and left the house with only a thermos of coffee, much to Mrs Mc Millan's annoyance. He jumped in his car and sped off heading for Northup University's Music College. He stopped a Louie's for a bagel and Morton News for his Saturday morning paper.

This was the final rehearsal before tonight's performance at the Craft's Fair. Although he had not played in public for many years and then only at a charity function with Margaret, he was confident that he would play well tonight. After all, he thought I made that speech at the AGM in the Rhett Butler costume. If I can do that I can do anything. He had thanked Barry for his help, who in turn asked for the costume, which he said he wanted to incorporate into his next performance. His tuxedo was more comfortable and Mrs Mc had had it dry cleaned and would have it laid out for him when he returned.

He entered the auditorium from the rear entrance and made his way to the front of the stage where Kevin McNally, the Director of the Music School, and Barry were having a serious discussion.

Barry: "Kevin, I don't feel good about this."

Kevin: "Well eventually everyone will know."

Geoffrey: "Hi guys, am I interrupting you or am I early."

Kevin: "Sorry Geoffrey, we were just going over the presentation."

Barry: "Have you seen the program?"

The World Premiere of

"The Morton Suite"

By

Ulysses Barry Oliver, Composer and conductor

Featuring

Geoffrey Hamilton, pianist

And Orchestrated

For the Northup Chamber Group

By Kevin McNally

Kevin: "I am sorry I forgot to tell you that we would be starting 30 minutes later, since the Chamber Group had classes until 8:30 this morning."

Geoffrey: "That's OK, I brought a thermos of coffee and bagels from Louie's. Would you like to share some with me?"

Barry: "Thanks we ate before we came."

Geoffrey took his newspaper and his coffee to the front row and munched on the bagel, while Barry and Kevin continue the interrupted discussion. Geoffrey, turned the page and came to Julian Day's column entitled "Who Is the Mystery Author and who is Ulysses". It went on to say, "**Mystery surrounds the Wilson Arts Fair announcement of the World Premier of the Morton Suite. Although a reliable source told this reporter that his first name was Ulysses and that he was Georgian. This reporter will want to hear more and learn more about the mysterious Russian conductor and author at tonight's Crafts Awards Ceremony.**"

Geoffrey: "You made the Newcastle papers, Julian Day's column." Barry came rushing over and Geoffrey handed him the pages.

Barry: "Who gave him that information?"

Geoffrey: "Who else has the most to gain from the publicity?"

Barry: "Robyn"

Geoffrey: "She does know how to plant a story and she has fed this one to Julian and she knew that he would print it. This will mean that the usual attendance at the Crafts Fair will increase by 30-40%."

The 5 members of the Chamber Group arrived and rehearsal began. Barry was more physically exuberant than usual and the rehearsal went without a break and everyone was pleased with the result. It ended with Barry thanking everyone for their efforts and everyone looking forward to that evening.

Geoffrey: "Well brilliant composer that went well."

Barry: "I think so. Did you think that Kevin liked it'?"

Geoffrey: "Of course, why wouldn't he?"

Barry: "Can I ride back with you? I need to talk to you." They pulled out of the parking lot and started back to Morton.

Geoffrey: "Do you want to talk about it now or later?"

Barry: "Now. Geoffrey I think I am in love."

Geoffrey: "I am flattered but…"

Barry: "Not you! Kevin. There I said it. I wasn't certain that I could tell anyone but I feel comfortable talking to you. Tell me I am I silly old queen who falls in love for the first time at 50."

Geoffrey: "Have you discussed your alcoholic problem?

Barry: "I did and Kevin said that he was an alcoholic but has not touched a drop of alcohol for 20 years. In fact, he met his lover at an AA meeting.

Geoffrey: "Does Kevin make you happy?"

Barry: "Yes"

Geoffrey: "Do you feel comfortable around him and do you trust him?"

Barry: "Yes"

Geoffrey: "Is the sex good?"

Barry:　　　"Yes, as good as it gets for those in their golden years. But it is not the sex, it is the feeling of finding the right person. Someone who shares your values and interests"

Geoffrey:　　"Does Kevin feel the same way?"

Barry:　　　"Yes, that is what we were discussing when you came in. We have been seeing each other for over 6 months. Now, he wants me to move in with him. His lover died 5 years ago and at 60, he did not think he would find love and someone who shared the same interests. He has had several opportunities with graduate students but does not want to go through that and beside it is automatic dismissal."

Geoffrey:　　"I have known him for about 8 years. Margaret and I both knew he was gay and met him and his lover at the theatre and concerts. I think he is a decent and caring person and someone you could trust"

Barry:　　　"Thank you for that. Now I have to break this news to Bryan."

Geoffrey:　　"Bryan will be OK with this. How are his negotiations with the purchase of the Kelly's Paddock going?"

Barry:　　　"From what I understand the Chinese have agreed to the Terms and Conditions and have set a deadline of the 23rd of December but even with the money you gave him for his shares, he is still $500,000 short. I could lend him the money, since I have that much in CBA but that would leave me with little in reserve."

Geoffrey:　　"Why not offer Bryan $500,000 for 20% of the business. You would handle the entertainment and the front of the house and hotel business and Bryan would handle the bar and the dining room plus build up his catering and food business."

Barry:　　　"I hadn't thought of it in that way but I can see that it could be a Win Win situation.   I am a hard worker and I would make my end it work."

Geoffrey: "And Bryan is a hard worker. So it would work. But what about your new relationship with Kevin?"

Barry: "I will discuss it with him. It might work out well, he has to be in Sydney each week for two days to conduct classes at the Australian Institute of Music and he has a one month music camp each year. I think that we can work something out."

They arrived at Kelly's Paddock.

Geoffrey: "Door to door service. Remember what Mrs Bower said "Be yourself." I will support you in whatever decision you make. See you brilliant composer."

Barry: "Thanks for the advice personally and with Bryan. See yeah brilliant pianist."

Geoffrey drove around the block and parked in the Wilson parking lot.
Upon entering the Centre he saw Russell and Bryan.

Bryan: "The new celebrity arrives."

Geoffrey: "What do you mean?"

Bryan: "You obviously have not seen the **Australian's** Business Section today? Not only has Robotic Solutions shares gone up 8% but you are featured as a cartoon character in your Rhett Butler costume."

Geoffrey: "No! I did not see it because I had to be at the University early this AM."

Russell: "Good morning Geoffrey. Don't listen to him. He has been manic all morning. He could not find you or Barry to help him. So he enlisted Mrs McMillan, Robyn and me."

Bryan: "I had prepared enough food for the usual number of people but the crowd is twice as large as in previous years and they all want "Healthy Eats". I called North Grange and Mrs McMillan said that you left in a rush for some meeting.

When I explained what I needed she volunteered her niece and nephew. She also called the Saas and Alice's two daughters are in helping as well. We just made it through lunch. However, I need to have enough ready for this evening."

Geoffrey: "Why not limit the variety of what you are serving and concentrate on just a few items."

Bryan: "I had thought I would give them the full range of what we offer but I can see that you are right, if I am going to mass produce I need to select a smaller range of foods."

Russell: "Or you could not prepare anything! You could provide the recipes and provide the ingredients and let people make their own. "

Bryan: "Russell when this is over, we can discuss that idea. I have already trialed all the recipes, all I need to do is to package them, provide the recipes and people could prepare them when they like."

Geoffrey: "I see that I am not needed. I can go home and enjoy my celebrity status. By the way Bryan, please talk to Barry. I think he has a proposition for you that you would be crazy not to consider." Bryan looked quizzically.

Robyn: "NO way Geoffrey, stay right where you are. "

With that, Robyn came sliding down the rope from the mezzanine.

Geoffrey: "Are you nuts! Do you realise that you could have killed yourself."

Robyn: "You do look cute when you are frustrated. Get out of your "old Geoffrey mode" and rejoice in the Rhett Butler mode. Race through burning Atlanta in your horse drawn wagon."

He had a momentary flash back to the day Margaret rode across the flooded Grove River and said something similar.

Geoffrey: "Has everyone gone mad. Or am I at a Mad Hatter's tea party."

Roby: "Relax and give us all a chance to do what you did at the AGM. I realised that you were trying to rid yourself of the past Geoffrey and find the new Geoffrey. Now, I need you to put on your thinking cap."

Geoffrey: "OK Miss Scarlett, I am yours."

Robyn to herself "If only that were true."

Robyn: "Let's go to my office"

They leave the hall and on the way she explains that Russell came to her and suggested that he would like to open a crafts shop and establish a training program for old skills.

Geoffrey: "That is a great idea and it does free up some of the space for other programs."

Robyn: "I have a crazy idea! I have money that Margaret gave us. We could break through the second floor of Russell's building. That area could be the training program for old skills. The crafts shop below would be for items that we regularly make and items that people would bring in and sell on consignment. The court yard between the two buildings could be cobbled over and be an outdoor restaurant area serviced by "Healthy Eats.""

Geoffrey: "Do I detect a Bryn Mawr education."

Robyn: "You're damn right. You made me see that Margaret wanted us to do what we do best and that meant taking chances. However, this is not a chance; it is an opportunity. I have discussed the logistics with the architect, David Leichhardt, who renovated this building, and he thought that it was a brilliant idea. The two buildings already complement each other and breaking through the 2nd level and putting in a glass enclosed bridge would not compromise the integrity of the heritage listing. In addition, he would recommend that we ask the Council to put heritage pavement in front of both buildings and extend it into and through the laneway and close the laneway to only pedestrian traffic."

Geoffrey: "I think you have sorted all this out. Why do you need me?"

Robyn: "Because I needed a sounding board and Margaret always said you had one of the best minds around."

Geoffrey: "OK. What is in it for Russell? Does he want to sell?"

Robyn: "He would sell for $400,000, which is $200,000 below market value, provided we gave him a 10 year lease on the ground level. We would split the profits, 70% -30%, I estimate that at a minimum we would net $20 000 per annum from the split. He would be the Director of the Trades area and paid from a grant that the NSW Government has given us. We would negotiate with either Bryan or Executive Catering for the food area.

Geoffrey: "I think it is a great plan."

Robyn: "Thank you."

With that, she opened a file folder pulled out her pen and signed the Heads of Agreement.

Geoffrey: "What if I said no, I don't like it?"

Robyn: "I would have gone back to Russell with a counter proposal. Sometimes we get so excited by a project that we allow the excitement to overcome our judgement. I thought I had it right but I needed and unbiased and uninvolved individual with an analytical mind to review it. And, that was you."

Geoffrey: "Thank you for your trust." As he started to leave.

Robyn: "Well, how is the **Morton Suite** going and how is Barry?"

Geoffrey: "I think everyone will be surprised by the music."

He thought about telling her about Kevin and Barry, but decided against it.

"Barry is fine, but a little nervous."

It was already after 2 o'clock when he arrived home. He saw Mr and Mrs McMillan in the kitchen, "A picture of domestic bliss," he thought. They had been married for 43 years and he had never heard them say an unkind word to each other in the 20 some years he had known them. They had had 2 sons, one had died when he was 18 in one of those unfortunate sporting accidents and the other two years later from a fall from a roof where he was installing solar panels. They had worked for the Bigelow family all their working lives and had met when Mrs Mc had been a maid in Hawthorne Manor and Mr Mc had been employed as a gardener.

His thoughts were interrupted by Mrs Mc.

Mrs Mc: "Have you had your lunch? I thought not, I suppose you did not have breakfast either?"

Geoffrey: "Guilty on both counts your honour."

Mrs Mc: "Here's a ham, avocado and cheese sandwich and a salad and one of your health food drinks. When you finish, Mr McMillan has something to show you in the garden."

Geoffrey: "This is good. I didn't realise how hungry I was. What's in the garden? Don't tell me that the gardenias have been attacked by aphids again?"

When he had finished, they walked into the garden but Geoffrey could see nothing.

Geoffrey: "What is it?"

Mr Mc: "When you came back from Summer Park last evening and had the 2 workman from the park deliver the branch from the Weeping Willow Tree, we wondered what you would do with it. I thought you might like to keep it intact, so I built a stone base next to the large oak, so that you could sit on the branch as you did In the Park with your head resting against the oak. While I cleaned it with water, I did not polish it, although I could do that."

Upon seeing the branch, a tear slip down Geoffrey's face and he turned to Mrs Mc and put his arms around her. She patted him on the back.

Mrs Mc: "That's alright." As he wept. She took him to the bench.   She motioned to Mr McMillan and they left him there.

A little later Geoffrey came back into the kitchen where the McMillans were enjoying a cup of tea.

Geoffrey: "I want to thank you for the bench. It will always remind me of Margaret and your thoughtfulness. I had a strange feeling when I was sitting there that it would be the last time I would speak to Margaret. No! That I would not need to speak to Margaret. I would think of her but not need to speak to her. Does that make any sense?"

Mrs Mc: "Yes, you no longer need Margaret."

Geoffrey: "I am not certain but I don't miss her in the same way. I think I will go up to my room and have a nap before I leave for Wilsons."

Mrs Mc: "We will see you there, since we want to hear you play Barry's music. I have left your tux in the closet along with your dress shirt."

* * *

Geoffrey arrived just in time to hear the University Chamber Group play their last piece, the Shostakovich's Piano Quintet in G minor, Opus 57, which meant that **The Morton Suite** would be on in about 7-8 minutes. Kevin McNally felt that the Shostakovich would be a good introduction for **The Morton Suite** and about the same length, 5 minutes.

He looked around for Barry but could not find him. He did see Bryan, who gave him a thumbs up. As the Chamber Group concluded and filed offstage and the lights went up but still no sign of Barry. What is the worst that can happen? Barry could not show up! However, the music did speak for itself and a Chamber Group did not need a conductor.

Fifteen minutes later, The Chamber Group's, first violinist, Helen Aviary, signal that they were ready. They heard the announcement from Robyn:

Robyn: "Ladies and Gentlemen I am pleased to present the World Premier of **'The Morton Suite'** as played by the University Chamber Group with Geoffrey Hamilton on the piano. Conducting his own composition, Ulysses Barry Oliver."

The four members of the Chamber Group and Geoffrey walked on stage as the lights in the hall dimmed.

"Where the hell are you Barry?", said Geoffrey to himself.

In the back of the hall, there was a commotion and a figure dressed in black with a long black cape with a red lining strode through the crowd and up the stage. It was Barry, devoid of makeup and every bit the maestro. He removed the cape with a florish and placed it over a chair revealing the Rhett Butler costume but with a black silk shirt.

Geoffrey: Quietly "You certainly know how to make an entrance."

Barry: To the University Chamber Group "It's show time. Let's make beautiful music together." And so they did.

The music painted a picture of Morton from the string instrument's softly reflecting the early morning rising sun touching the dew laced trees and the rushing river to the rising tempo of the day's activities until the final setting of the sun and the closing of the day with only the piano riffing a few chords and then a rush of the strings fading into silence. At its conclusion there was silence until Barry turned around and bowed to the audience. Then the audience burst into applause and rose to their feet and clapped vigorously.   He turned to the Chamber Group and mouthed the words "thank you," they in turn applauded him.

He turned to the audience and raised his hands for silence.

Barry: "This piece would not have seen the light off day, had it not been for the encouragement of Geoffrey Hamilton, AKA Rhett Butler, our brilliant pianist, who is making his debut. There was general laughter. He invited Geoffrey to come forward. "Finally the orchestration which enhanced my otherwise mundane offering was the work of Kevin McNally, my partner". Kevin came out and Barry kissed him on the lips.

Geoffrey said to himself "Talk about making a statement!"

Following **The Morton Suite,** Robyn announced the winners of various prizes and raffle winners. Finally, the announcement of the "People's Choice" for the Quilt.

Robyn: "The winner of this year's People Choice Award is Quilt #7, the Morton Heritage Quilt. I am pleased to announce that the Quilt has been bought by Robotic Solutions to be hung in their new foyer. The Retirement Quilt book describing the making of the Quilt is on sale today. Also, the total from our Annual Crafts Week is $76,000, far surpassing anything we have raised previously. A portion of this will be given to the Farmer's Drought Relief Fund.

My personal thanks to all who contributed to the success of this Week and to those who have attended and given so generously."

Seeing Maisie talking to Russell and Bryan, Robyn went over to them.

Robyn: "You boys must be happy with yourselves. People's Choice to be added to your other Award and then the trip to Sydney for entry into the National Competition."

Bryan: "We were actually discussing Barry. He has a boyfriend, which he let everyone know by the kiss he gave Kevin McNally on stage and Barry is my new partner in Kelly's Paddock, which allows me funds to removate the pub."

Robyn: "Boys do you mind if I steal Maisie away?"

They shake their heads NO and Robyn led Maisie to one side.

Robyn: "Before Russell blurted it out, I have news. I have signed a Heads of Agreement with Russell to buy his building as a crafts centre." She repeated everything she had told Geoffrey. "I will have to seek Board approval but you and I control over $600,000 of Margaret's money and I think this is the right decision and so does Geoffrey."

Maisie: "I think that is a great idea and it will free a lot of space for me and provide an outlet for locally made crafts, which should benefit the farming community. It will also provide a space for training in traditional skills. I will support you and go to the Board with you."

Robyn: "How do you think our little plan for Geoffrey has gone?"

Maisie: "Aside from the fact that you are in love with him, I think you fulfilled all your promises to Margaret. So girl, make your move before someone grabs him. It is not every day that you can snare Rhett Butler."

Robyn: "But I am not Scarlett O'Hara."

Maisie: "And he is not really Rhett Butler."

Robyn: "What would Margaret say?"

Maisie: "Ask her when you see her! Do you think that she would like to see you happy?"

Robyn: "Yes."

Maisie: "Do you think that she would like to see Geoffrey happy?"

Robyn: "Yes."

Maisie: "Do you think you could make Geoffrey happy?"

Robyn: "Yes."

Maisie: "Do you think he would make you happy?"

Robyn: "Yes."

Maisie: "The 20 questions are over. Margaret would want you both to be happy, you would be happy with Geoffrey and Geoffrey would be happy with you."

Robyn: "OK, suppose you're right, what do I do?"

Maisie: "You need to read Mills & Boone novels. If you want your man, you go after him. I assume that you are going to Geoffrey's party on the 23rd that gives 2 weeks to have him wrapped and put under your Christmas tree. I am off to a party at the Kelly's Paddock. Are you coming?"

Robyn: "No I have a few things to do and, frankly, I don't feel like a party."

Maisie departs and Robyn goes to her office and sits quietly at her desk. There is a gentle knock on the door. She looks up and it's Geoffrey.

Geoffrey: "I am going to the party at Kelly's Paddock and I thought you might like to go with me." She thinks for a moment.

Robyn: "I would like that." They leave together.

25. GEOFFREY'S CHRISTMAS PARTY

* * *

Geoffrey had had a busy week. He had settled the purchase of North Grange with Quinton's solicitors from funds he had obtained from the sale of shares in AAC on the advice of Paul Gallant. He now owned North Grange outright. He exercised the Trust's option to acquire Bryan's shares in Robotic Solutions, which allowed Bryan and Barry to meet the deadline for the payment to the Chinese. He had held meetings with the University and Sir Humphrey and reached agreement on a joint venture which would see Robotics Solutions being the conduit for providing research and development funds and sharing the intellectual property rights of Artificial Intelligence discovered by the University and he had agreed to serve as Chairman of the new School of Artificial Intelligence. Finally, he had found love.

He sat on the terrace in the late afternoon sun day dreaming when he was startled by the ringing of his mobile.

Geoffrey: "Hello Barry. How are you? No, I am not doing anything and I would be pleased to see you. Where are you now? That close? I will see you in 15 minutes."

Geoffrey checked to see, if there was anything in the refrigerator, in the event that Barry decided to stay for dinner. There was left over chicken and half an apple pie and salads, so he knew that he could feed 2-3 people.

Barry: "Yo Geoffrey, are you there?"   Barry had come through the back gate rather than the front door.

Geoffrey: "I am in the kitchen arranging lemonade and Mrs McMillan's sponge cake. Have a seat, I will be right with you,"

Geoffrey arrived with a tray and plates of sponge cake and a carafe of lemonade and 2 glasses. He was startled by the change in Barry.   Gone was the peroxide hair, the painted nails and the makeup. In its place, a crew cut, no makeup but well-groomed fingernails but no coloured polish and dressed in a Crew shirt and CK jeans. He was more preppy than Geoffrey ever was.

Geoffrey: "What happened to you? As Michael would say, did you fall in or out of Brooks Brothers?"

Barry: "Too butch?"

Geoffrey: "That's not it. I like it. It is you but it will be a surprise for people used to the old Barry. Did Kevin have something to do with this or is this the real you?"

Barry: "Kevin had something to do with it but he told me what Mrs Bowers said to me when I met her last year, "Barry be yourself and everyone will see the true you. I can live with you because I see who you are, not what you're wearing or how you camp it up."

Geoffrey, I am gay but I do not need to highlight the gay stereotype, nor do I need to pretend to be straight.   For years, the theatre was my cover, my way of hiding behind characters but the characters took over and I was suddenly on stage 24 hours a day and playing the gay role. And, I did it well to the point that I did not know who I was. I think this is the true me beneath the other me."

Geoffrey: "That is really a wonderful insight. Not that many people could be that honest. I am really proud of you. The new you began to emerge during the

Morton Suite.   I probably saw this metamorphous before others and it was wonderful to see"

Barry:	"I still will perform in drag at Kelly's but that will be my stage presence, not the real me."

Geoffrey:	"This would normally call for a bottle of champers but let's toast the new Barry."

Barry:	"Let's also toast the new Geoffrey. It took guts to wear that Rhett Butler outfit but you did wear it well. I had two different thoughts would you come out of the closet and announce that you were gay or would you emerge as a new person."

Geoffrey:	"A toast to the brilliant composer."

Barry:	"And to my brilliant pianist."

They laughed.

Barry:	"I almost forgot why I came. The first, is to thank you for your thoughts about Kelly's pub. It was the right thing to do. Without too much trouble, I was able finance the $500,000 and both Bryan and I are happy with the arrangement. I am particularly happy with owning 20% of the pub. The second reason, is that I wondered, if I could bring Kevin to your Christmas Party? "

Geoffrey:	"Of course and he will know many of the people coming.

Barry:	"Is there anything that Kevin and I can bring on Friday?"

Geoffrey:	"No, I have asked everyone not to bring presents but to donate something to the Farmer's Relief Fund."

Barry:	"Bryan has been very active in raising money for the fund. He says that his Hunter Valley Organic Farmers Association has proven that they can grow crops with 50% less water."

Geoffrey: "That is interesting I will talk to Bryan about how the University and Margaret's Trust might be able to help. Incidentally, he asked if he could bring Ava Mc Manus."

Barry: "Yes. Bryan left the DADs program just before the Crafts Festival and they started seeing one another after that. I think they would have gotten together earlier, but Ava was worried that the University might consider it a breach of professional ethics by dating a client."

Geoffrey: "Speaking of telling people, did you tell Bryan about Kevin?"

Barry: "Yes. I told him about us."

Geoffrey: "What was his reaction?"

Barry: "He said he was happy for me and that he was happy it was someone like Kevin. He knew Donald, Kevin's partner, and said that he was a fine person, unlike me more academic then theatrical. What he meant was Donald was quiet and I am flamboyant or as I used to say 'a screaming queen.'"

Geoffrey: "I like the flamboyant moniker better, since it represents where you are now."

Barry: "You are right. I must be going. I have a show this afternoon. I have a new number based upon that well known play "Portrait of Geoffrey Hamilton.""

Barry smiled and watched the look of shock on Geoffrey's face.

Barry: "I am only kidding Geoffrey. It is based upon Oscar Wilde's "Portrait of Dorian Grey. I play both the portrait and Dorian. The costumes are quiet stunning. I thought it was an appropriate way to introduce the new me."

Geoffrey: "Except that in the end you die and the portrait reverts to its youthful self."

Barry: "I am certain that the irony will not be lost on the audience. Kevin and I will see you on Friday evening at around 6-6:30. Thank Mrs Mc for the cake. Bye."

After Barry left and Geoffrey had washed, dried and put away the glasses and plates, and since it was early evening, Geoffrey decided to go to the garden and sit on the new bench that Mr Mc had created from the Thinking Tree. It had been sanded and stained but Geoffrey could still trace his and Margaret's initials. He still felt her presence whenever he sat there. He had allowed Robyn to sit there without him and she said that it was the most wonderful feeling. She said she had talked to Margaret and felt that Margaret had given her blessing.

The next day, he was in his office wrapping presents with Mrs McMillan when Stephen from Executive Caterers arrived to discuss the food for Friday night.

Stephen: "Hello Geoffrey, Mrs McMillan. What are you two up to?"

Geoffrey: "Hi Stephen. We are wrapping presents for Friday night."

Mrs Mc: "Hello Mr Stephen. Would you like some coffee?"

Stephen: "That would be lovely, thank you. Geoffrey, I thought that you told everyone that they could not bring presents but donate to the Farmers Relief Fund." Now, I find you wrapping presents."

Geoffrey: "It is only for the Quilt Team – Robyn, Maisie, Russell,

Barry and Bryan. I thought that a framed picture of the Morton Heritage Quilt would remind all of us of what brought us together."

Stephen: "They will really love that Geoffrey. You are really a thoughtful person."

Mrs McMillan returned with a carafe of coffee and a plate of assorted cookies.

Mrs Mc: "Here you are Stephen, Mr H."

Stephen: "Thank you Mrs McMillan. Here is a copy of what we planned to supply on Friday, if you agree."

Geoffrey: "Let Mrs Mc decide." He passed the details to Mrs Mc.

Stephen: "We think that 4 people will be able to cover the party, since Mike and I are guests, we can always back up the staff. We will arrive at 5 to set up. We will have the bar on the terrace and use the barbeque to keep the hot dishes warm. One waiter and the waitress will circulate with the canapes from 1830 until 2100. How does that sound?"

Mrs Mc: "Mr H, I think we should have champagne at the start and light canapes and after everyone has arrived move to something more filling."

Geoffrey: "I agree, the waiter and waitress should be serving champagne to start and then the waiter can start with the canapes and bartender can then serve drinks. I will have to show the bartender how to make my famous Collada Daiquiri."

Stephen: "Have you confirmed the numbers Geoffrey?"

Geoffrey: "Why don't we plan on 25, since Russell may have his son and daughter-in-law? I have invited Fred and Jane Russell but they were not certain they could come, since their son is expecting his second child anytime this week. "

Stephen: "I think planning for 25 will cover a few more. Geoffrey, Mike and I cannot stay for the entire evening, since Christmas is our busiest season and we have 2 other events to cover before midnight."

Geoffrey: "I totally understand and I am flattered that you were able to squeeze us in."

Mrs Mc: "Stephen come with me into the butler's pantry and decide how you want to use it."

Stephen: "See you around 5 on Friday."

Mrs Mc: "Mr Geoffrey, Mr McMillan and I have to go to Newcastle for some last minute shopping for our granddaughter. Do you need anything?"

Geoffrey: "No thank you Mrs Mc."

While Mrs McMillan was shopping, Geoffrey started to decorate the Christmas tree. A small well-proportioned spruce that came from the acreage still owned by the Bigelow Trust. He enjoyed trimming the tree and the smell of the spruce brought back so many memories of youth and Margaret. When he was finished he stood back and admired his handiwork. He was certain that Mrs Mc would appreciate the tree and the decorations. He arranged the presents he had for the Quilt Team under the tree, as well as his special present for Robyn, Alice and Michael and the McMillans.

It was a lazy early summer afternoon and he was free of any commitments. There was time for him to practice the piano. He did not want to do scales, in fact he hated scales. He wanted to play something more interesting. He found what he was looking for in the piano bench. His usual choices were Mozart and Beethoven and more recently Saint Saens, especially his Piano Concerto No 2 in G major but on Barry's recommendation he had discovered] the world of Gershwin. When he first played Gershwin, he felt that he was being disloyal to Mozart and, perhaps to Margaret. He did associate the Mozart pieces with Margaret and the times that they had played four hand or she listened to him as he played for her. He was reminded by Barry that had Mozart lived in the 21st century that his music would have been different and that Mozart might have been a rap artist.

An hour or so later, he sat back from the piano, checked his Fitbit and decided that he better take a walk, if he wanted to achieve his 10000 step daily goal. He had altered his mornings and now bicycled into town three days a week to his gym session with Euan and would follow this up with an early breakfast at "Healthy Eats" which was the pop up café between Wilson's and Russell's building. He met Robyn there each morning, just after she finished her Pilate's session with Yung Ok Oh.

Robyn: "That women will kill me yet. Each time I go, I say to myself, you are too old for this. Then I see an 80 year old and say to myself, if he can do that so can I. You already know how stubborn I can be."

Geoffrey: "You have been going for over 1 month and I can already see the difference and you are not stubborn only determined."

Robyn: "Yes, I have lost 5 kg and I do feel fit. My goal is to be able to run up the 3 flights at Wilsons without tiring, I am not there yet. How are plans for your Christmas party?"

Geoffrey: "Between Stephen and Mrs Mc and Alice everything is fine. For over 28 years, Margaret and I hosted a Christmas Party, last year I could not bring myself to host one and I spent the evening at home alone. This year it will be an emotional evening surrounded by people who have made a difference to me and help me redefine who I am."

Robyn: "Geoffrey, you and Margaret made a difference to them as well."

Geoffrey: "And then there is you! After Margaret died, I never thought that I would find another person to share my life."

Robyn to herself, "But Margaret did."

Robyn: "But Geoffrey, I have been sharing your life with Margaret for the past 25 years. You don't think that after seeing you in your Rhett Butler outfit that I was going to let you go."

Geoffrey: "Blame that on Barry, although I did enjoy playing the role. I understand what Barry said when he said that you can let the role takeover your life and you become the character.

Robyn: "Sort of like the movie, "The Mask"?"

Geoffrey: "Exactly, although not with such dramatic consequences. Will you come over around 5 o'clock this evening, now that you are practically a neighbor?"

Robyn: "I will walk over and probably meet Alice and Michael on the way. Anything special?"

Geoffrey: "No, I just want you to be there when people arrive."

Robyn: "For moral support?"

Geoffrey: "No because I want you to be there before anyone arrives, while I am not distracted by other people and I can appreciate you."

Robyn: "Geoffrey you are positively poetic at times. This is a new you."

Geoffrey: "I hope so! See you around 5." With a kiss on her cheek, he left and bicycled back to North Grange.

He decided to go through Summer Park and past the place where the Willow Tree had been. He expected a gaping hole. Much to his delight, he found a new Willow Tree and a bench underneath it. He alighted from his bike, walked over to and sat on the bench and looked over the Grove River. He closed his eyes and remembered the many times he had sat here. When he stood up to leave, he noticed a small plaque which read:

He wiped a tear away as he rode away toward North Grange.   The McMillans were there when he arrived. They were having tea in the kitchen.

Mrs Mc: "Mr Geoffrey would you like some tea?"

Geoffrey: "I would love one. I had a wonderful experience today at Summer Park."

Mrs McMillan poured the tea into a ready cup.

Mr Mc: "You saw the tree and the bench and the plaque that the boys from the Park's Department placed on it."

Geoffrey: "Yes."

Mr Mc: "Miss Margaret was always generous to them at Christmas, birthdays and other times. They saw how emotional you were when the tree collapsed into the Grove. So they decided to remember Miss Margaret in their own way."

Geoffrey: "It was a lovely tribute. Should I write someone or do something?"

Mr Mc: "They said that when Miss Margaret gave them a gift or remembered their birthday or their children's birthday, she said that she did it on the basis that no one would ever know what she had done. Therefore, they wanted to honour that kind of giving."

Geoffrey finished his tea and went up to his room, his clothes were laid out for the evening. He still had 3 hours before anyone would arrive. He thought he would lie down on the bed and take a nap before he showered and changed.

Two hours later he awoke and felt rested and hungry. He showered, shaved and did a Euan inventory. Well 10 kg lighter and more muscle than previously, not bad. What would his grandmother have said "hot"? He laughed at the thought of his grandmother saying anything like that. She might have said "better", instead of passable.

He went downstairs around 4:30 and Mrs McMillan had a plate of finger sandwiches and milk for him.

Geoffrey: "Sandwiches and milk"

Mrs Mc: "You need to fortify your stomach. The sandwiches will take the edge off your appetite and the milk will coat your stomach before you consume alcohol."

Alice: "She's right you know."

Geoffrey: "OK, I'll eat it without and grumbling."

Alice: "How are things going with Robyn?"

Geoffrey: "We are taking things slowly, one step at a time. This is something new for both of us."

Suddenly, Robyn arrived with her usual exuberance.

Robyn: "Well here I am. The new me!" She twirled around allowing the pale blue figure hugging chiffon dress to billow out.

Alice :   "That is a divine dress. Is it a Saba?"

Robyn: "Yes."

Alice: "It is perfect for you."

Mrs Mc: "Well, when you want to, you really scrub up well."

Robyn: "Geoffrey, this is in your honour, at least give a girl a signal that you appreciate the effort."

Geoffrey: "I am gob smacked by this vision of loveliness before me."

Robyn: "Don't get poetic on me. So you like it?"

Geoffrey: "Most definitely." He takes her in his arms and kisses her on the lips.

Michael: "Get a room you two. This is a respectable Christmas Party."

Alice: "Ignore him Geoffrey/Robyn."

They all laugh.

The guests begin to arrive and the waiters begin serving the champagne and apple juice. Geoffrey checked on the guests. He noticed that Barry and Kevin were talking to Stephen and Mike and Bryan and Ava. Maisie was talking to Mrs and Mr McMillan, Russell with his son and daughter-in-law were laughing with Fred and Jane Russell.   Sir Humphrey and Lady Humphrey were talking to Robyn, while Larry and Barbara Abbott were talking to Alice and Michael. His health support team Bruce and Sue were laughing with Yung Ok Oh and Tim and Euan and Micha.

Geoffrey wandered on to the terrace, away from the happy voices and laughter. Suddenly, he was aware of Robyn by his elbow.

Robyn:　　　"Penny for your thoughts? You look as if you expected someone else."

From the lounge room came Barry's voice: "No Ava this is the Elvira Madigan theme. Listen." Barry sat down at the piano and began to play Mozart's Andante Concerto 21.

Geoffrey:　　"Not anymore, everyone is here." He kissed her tenderly on the lips and they went back into the lounge.

The End